D0621671

Quantum Souls
(The Cleansing)

By

Max Holland

We instinctively know the reason for our existence,
yet the awareness is so inconvenient to our narcissistic
life style that we purposely ignore it?

Dedicated to the artist who created the cover of the book, my

Soul Mate.

Maggie Holland

TOC

Prologue

Who are we, where do we go to next, if we go anywhere at all? The world of quantum physics tells us there is nothing here except atoms, are we just that, a single atom of intelligence in a Universe of atoms? Our DNA code is the intricate structure that ultimately designs us and there is little difference between single cell organisms and complex animals like humans.

If you go back in time you will find there is one common ancestor between all living things, one family tree, and one blue-print of life. So were we designed by a scientist a Creator from a different dimension, is life a virtual reality game that we play, if so how do we play it and how do we win.

CIA agent Matt Stone aboard an aircraft on his way to London to embark on a mission of urgency has a near death experience and a revelation of our extraordinary creation. In London he learns more of the evil presence that stalks the Earth in the form of Don Vinchenti the Italian President of Italy, the European Union and puppet of the mega wealthy ruling elite, the Wed group. They are the people you never hear about, who spend their lives in the shadows and are the real power, the real ruling class. They plan to destroy the countries of the Middle East in order to take control of the oil.

Meanwhile China and Russia look like being forced into a world conflict to preserve their claim on the regions oil production. The lack of employment in Europe and the United States is the cause of violent political demonstrations in the streets. As the planet Earth goes into meltdown Matt meets his soul-mate Louisa Vinchenti the step-daughter of Don Vinchenti. With her help, Matt and a small team of experts attempt to disrupt the timing of the war as the conflict could destroy the planet.

Chapter 1

California

Streaking within feet of the Mojave Desert an F16 sparkled in the bright sunlight as it accelerated toward the rock pinnacles of Trona leaving a long trail of curling dust rising slowly into the still air.

In the cockpit Colonel Matt Stone flipped up the dark visor of his helmet to scan the rapidly closing hills. Carefully, with the precision of a surgeon, he manipulated the control stick aiming the powerful craft between two of the ancient rock sentinels. With the aircraft tipped on its side he guided it through the narrow gap within feet of the rock, then flicking the wings level he continued his low flight across the scorching desert floor. Gently he applied a little back pressure to the stick and with a quick snap of his wrist he put the fighter on its back. Now with the craft inverted he flew within twenty feet of the surface. From this reversed attitude Matt thought of the microsecond of time that stood between him and death. He had seen a young pilot killed practicing this maneuver. The youngster had died in a cartwheeling tangle of hot twisting metal, finally exploding into a rasping ball of fire. As Matt had driven towards the scene he saw just the smoking remains of the craft rising from the barren landscape signaling a solitary beacon of death.

Now his attention focused on his inverted fighter as it screamed over the desolate land with rocks, boulders and brush passing in a blur of color above his head. Carefully his left hand pushed the stick forward, while his right hand curled around the throttle easing it smoothly in until the engine reached full power, then as the craft curved up toward the sky a film of red began to blur his vision taking him to the edge of consciousness, with the negative Gs' numbing his mind the powerful jet roared away from the desert terrain sending a billowing cloud of dust hundreds of feet into the air.

A second later, with his sight clear, Matt climbed the craft vertically up blasting through the white clouds set three dimensionally against the blue sky. Leveling the fighter at thirty five thousand feet he called Center.

"Edward's approach, red one, over"

"Red one go ahead"

"Approach red one, level at three five zero, request one thousand through the valley, over"

"Red one, you are cleared to descend through the valley, not above one thousand"

"Red one cleared through the valley, not above one thousand, roger"

Matt eased the power back putting the plane into a gentle descent, flying down between the mountainous clouds until he could see the small towns below. He descended to five hundred feet above the ground then glanced out the side of the cockpit, he saw the little towns, roads, and fields zipping by like a pack of cards in a dealer's hand. A flash of color caught his attention. He brought the fighter round in a tight turn until he was able to catch a brief glimpse of a brass band marching through a small town. He imagined there would be children happily running alongside the band with musicians dressed in candy striped uniforms gaily swinging their arms to the beat of a drum.

A lump of compassion formed in Matt's throat as the snapshot scene flashed by. It was these people he cared for, the simple folk, the innocent whose lives were so often shattered by governments taking them into unnecessary wars.

Although it had been two weeks since he had flown an F16, he was relaxed with the aircraft. The cockpit was small, tight like a glove, with a familiar array of instruments that made him feel comfortable. He looked down to see the ground sweeping by as he flew the aircraft between the low brown hills bordering the valley.

Somewhere in the back of his mind he could hear a choirboy singing. It was then he knew it was about to happen again. For the past few weeks he had been having strange visions, maybe premonitions, he wasn't sure which. They were often disasters of one kind or another, many occurring in other parts of the world. The events were so real it seemed as if he had actually been in two places at the same time.

He had noticed a pattern building, almost as if someone was giving him an overview of a degenerating world of crime, pollution, famine, terrorism and viruses. He knew the greed of mankind was spreading its own lustful infection across the planet, everyone was aware of that. So what's the difference now he thought? It had been this way for thousands of years?

First he had wondered if the visions were caused by stress, but it wasn't long before he caught reports of the incidents in newspapers, confirming his visions of the future were actually real. The experiences always left him with a feeling of anxiety that was hard to shake. He had asked himself the same question many times, why me?

Now he felt that same feeling that came over him just before a vision occurred, he knew something strange was about to happen. Just at that moment the sunlight caught the edge of the aircraft wing and the reflected light flashed into the colors of the rainbow. The pattern rotated faster and faster like a child's kaleidoscope. The choirboy's voice filled the cockpit. He could see the inside of a church where a wedding service was in progress. The groom stood proudly with his bride. Rays of sunlight streamed down through a stained glass window onto the pallor face of the young choirboy. The eloquence of a Latin hymn pitched high into the echoing chamber seemed real, too real. Was he actually there?

Outside in the vestry Matt saw a squad of troops pressing themselves against the cold stone walls. A soldier stared into the eyes of an officer his high forehead and greasy face broke into beads of sweat. He didn't speak, his face wild with anxiety stared back at his subordinate. The officer remained still, waiting for the singing to stop, to give the fatal order. Then a few moments later, with lips curled back, he screamed the order: "Avanti"

The troops burst without mercy into the church, their guns ablaze, chewing the pews to pieces in seconds. All those who had been seated lay mutilated or dead, strewn amongst furniture, now blood-soaked and splintered into match-sticks.

Only the boy was left standing his small hands gripping the pew in front of him. Tears filled his eyes before slowly rolling down his angelic face. The boy looked up to a stained glass window where the image of Christ's crucifixion was set in a dazzling array of color. The colors blended into one, spinning faster and faster until they sparkled off the wing of the aircraft.

Matt shook his head and turned the aircraft in a long lazy curve away from the dazzling rays of the sun. With the choirboy's hymn still echoing through his mind he headed back towards the base.

He was angry that he had allowed himself to be distracted from flying the aircraft and wondered if his imagination had run wild? Or could it be, for just a briefest moment in time, he had actually been there?

He listened to A.T.I.S the Air Traffic Information Service giving out its continuous recorded landing information: wind, runways in use, quoting the information update with a phonetic letter of the alphabet, in this case Tango. Matt pressed the transmit button.

"Approach, red one five November, twenty north, one thousand, inbound I have tango, expect two four."

There was a short pause then, "Red One, you are cleared for a straight in on two four. The wind is, two, two zero, at ten, call tower on one one niner seven, good day Sir"

As the F16 continued on its final approach over the Mojave Desert into Edward's Air Force base, Matt's thoughts were on the telephone call he had received at 6 am that morning. It had been from his C.I.A director and friend General Ichner.

"Matt, something serious has come up.

"OK"

"Get your bags packed for a trip, then go relax for the morning, I have a mission for you, I'll contact you later.

Matt knew when his director said "Go relax" he was really saying "Go do anything that you want, it may be your last chance."

His role in the U.S.A.F, between assignments for the C.I.A, was as an instructor at the 34th pilot training school. So, after an early breakfast and packing a suitcase, he had driven to the base. Then it was just a simple matter of paperwork to do the thing that relaxed him the most, so he had filed a flight plan, climbed into his favorite F16 and powered down the center line of the runway. The feeling of freedom that always overwhelmed him had returned that morning as the powerful craft thrust him high into the deep blue sky.

Now his mind returned to the vision that had occurred a moment ago. Had it really happened had he really been there or was it just an illusion, just a trick of light and sound? Yet he thought he could still hear the choir singing somewhere off in the far distance.

Rolling to a stop on the hot tarmac Matt looked down from the open cockpit and saw an officer in a bright blue uniform walking with some urgency toward his plane. He climbed down and turned to be greeted by an unusually stiff looking individual.

"Sir, Col. Stone?"

"Yea, that´s me," Matt said unbuttoning his flying suit.

"Sir, the jeep is waiting for you. Could you follow me?"

"Excuse me! Follow you?"

"Yes sir, to General Ichner? I have orders to take you over to him"

"OK" Matt said. Then at his own pace he followed the young man to where a jeep and driver was standing waiting.

"So, we're we going guy"

The young officer just pointed to a large airplane sitting on its own at the far end of the airfield. As they came closer to the aircraft Matt recognized it.

"Air force one, I'm impressed," Matt said, at the same time tipping an eyebrow toward the younger man.

The officer who was sitting rigid on the edge of his seat never acknowledged the comment but Matt felt the man's eyes turn toward him. The officer nervously fumbled to open the door as the jeep came to a stop.

Matt climbed up the stairway behind his escort, as they reached the top the door swung open. Inside there was a sense of peace. A man in uniform who he recognized as General Ichner's aid, Major Oldfield, was waiting to greet him. He was tall elegant with dark sinister eyes and disgusting habit of constantly sniffing. Matt knew and disliked the man, but never the less managed a smile as their eyes met.

"Good morning, Col. Stone, this way please"

Matt could tell from body language a great deal about what a person was thinking and for that reason he had a bad feeling about Oldfield. He knew the man had been in Special Services and had heard he was a clever strategist but personally Matt would not have trusted him to make coffee. He waived his hand toward a closed door. "In there, Colonel Stone"

He smiled and walked across to the door, pushed it open and entered the empty room. It was hard to believe he was aboard an aircraft. The room was furnished with settees and large comfortable armchairs it looked like the lounge of a first class hotel. It was bathed in soft lighting with music in the background. The air-conditioning gave a pleasant relief from the temperature outside. He took a seat and waited.

Twenty minutes past before the door facing him opened. A stocky man dressed in striped business pants, braces and a white shirt with sleeves pulled back by arm-bands, walked into the room.

"General." Matt said as he stood up to attention and saluted.

"Matt, how are you?" The General said returning the salute with a casual wave.

"Fine Sir, just fine"

They shook hands. The General waved him toward an armchair, and then took a seat himself. "Did you take the time to relax?"

"Yes, thank you"

"Good." He paused, "Matt, as I indicated on the phone earlier, we have a major problem. The British have supplied us with their intelligence reports that suggest the President of Italy, who as you know is also the current President of the EU," he paused, "that lunatic Don Vinchenti."

Matt nodded.

"Well, we believe he is about to instigate a war in the Middle East."

"Are you serious?

"From the information we have, I'm very serious.

"But why would he? What's his angle?"

"One word Matt, oil"

"Surely if China or Russia get wind of this they won´t be happy"

"You're right they are just as interested in controlling the oil as anyone else. China is power hungry she is already working in most of Africa and particularly in the oil producing countries from Sudan down the eastern seaboard and as far over as Nigeria.

We do know that Vinchenti is totally insane and very dangerous: we are pretty certain that he is going to launch a nuclear attack on Israel from a location somewhere in the Middle East. Then on the pretense of helping Israel he will use nuclear weapons to wipe out most of the Arab states, then afterwards go in with the EU army, of which he has total control. With them he can clean up and take over"

"Where the hell did he get nuclear weapons from?"

"Believe it or not Iraq, that´s why we couldn't find them there. Our brilliant intelligence agency finally has evidence that Saddam shipped them out a month or more before we got there."

"Great, too bloody late" Matt said.

"Anyway his intention is to have Israel perceive wrongly, that the strike was launched from one of the Arab countries, almost certainly from Iran."

Matt drew his breath in sharply and uttered a short. "Wow"

The General continued. "By the signature of the launch, Israel will identify where it came from and will reply with an immediate nuclear response. That will almost certainly bring in the new coalition of Islamic States and God knows whom else. We can't inform Israel until we have positive proof because if it turns out that the information is not legitimate it will put the so-called peace negotiations with the Palestinians, which are already fragile to say the least, at risk."

"Is there some question about the information then?"

"The British have a mole deep in Vinchenti's organization but he hasn't been able to gain all the facts just an outline. We desperately need more information. To make things worse we've received satellite shots which show that China is mobilizing"

"Maybe, they do know something"

"Yes exactly, so it is imperative that we get a look at Vinchenti's plans which we know are kept at his estate in northern Italy. He uses the home as his personal headquarters away from his government. If he's to head an attack on Israel then we need to know how and when. The British are preparing to send a small team in to the building and you are going in with them."

"With them"

"Yes Matt, with them"

"I'm not happy working with people I don't know. What about using my guys?"

"No, it's not possible" He turned, indicating the door he had just come through. "I've just come out of a meeting with the President of the United States, the Vice President, the Chief of Staff and the Secretary of State." He paused. "We go in with the British, its politics."

"OK, whatever you say boss" Matt said.

"Anyway, one of their people you already know from your days behind the Wall, Paul Johnson-Smith, plus they are supplying an electronic and explosives expert who they say is the best there is, and a chopper pilot to get you out. We are also going to employ a minder to keep an eye out for you. It'll be better if we don't let the British know that we have an extra team member.

"Will he be somebody I know?"

"We haven't decided who to use yet, but you'll know in good time. Another thing, the Brit's are trying to recruit Vinchenti's daughter. She is currently working with a medical relief organization in the Balkans. If they can pull it off, we'll be half way there. I told them in the meeting that you know your way around Europe more than anyone else with your expertise, so you got the assignment."

"Thanks, friend" Matt said with a grin.

"You're welcome," he smiled. "Anyway, you're to fly to London tonight and you probably have an hour before your paperwork comes through Major Oldfield will deliver it to you just as soon as it's ready. Meanwhile update yourself on Vinchenti. The research library has the file on Vinchenti and it is ready waiting for you. Also you need to go down and pick up a piece of equipment from the widow-maker. So you had better get going."

"Right" Matt said as they both stood up

"Good luck Matt"

They reached out and shook hands. "Thank you" Matt said, as his eyes joined the others, a tiny smile broke on his face. "It'll be interesting"

Outside the air was hot the young officer who had been waiting for him looked relieved that he could now get out of the heat. Matt jumped in to the jeep then as the driver turned the vehicle around he looked back at Air Force One and wondered about the panic going on inside. Would this be the beginning of a major world disaster or could this ego-maniac be stopped.

The jeep pulled up next to the F16 Matt had just flown. The chief mechanic, Flight Sergeant Fred Balding, was standing by the wing of the aircraft twisting the end of his handle-bar mustache. The mechanic's red face grinned at Matt, who smiled back as a way of recognition while they waited for the deafening noise of a departing helicopter to cease. Fred ran his fingers along the metal of the aircraft, and then nodding his head at the craft. "It went well, Sir?"

"You asking me Fred or telling me?" Matt laughed.

"Asking Sir?"

"Fred, this bird is in great shape and you know it"

Matt climbed onto the aircraft pulled a small bag from it, then jumped down. He was walking away when he heard Fred speak to him from behind.

"Hear you are going on a trip sir"

He turned abruptly, looking at the Flight Sergeant in utter disbelief. "What did you say Fred?"

"Sorry Sir didn't mean to surprise you. It's just that I have orders from Major Oldfield to have a chopper standing by to take you to L.A Airport"

"Oh, Ok Fred"

"Going on vacation, Sir?"

"No just a long week end"

"The chopper is ready when you are Colonel"

"I'll let you know Sergeant"

"I'll be in OP's if you need me but I think that Major Oldfield will be running you over to the hanger"

"OK"

They walked towards the operations room together. Fred held open the glass door, and then with a casual salute walked off. Matt watched Fred's short legs carry him off toward the maze of corridors that bustled with military personnel. The hallway was crowded with people rushing in every direction. He turned and almost collided with a young female officer. For a moment her eyes flashed in anger then changed to a look of recognition. "Excuse me," he said. "I'm sorry but what's the panic about, why is everyone flying around like lunatics?"

She put her head to one side, as if she was trying to remember why he seemed so familiar.

Then she smiled, "Don´t you know? China is mobilizing it was just on CNN,"

"So now the military get their information from television," he said laughing.

She smiled once again then turned away. He watched as her neat figure dressed in a navy blue uniform disappeared into the melee of people. Somehow he knew they had met before, but was it in this life, could she be a soul-mate, had their paths crossed for a brief moment bringing back the memories from a previous existence?

He entered the huge bright elevator that would take him down to Hans Munson's laboratory. He pushed his way in-between the white faced occupant's standing nervously in contagious silence. The lights on the board indicated they were going down fast. It stopped many times at different levels, allowing several of the passengers off, before finally stopping at the last level. The doors slid open and the remaining passengers quiet with obvious apprehension hurried off to their respective posts. Matt walked across to yet another elevator. Two security guards were sitting behind a desk beside the doors.

He took his wallet from inside the flying suit and produced a plastic card which he handed to the younger man. The clean-shaven young guard studied it thoroughly, looking first at the card and then back to Matt. Finally satisfied, he pointed to a small electronic finger print identifier, Matt placed his forefinger on the little screen, at the same time pressed the button next to it, the elevator doors slid open.

He felt the elevator descending going down it seemed to almost the center of the earth. At that moment the doors opened and a cold blast of damp and musty air greeted him, bringing back the memory of his first visit to this deep labyrinth below Sat Net's control center, the heart of the CIA's west coast operation.

It had been at the time of the first Libyan crisis he had been summoned to the operation room and given precise instructions regarding his target. It was then he visited Hans Munson's laboratory, where he was supplied with several, small but deadly, heat seeking arrows with explosive tips, plus five compact cross-bows.

Having assembled his team, the operation was called off. Washington decided to go ahead with a bombing raid instead. The bombers had been given permission to fly from their bases in England. France and Spain had refused to permit the bombers to use their airspace this meant taking a longer route over the sea making their chance of success even more tenuous. Nevertheless their accuracy had been good, but unfortunately Kaddafi had moved from the target area before the aircraft arrived.

Matt was sure, had his team been allowed a go at Kaddafi, he would have been killed many years before, which as it turned out would have saved a lot of Libyan lives. He often wondered why Washington had a change of heart at the last minute.

He turned many corners until he arrived at the old laboratory which looked as if it had been recently painted. The aroma of the new paint hung in the air. Inside Hans Munson was waiting in reception. Matt knew that the man was named the Widow-Maker for all the innovative electronic gadgets he produced for killing people. Hans peered over the top of his bifocals, "Matt Stone welcome, come in, come in"

Matt nodded giving him a knowing smile. He followed the older man through a set of doors and into his workshop. The room was long and narrow with a low ceiling which gave the appearance of an engineering factory at one end, and an electronics laboratory at the other with people in white coats going about their business paying no attention to the visitor.

"Sit down, sit down, I'll be with you in a moment,"

Hans Munson went over to a bench Matt followed him and took a seat next to him then watched as Munson peered into a small microscope and carefully manipulated the tiniest of tools. He saw that he was putting a battery into a watch transmitter he knew that the life span of a battery in such a transmitter would be fairly short, just a few minutes. This meant it could only be used when really needed.

"OK Matt, this piece of equipment is a scanner, reader and transmitter. This little baby can patch a signal through to our satellite network from anywhere in the world. What you do is pull out the winder like this." His fingers gripped the small winder and he pulled it out from the watch. Matt could see it was attached to a fine wire which was spring loaded.

"Now, as you can see the winder looks like a diamond, it isn't, it is in fact the scanner head, and each of its facets is a lens. You hold it like this, four inches above the text, press this button and it will

19

scan up to an A 4 size paper, here, put it on." he said handing Matt the watch. "Then just push this button and it'll transmit," he said pointing to a button on the side of the face. "Also if you plug in a small memory stick, just here, you can read the info on the face."

"Is that all it does?"

Munson gave him a look over the top of his glasses. Matt smiled back at him. "Just joking," he said.

He left the laboratory, went back up to the next level and found his way to the room marked Library. A guard took a look at the security card Matt offered him before allowing him to pass. Inside the musty room a uniformed attendant was seated at the inquiry desk.

"I'd like to take a look at the file on Don Vinchenti?"

"Don Vinchenti sure I have it ready for you Colonel Stone, I've been expecting you" The pretty girl passed a folder over to him. She pointed at a plastic topped table with a hard molded seat. "You could take it over there Colonel"

"Thanks" Matt said hardly noticing the girl his interest in the document had become paramount. He opened the cover.

Top Secret:

Don Vinchenti.

Born 6am. 6.6.1946, Milan Italy..

Father: Italian.

Mother: Italian.

Married.

Family: 2 Stepdaughter's one deceased, no natural children.

Sister Marina, married to Mario Lousioni

Profile: Ranks in the top ten of the wealthiest men in the world.

From the age of three showed an incredible flair for mathematics and an uncanny almost inborn knowledge of science. Studied Mathematics and chemistry at the University of Milan and was awarded student of the year three years running. Then After leaving University he took a position with Delinco Chemicals a major pharmaceutical company in Rome. After four years with the company a row with his superiors occurred and he was fired. A week after he left the factory it burned to the ground.

In the slums of Milan he started his own biochemical factory, Bicemco International.

At the age of forty he owned outright Italy's largest pharmaceutical empire: which included a vast heavily guarded facility built on a thousand acre site in Uganda. In 1996 he sold the company and retired to his home in Milan.

In March 1998 he became a Minister, ordained in the Church of the Lyonesse Group a right wing bigoted sect of the Roman Catholic Church opposed to many of the Vatican's polices including celibacy.

Within a year news spread of a miracle worker priest who had the ability to cure the body of the HIV virus. People flocked to drink the sacred water, blessed and given to them by Father Vinchenti. Within weeks of an infected person taking the holy sacrament from Father Vinchenti the virus would disappear from their body.

After years of government disasters political unrest was rife in Italy, the country was ready for a savior Don Vinchenti became that person. With the help of the Church and his brother-in-law a new party was created, it became the political wing of the Lyonesse church. Then with his earlier fame as a miracle worker and an outspoken critic of the government, his party took a landslide victory at the polls and Don Vinchenti became the President of Italy.

Soon after he came to power he declared himself the 'Son of God', from his work as a Minister in Milan the Italians believed it. His rise to power came as a result of bribery and bully boy tactics and probably worse.

<UPDATE> NOTICE 5155-297 CIA. As president of the EU Don Vinchenti is also the head the European Defense and

Security Protection the ESDP, which has direct control over the newly formed, European rapid reaction force.

Matt flicked through the other documents but as far as he could see there was nothing much that would help him. The latest reference was to his wife who had not been seen in public for ten years. She had two daughters by a previous marriage. The eldest daughter had been killed ten years ago in a skiing accident along with her young husband. The other daughter, a doctor, works for IMCO the International Medical Charity Organization based in London which sends medically qualified people to help the sick in war zones throughout the world. There were recent photographs of Don Vinchenti, but the photographs of his wife and surviving stepdaughter were all over ten years old.

Matt read to the end of the report. Don Vinchenti's psychological profile was described as psychopathic personality.

He closed the file and handed it back to the attendant. At that moment he felt a tremor in the pocket of his flying suit, it was his pager vibrating. He took it out, it read, Colonel Stone. I am in reception. Major Oldfield.

Matt returned in the crowded elevator to reception on the first floor. There he found Major Oldfield standing waiting for him.

"Please follow me Colonel I have your orders"

They walked along the corridor and stopped at an office. The General's aid put a key in the lock and opened the door. His hand reached inside switching the fluorescent lights on, then stood aside allowing Matt to enter first. The room had obviously been used recently for a meeting. There was a stuffy odor of stale smoke, empty coffee cups stood on a large desk amongst the piles of paper left behind by the coffee drinkers. From the bustle outside Matt was not surprised that they had left in a hurry.

Major Oldfield opened his briefcase and handed a tiny memory stick which could be inserted into a watch. Matt was wondering why it bothered him so much that the man had anything to do with his travel, arrangements. He took the memory stick held it for a moment while he looked into Oldfield's eyes. Then in case his suspicious nature became too obvious he turned away but not before he had read something strange in the other's eyes. He slit open the envelope and pulled out a letter, it read.

Col. Matt Stone. These are your travel documents the memory stick contains your mission information and is not to be read until you are aboard your flight out of Newark. More instructions will be sent to you when you pick up the signal in Italy, act on them after you have transmitted the information we need. Good luck Matt, General Ichner

Before slipping the papers into his pocket he opened the packet marked (Travel Documents) and flicked through the papers checking to see if they were complete. He had been routed on a commercial airline out of Los Angeles to Newark then on to Gatwick, London with Virgin. Interesting, he thought, traveling on a British airline. The memory stick he slipped into his flying suit and zipped up the pocket.

He looked across to Oldfield who was busy locking the office, "Well Major we had better get going."

"Now, if you would like to follow me Colonel, I'll take you over to your transport" Oldfield said.

"OK Major, let's go."

As they walked back along the busy corridor he wondered what instructions the memory-stick contained. They stopped at reception to pick up the luggage that he had left there earlier that day.

A blast of hot air greeted them as they walked out of the building into the bright sunlight. A jeep was waiting for them, but just as Matt was about to climb in, a voice from behind called out.

"Matt, you old son of a bitch" It was Ed Wheeler a CIA friend from many years past. Matt quickly threw his luggage in the jeep, then much to Oldfield's obvious annoyance he walked over to his friend and shook hands.

"How yer doing Ed?"

Ed was dressed in shorts, sandals and a straw Mexican style hat that was pushed to the back of his head. Matt noticed the stocky man's dark crocodile skin was now showing the results of many years living in the sun Matt knew Ed had spent most of his service life in South American.

"I'm Ok, what about you Matt, you good, what are you doing you still fly those birds?" He pointed towards the aircraft Matt had just flown, which was still sitting on the apron.

"You know how it is, no rest for the wicked." Matt said finally releasing his hand from the others equally strong grip. "So where are you off to Ed, you look like you are going on vacation"

"You kidding me, no, I'm on my way to L.A, going south, Bogota." Then with a huge grin and sparkling eyes he asks. "You Matt, what are you up to?"

"I'm going to L.A as well, how you getting there, wan 'a lift?" Matt said nodding toward Oldfield and the jeep.

"That's my chopper, over there," Ed said pointing to a helicopter sitting nearby with its engine running and the blades slowly turning. "I have got a lot of equipment and baggage it would be easier if you come with me"

"OK, great, I'll get my things" Matt walked over to where Oldfield was waiting with the jeep.

"I've got a lift with a friend Major, I won't need the chopper," Matt said as he reached in the vehicle for his luggage.

"But Sir, your orders"

"Yes" Matt said not amused.

"You are expected to travel on that transport. It's been sent empty, especially for you. It also has to pick-up the Presidential courier bag which is coming in from Washington, so it must leave right away and you should be on it"

"Should I now?" Matt gave the man a look, then slung the heavy canvas bag over his shoulder turned his back and walked over to Ed's waiting chopper. Once aboard Matt leaned over to the pilot. "Would you call the tower for me? Ask them to inform the chopper sitting outside D hanger that Colonel Stone has made other travel arrangements, thanks."

Matt sat back and looked at Ed. "It is really great to see you it's so rare that I see anyone from the old days."

The helicopter rose and with a forward motion began its climb across the airfield gaining height until it began a long turn to fly back parallel with the airfield in the direction that would take them toward the coast. After a while Matt glanced out of the window and saw the helicopter that had been sitting outside D hanger was traveling in the same direction as themselves, just ahead and about two hundred or so feet lower. Suddenly it started a turn and then surprisingly continued in a flat turn until it had completed a full three hundred and sixty degrees. Matt was fascinated by this maneuver and wondered what was going on. It went round again, this time faster, then another turn even faster, it was then he realized it was not turning but spinning on its own axis in a flat elevation. Matt watched as bits of the aircraft began to come off, it was obvious that the helicopter was totally out of control and falling apart, now spinning faster and faster until it became an unrecognizable blur of parts.

Matt nudged Ed who was sitting beside him. "Ed look, I'm sure that's the chopper I was supposed to be on."

Ed leaned over him for a better view. "What the hell is happening to it?"

Before he could answer, Matt saw the body of the pilot fly out from the breaking wreckage and down toward the ground he waited for a parachute to open, but the body just kept plummeting toward the ground...

"Looks like the tail-rotor came off," Matt said, and then quickly unbuckling his seat belt to leant forward to speak to the pilot. As he did, he realized it was unnecessary; the pilot had seen the catastrophe and was relaying the information to Edward's control tower.

"Shit man, you were lucky"

Matt nodded and re-buckled his seat belt. He was wondering why the tragedy happened. From his experience he knew the maintenance on the aircraft at Edward's was above exception, tail-rotor failure was almost certainly the cause of the problem, and the chances of that happening by accident would be extremely low.

Matt watched as the last parts of the disintegrating helicopter fluttered like the leaves of a tree toward the distance ground.

"Well Ed, I guess I'm in your debt. If you hadn't given me a lift, -------"Matt never completed the rest of the sentence, the obvious conclusion spoke for itself.

"Who thought you would be on that chopper?"

Without saying anything Matt turned his eyes toward his old friend. Then deep in thought they both remained silent for the rest of the journey. Matt looked out to see the sprawling city below and decided it was time to change his travel plans. He pulled his cell-phone out and called Oldfield.

The call back directed him into Burlington Vermont, and then by hire car on to Montreal.

Chapter 2

Montreal Canada

Inside the waiting lounge Matt sat with his briefcase on his lap studying his fellow passengers. There were a number of businessmen in drab suits each sitting staring ahead making no eye contact with each other. A fat lady with three children looked frustrated she cradled one in her arms while another cried for attention in a carry-cot situated on the floor between her legs. The third, a boy, imitating a jet, ran up and down the aisle much to the annoyance of some of the passengers.

Feeling somebody staring at him, Matt looked down the aisle and saw a man in the opposite row instantly turn his gaze away. Although he didn't recognize the dark skinned man but the incident caused a feeling of apprehension in Matt's stomach. He wondered if he had been right about Oldfield, did someone know of his mission were they following him, even though his route from L.A had been changed. The helicopter accident was continually in his thoughts, had it just been a coincidence.

Matt looked out of the window and saw the baggage handlers dressed in thick coats loading the aircraft in a deluge of swirling snow. The passengers stood up and shuffled towards the doorway. The swarthy-looking man had slipped past the others and disappeared ahead.

"Good evening sir" A slim blonde with a permanent smile sitting on pencil lips held out her hand for his ticket.

"Oh, that's on the right side, near the back" she said.

He found his seat, placed his briefcase in the overhead locker, clicked it shut, sat down into his seat and snapped his seat belt together. Matt opened the Wall Street Journal that he had chosen from a pile of papers and magazines offered to him by a passing flight attendant. The front page had headlines that read `Massacre in Italy' plus a picture of the remains of the gunshot shattered pews inside the church. It stated that Francisco Gurino the leader of the left wing Christian Socialist Party had been killed in Milan while attending the wedding service of his daughter. It went on to name some of the guests who had also been killed, nearly all being the executive membership of the C.S.P. Matt shuddered remembering his vision then leaned back and closed his eyes.

Soon the engines where whining up to a frenzied pitch. Given a final flood of power, they gradually calmed down into a silken repose. The huge beast bumped along the dark taxi-way while a video explaining the safety features of the aircraft played. Included in the instructions was all the usual cheerful information, such as the location of life jackets in the event of water landing. The thought of the cold Atlantic water, did not exactly excite him.

Then the lights dimmed and with the sound of the engines now at full power the great aircraft moved forward gathering speed as it rumbled along the runway finally giving way to a more gentle motion as it lifted off into the dark night. A bleep and only the no-smoking signs were left illuminated.

A couple of hours later Matt was feeling warm and comfortable after dinner. He had chatted to an old French woman seated in the isle across from him and enjoyed a cognac which he had ordered for the two of them, now he felt slightly drowsy in the peaceful environment. A short while later he listened to the Captain explaining to the passengers that the bumpy ride they were experiencing was due to clear air turbulence. Then as his thoughts drifted to his forthcoming mission he slipped into unconsciousness.

The blonde flight attendant with pencil lips who had delivered Matt his drink bent down to whisper in the ear of the man with the dark skin. "I washed the glass after he finished the drink."

"Good, did you dissolve both pills?"

"Of course, will it take long?"

"No, just a short time, it affects everyone different. Although I'm surprised he hasn't called out, that drug can be painful when it hits the heart. He's probably dead by now, go back and look."

She straightened up, and then walked casually along the aisle past Matt, giving him just a cursory glance as she passed by.

#

Major Oldfield's body lay crumpled on the desert floor with the last of its life blood draining into the hot sand. The hands of the body still clutched the remains of the Judas money. In the gathering darkness the rest of the hundred dollar bills swirled in the dust, racing with the tumbleweed, towards the deep red setting sun.

Chapter 3

Vlado Bolvic sat racked in pain propped against a wall in the bombed ruin of his home. Surrounded by broken furniture he cradled his lifeless wife in his arms and wept at the sight of his young daughter sitting frozen in shock among the wreckage that had once been their living room.

In the distance he could hear the explosions of bombs raining down on his homeland. Although he felt concern for the safety of others, he was thankful for the moment of peace that it afforded him. He glanced up to the grey overcast sky it was snowing again. He tried to rub the tears from his eyes but his hands were frozen.

"Yola come, come to daddy." The child didn't move or show any sign of recognition. Vlado looked down at his wife and wiped the snow away from her face. He rocked back and forth with grief as he stroked her forehead and pushed the strands of hair away from her colorless features. This would not be the first time he had lost a loved one in this long war. A year had passed since a shell had killed his aging mother while she stood in line waiting for bread. Then a week ago his eldest daughter had been killed by a sniper while she waited in vain for a United Nations supply truck to come.

The name, United Nations, struck cold in Valdo's heart. To him they were united only in word not in deed. He thought of the atrocities that had been committed in the last conflict before the so called peace that had given each side time to re-group. A year ago the war had started again after the Republika of Srpska held a referendum for independence to break-away from the Federation of Bosnia and Herzegovina. Now the entire Balkan region of central Europe was back in turmoil. The U.N had done little to bring the murderers to trial for their previous war crimes and now with the new hostilities started the U.N just looked on as the same thing was happening again.

When Yugoslavia broke into civil war in the last years of the twentieth century, the elders of the village had believed that after the Nazis ethnic cleansing of World War Two, the U.N would never allow genocide to be committed in Europe again. Yet he had heard that around a hundred thousand people were killed during the nineties war and more than twenty thousand women were raped. The elders had been wrong, that time the world leaders had waited until it was too late, and this time it would be no different. No one would come to stop the slaughter.

He knew the leader of each country represented in the U.N would not be willing to help criticism from their home media would send their political ratings tumbling if they allowed their troops the use of force and were then killed in action. The snow was heavier now he looked at his child staring vacantly ahead. He could do nothing his wounds had paralyzed him. "Yola, come to daddy." Again the child failed to move, just continued to cuddle the doll, her eyes glazed, blank and filled with frozen tears.

A shell whistled overhead, instinctively he ducked. He hoped it would fall harmlessly in the fields beyond the village, but he knew better. It would almost certainly hit its target with precision. Within seconds there was a deafening roar, followed by blood chilling screams coming from his neighbor's homes. He felt for them, wanted to help, but he was unable to move. He pushed their screams to the back of his mind and thought of God.

In the early days Vlado had prayed that someone from the West would come to his aid. As a student he had traveled through Europe and enjoyed visiting the United States. He had been in New York one Christmas there he remembered the sparkling lights and colorful windows of the magnificent shops. He had seen stores packed with shoppers, desperate in their endless quest to satisfy their own materialistic needs. He wondered about the shoppers, did they like their government, lack compassion for humanity and were their lives only satisfied by the trappings of materialism? Tears rolled down his cheeks as he cried for the unconscious body of his wife who had never seen the tinsel cities of the west and now never would.

He looked down at the snow covering him, surprised see that the blood still showed through the heavy snow. He wanted to call Yola again but his throat was too dry. He looked at her; she was sleeping now her tiny hands frozen white still clutched the rag doll.

There was the rattle of gunfire again in the distance. Vlado knew that it would not be long before the artillery shells would be dropping around him. But for the sleeping child, he wished a shell would fall on his home, and take him with Gilda and end it all. My God he thought what a relief that would be after all these years of torment. He felt weak and dozed off into a dreamlike state. He seemed for a moment that he was looking down at his body from a few feet above and he saw the heavy snow had finally covered his bloody wound. It was strange to have no feeling in his body, no pain now, he could see his hands like his body, were frozen stiff. It made him sad that he could no longer wipe the snow from Gilda's face.

Suddenly, he heard a noise and watched as if in slow motion a soldier that had appeared in the broken wooden frame that had once been the doorway to his home stubble towards him. He wore a blue beret with the insignia of the United Nations. The soldier viewed the scene, and then he turned to call to a hidden companion. "In 'ere Dave" he called, 'there's more bodies in 'ere mate."

Vlado realized the snow covering them must have given the soldier the impression they were all dead.

"Too bloody late again" the soldier went on. "If the bloody government won't let us fight the bastards, how the hell can we protect the poor sods?"

The soldier bent down on one knee with tears in his eyes. Vlado thought he was about to help him, but no, he reached to the ground and picked up the shawl Gilda had been wearing when the shell exploded. The soldier stepped carefully through the debris and then bent down placing the shawl over Yola. Then with just a glance down at him he walked back to the opening.

Vlado wanted to cry out to the soldier, tell him that she wasn't dead, neither was he, it couldn't be, he knew Yola was still alive life just could not be that cruel.

At the doorway a young woman appeared. She was dressed in worn khaki drill and wore a red cross on her arm. Although her face was dirty, it was obvious she was beautiful and she looked out of place among the devastation. Vlado thought she could have been a film star. She pushed aside the English soldier and climbed over the rubble to stand looking down at them.

It was at that moment Vlado realized for the first time he too was dead. When he had prayed earlier his hands had frozen together. Now he looked down on his own body and prayed one more time.

He saw the young woman crouch down and put her hand around Gilda's limp wrist feeling for a pulse. Vlado knew there would be none. Then she gently brushed the snow from her forehead, and closed her own eyes. Vlado could hear the young woman whispering a prayer.

"Oh my Father, forgive them for the iniquity of their soul and let them live," were the words Vlado believed he heard her say. Then she stood up and seemed to be waiting for something to happen.

As if in a dream Vlado felt himself return to his body. A smile flickered across the girls face and then she turned and spoke to the soldier. "Get them into the ambulance, I think they're alive." She winked at Vlado then climbed back across the rubble and out into the street.

Vlado twisted his stiff neck to watch her climb into an old rusty land-rover before pulling away skidding along the road, sending a spray of slush flying high before disappearing out of sight.

Vlado looked back to see the astonishment on the face of the young soldier he was staring at him in disbelief. It was then, at that very instant, and beyond all possible hope, Vlado felt Gilda's body stir. His heart jumped. An incredible feeling of excitement swept over him, bringing a rush of emotion so great, that he began to sob out of control.

"Dave" the soldier called to his unseen friend. "Quickly, come here, I think she's bloody right, I can't believe it mate, they are alive"

Then he bent down and picked Yola up. The soldier brushed the snow from the child's face she was still sleepy, she looked down at Vlado and gave him a weak, but definite smile.

Gilda's eyes were smiling up at Vlado. Warm tears ran down her face melting the snow. He bent forward and kissed her lips.

As they were lifted into the military ambulance Vlado felt his voice returning. He spoke to the male nurse. "That relief worker the girl that was here"

"Yes mate?"

"I want to thank her. I think she must be an Angel."

"Louisa Vinchenti" He laughed. "Some other time mate, knowing her and the way she drives, she'll be half way across the country by now."

Chapter 4

Selva Italian Dolomite's

A long black limousine wound up the icy road towards a sinister granite-walled estate. Snow laden pines lined the route like guardian soldiers their long branches swept the passing car, causing small explosions of snow to cascade across its roof in showers of glittering particles.

Finally it came to a standstill at the tall iron gates, the only entrance in the granite walls. Attached to the gates was the ominous sign "PROBITIO". The driver sat patiently smoking a cigarette, while in the back of the limousine Louisa Vinchenti wiped the window with her sleeve. She peered out at the stony-faced guard his ill-fitting woolen uniform gave him a comical clown like appearance.

She smiled to herself and curled deeper into the long coat wrapped around her slender body. Finally she felt clean for the first time in weeks now that she had left the war zone a few days earlier and returned to her London apartment. Her tour with I.M.C.O was over for the moment and now for the first time in weeks she was going to see her Mother. Her face was drawn as she watched the steam from the exhaust curl past the window rising into the cold afternoon air. After what seemed an eternity, the gates opened.

The car moved slowly along the inner road, allowing Louisa to catch glimpses of the old chateau through the stands of tall trees surrounding it. The great estate was a family heirloom. From her earliest memories the family had come from Rome to these mountains for their summer vacations. The Chateau had been an enchanting place for her and her sister Gina to play in and explore. Fantastic stories and Games were conjured up by their young imagination. Since Gina death her Mother had become mentally ill, or at least that was her stepfather's story. Now her feeling for the place was different, the sight of it just brought cold shivers to her body especially knowing her Mothers predicament.

She stared at the soldiers as the limousine passed by them some had dogs, all carried guns. God, she thought, how this place has changed!

The car came to rest at the granite steps leading up to the building. She paused for a moment to draw the coat tightly around her shoulders she pulled the collar up over her long dark hair to veil her face then stepped out into the cold air. She ran up the steps toward the huge Gothic door. The door swung open as if aided by an unseen hand. When she entered the great hallway she looked around the familiar surroundings with a feeling of bitterness. In her childhood this had been a happy place, now because of the miserable incarceration of her Mother it was nothing less than a prison. As she walked toward the center of the hall her high heels echoed on the hard marble surface reminding her of the stark cold of the Chateau. At the end of the hallway a magnificent staircase swept upwards, splitting at the top to form a gallery on either side. She saw a movement on one of the galleries. She strained, squinting to see into the shadows cast by the flickering candles of the enormous chandelier hanging high above her head. The figure withdrew further into the background. Good start, she thought, now I know I'm home, this place gives me the creeps.

Pushing any apprehension aside she walked quickly toward a doorway that she knew would offer a warm retreat. Without hesitation she pushed open the great door and entered the warmth of the dimly lit room. A fire was glowing in the hearth of a wide and ornate marble fireplace. An old man dressed in a green porter's uniform was bent on one knee carefully placing logs onto the fire. The logs, wet with snow, hissed and spat at him. He placed both hands on one thigh and pushed himself up, then turned toward her.

"A! Signorina Louisa, welcome to the ouse"

"Ciao Hubert" Her eyes smiled at the old man. Hubert's wrinkled face grinned back sheepishly.

"Hubert, please would you inform my father that I'm here"

"He already knows," he said with a shrug of the shoulders that spoke volumes."

Without another word he made his exit silently across the deep pile of the Persian carpet. She watched the glow of the fire flicker across his stooped form disappearing through the tall carved doors. She would have liked to question him about Mother, but she knew the old man was loyal to her father and wouldn't be helpful.

Drawn up beside the fire was an overstuffed armchair with inviting arms. Louisa collapsed into it. She snuggled down in her coat, kicked off her shoes, flung her head back and sighed as she closed her eyes.

Some while later the door opened causing her to wake from a dream in some confusion. Even before she could take in her surroundings the tall immaculately dressed figure of her stepfather walking towards her, brought her quickly back to reality.

"A, Lou, you're home"

There was no escape. She stood up and moved cautiously towards him.

"Come, my baby, come here"

She felt the clammy skin of his arms around her. His garlic breath revolted her. She pulled away.

"So where's Mother?"

She asked this as a defensive action as well as wanting to know.

"A! What kind greeting is that?" he said. He was angry his shrill voice rising. "Your mother, she's in her quarters"

"Why after all these years is she still locked away like a prisoner?" She could feel her own face reddening.

"My dear daughter" his voice now controlled and patronizing. "Your mother is not a prisoner. As very well you know she has her psychological problems the doctor, he wants that she rests, that's all."

"For ten years, that's a pretty long rest wouldn't you say Father?"

"I see, London, it's done nothing to improve your manners."

Louisa moved away from him, walking closer to the fire.

"May I see her then?"

"I'll have Carlo take you to her"

"I don't need your servant, thank you very much, I'll go by myself"

"No you won't, Carlo, he has the key to your mother's apartment."

Louisa fought to control herself. "Oh! I must be mistaken I thought you said she wasn't a prisoner"

"She's not it's for her own good and you had better keep your insolence to yourself."

She could not contain her hostility toward him any longer. "I'm not one of your religious soldier nuts! I'm supposed to be your daughter"

"In name only, so be careful my dear. Your little demonstration of temper it could be the beginning of the same sickness that has stricken your mother."

She knew him well, and knew there was an underlying threat implied by the statement.

He turned away saying, "I'll call Carlo" then walked to the side of the room and pulled on a long cord hanging from the high ceiling. Then he gave Louisa a long penetrating stare. She could see his satanic eyes suppressing his annoyance with her and felt them penetrating deep into her very soul.

A moment passed before the door opened, a man with a swarthy complexion and black curly hair entered. He was dressed in the same porter's outfit as Hubert he waited quietly while Louisa strode defiantly to the door.

"I'll expect you for dinner, Louisa," Don Vinchenti commanded as she left the room. She nodded in answer but didn't look back. Instead she followed the servant out of the room and along a series of corridors until they reached the end of the wing, there he unlocked a door that led up a stone spiral staircase. Good and bad memories of the old place came flooding back. She had trouble with them, but the wonderful anticipation of seeing her mother swept them aside. After climbing the stairs she followed him along a hallway lit by oil-lamps hanging on rough stone walls. She remembered from her childhood that these lamps were the only form of lighting in this older part of the chateau. Carlo stopped at a doorway. Taking a large key from his vest pocket, he opened the door and stood back.

When Louisa entered the room she found her mother sitting reading by the light of a single lamp. She felt relieved that her mother looked well, in spite of the fact she was a captive in her own house, her great beauty still radiated from her aging face.

"Louisa, is it you?"

The door closed behind them, and then with tears in her eyes she crossed the room and put her arms around her mother.

"How long has it been?" her mother asked, wiping away the tears from her drawn face.

"Too long Mummy. I've been calling and calling. Every time I called Father told me you were fine, but you didn't want to be disturbed. I knew it was rubbish, but he wouldn't let me come over from London. He put me off time and time again, telling me that he was too busy running the country to have me here. If he is so busy, why is he tucked away here and not in Rome? That's where the head of the state should be. Anyway, I eventually drove him mad. I called on the hour, every hour, day and night, until he answered my call and agreed to let me visit. I don't understand his problem he has never prevented me from seeing you before, what's the difference now? I wonder what's been going on it's strange that he didn't want me around?"

She paused. "Anyway enough of that how are you? God I've missed you."

Her mother had tears in her eyes. "My darling Louisa, it's so wonderful to see you. I'm so glad, just so glad you're here, I can't tell you." She wiped her tears away.

"Are you well, do you need to see a doctor Mummy? I've been so worried."

"No Darling. I'm fine."

"Are you really?"

"Absolutely, I'm fine honestly"

"It must be awful for you, stuck in here"

"It's not a problem, I promise you. Now tell me how's London? What are you doing there? Are you still helping in that relief organization?" she said, regaining her composure.

"Oh yes Mummy. I only came back from the Balkan's a week ago."

"The Balkan's my goodness! I didn't know you were actually there. I thought you worked in their offices in London."

"Don't worry, I love it. I don't know how but I seem to have a gift, I'm able to help people just by praying for them. It is wonderful"

"I'm sure you were born to do that, Lou. It's probably the reason you came back."

"Came back, Mummy, you mean reincarnated?"

"Yes darling that's right. Now do tell me how is that young man what's his name, Roberto?

"That's right Roberto, but I'm afraid we've split up. It's been some time now, in fact it was just after we split that that I decided to go out to the Balkans and help those poor souls."

"I didn't know your relationship had ended. What a shame."

"Not really Mummy, I don't believe that I loved him. He was just a good friend and probably always will be, but you know, that job of his was the final straw. He was spending more and more nights at the newspaper and I spent most evenings alone, plus he was continually questioning me about father. I often wondered about his motives, perhaps he was more interested in father than he was of me. Anyway, to cut a long story short, we parted, now I'm independent and I prefer it, I love my work"

"I'm sorry Lou, from what you told me, he seemed such a nice man."

"Yes he probably is. But it's for the best and its all water under the bridge now. Roberto certainly wasn't the soul-mate you promised I'd meet one day." She paused. "Do you remember when I was a little girl, you told me about soul-mates and reincarnation?"

"Yes darling of course, why?"

"I was wondering, how will I know my soul-mate?"

"Don't worry Louisa you'll know when you meet."

"Why is it so important to have a soul-mate?"

"If you remember, I told you we are here on Earth to learn how to live together, to become altruistic. Friendship and the intimacy of a relationship with a soul-mate is part of our learning experience."

"Is father your soul-mate?" She hesitated, "God I hope not"

"No." her Mother smiled. "No Louisa, he is definitely not my soul-mate"

"God, this is disgusting Mother leaving you in this apartment, it's no better than a prison and Father thinks he's the Son of God, like hell he is. Why he keeps you locked up here is beyond me there's nothing wrong with you, you're as sane as I am" Louisa looked into her mother's eyes there she could detect certain anguish.

"Louisa, I'm sorry I can't tell you why, but he's afraid to let me out of the Chateau. Actually it suits me, please believe me, when I tell you that my life is not wasted and I need this time of solitude.

I will explain one day when it is time, for now you must just trust me."

Louisa felt hurt by her mother's resistance to confide in her. She shook her head. "Mummy I don't understand"

"Darling, it would only make matters worse if you did. Don't worry, I'll be all right"

Louisa's eyes were now becoming accustomed to the dim light, so she took a moment to look around the room. There was a bookcase covering the whole of one wall. Against the other rough-cut granite walls there were large pieces of painted furniture, each one was covered in green and blue flowers. Exaggerated by shadows cast from the oil-lamp, they gave attractive warmth to the otherwise austere surroundings.

She shuddered at the thought of mother being confined to this prison. Time passed as they chatted, eventually there was a rapping on the door, Louisa walked over to it. A key turned in the lock from the outside and the door opened. Carlo was standing there, key in hand. It was the first time she had noticed how ugly he was. His pocked-marked face wore a permanent grin that almost divided his face in two.

"Signorina Vinchenti"

"Yes" she said, not amused by the unwanted intrusion.

The manservant was undeterred by her surliness. "It's seven o'clock the Master suggests dinner at eight"

"Yes, yes, I'll be there in good time" She pushed the door closed and walked back to her mother, she felt annoyed by the servant's attitude towards her.

"You must go Lou your father expects you"

"I have one more question Mummy"

"What's that my darling?"

"When we come back each life-time, are we always the same sex, or can we be either?"

"I believe you can be either, although it´s more usual to be the same sex each time"

44

"Oh, really" she said thoughtfully. Then she forced a smile, knowing that her mother was also putting on a brave face for her. They kissed and held each other for a moment.

"I'll be back in the morning Mummy." She looked at her watch. "God It feels like I've only been here a few minutes, never mind I can spend the day with you tomorrow"

She turned away and walked toward the door pushing her hands firmly down into her coat pockets while her eyes filled with tears.

Outside she came upon Carlo standing waiting in the shadows, a lecherous stare emanated from the sunken pools of his eyes, making her flesh creep. He walked ahead with his shoulders swaggering. She composed herself and wiped away the tears with the back of her hand before following him down the hallway. They passed antique oak furniture standing like great statues along the corridors, the light from the candles high on the walls flickered as they passed by. Between the furniture large oil paintings in deep gilded frames hung on the stone walls.

This brought memories flooding back, memories of her and her older sister playing together in the maze of corridors, stairways, attics and basements on their summer vacations. Now Gina was dead killed ten years ago in a skiing accident with her young husband. They had been on a guided mountain tour there had been an avalanche, and their bodies had never been found. The guide had escaped with his life, only to be killed the next day in a car accident.

When they reached her room, Carlo mumbled something about not being late for dinner. He was standing between her and the entrance to the room, as she squeezed past him she felt his hot breath against her neck. She pushed him away, giving him a

45

look of disdain for his trouble. She entered the dark room, closing the door behind her.

She walked across the room passing the two tall stained glass windows to find her cases had been unpacked and her clothes for the evening had been laid out on the bed. The remainder had been put neatly away in the large armoire standing majestically against the wall. The only other light came from an oil lamp placed on a chest next to the bed. It cast eerie shadows around the spacious room, leaving great pools of darkness in the furthest corners. Louisa shivered, she wasn't frightened of the dark but it was something else that bothered her.

#

After leaving Louisa at the door of her room, Carlo walked across the hallway to wait in the guest room opposite. He waited in the darkness for a few minutes, his mouth dry and his hands shaking in anticipation of seeing Louisa undressing. He could tell from the way she wore her clothes that her breasts were large and her body slim. The thought of seeing her naked brought an uncontrollable wave of excitement to him. Silently he stepped back across the hall to Louisa's door. Carefully he entered the room, so quietly that Louisa seemed quite unaware of his presence. While his hand gently pushed the door closed, he held his breath in case the door creaked behind him. He stopped in the darkness of the doorway, hidden except for the filtered moonlight streaming down from the tall windows which caught the high cheek bones of his face, giving him an almost skeleton-like appearance. He looked across the dark room to the warm glow of the oil-lamp casting long shadows onto the wall behind Louisa. She began to unbutton her dress, putting her hands behind her back and fumbling to undo an awkward bra catch. As her clothes fell quietly to the floor he was unable to stop himself and gasped out loud. He heard her whisper in the darkness "who's that?"

Just for a moment he thought she would turn he prayed the howling wind outside had mingled with his gasp.

"God this place is really getting to me" he caught her mutter. Then she appeared to relax again, and continued to slip off her pants. She was bathed in the glow from the oil-lamp that highlighted the round curves of her full breasts. Carlo trembled, trying to hold every muscle still. As she turned his eyes ran slowly down Louisa's back stopping at and soaking in the beautiful sight of her protruding buttocks. The muscles stood firm and strong like a young athlete's. Louisa reached down picking up her fallen clothes. Time seemed to stand still for Carlo as the sight of her almost hairless body bent over in the most provocative position hypnotized him. It was too much for him to take his body vibrated with passion. He reached behind him, his hand frantically searching for the handle of the door. He had to get out he had to leave. With beads of sweat running down the nape of his neck, he took a last look, then stepped out into the hallway and walked away toward the kitchen. The palms of his hands were wet as he clenched them together imagining what he would do if he ever got the chance.

#

Louisa stepped into the shower. The sensation of the hot water touching her skin brought back a flash from the past as she imagined Roberto's arms around her body, gently caressing her with scented soap. The memory of showering with him in her London home was still strong and even a little sad. She shampooed her hair, and meditated on the day's events. The feeling of hatred for her father brought out the deep-seated loathing from the childhood misery she had suffered. Now, because of the devastating predicament of her mother, she felt the emotion of malice rising in her, a sensation she disliked yet was unable to fight off. She had to do something to help mother? Out of the shower, she began to dress in the dim glow of the lamp. For a brief moment she caught herself thinking about Roberto. If only he were here, if only — no, hell no, we're finished. I must forget him.

Looking at her watch she quickly finished dressing, and at eight o'clock, not a moment before, she went down to dinner.

Chapter 5

Rome

Earlier that morning Don Vinchenti's sister Marina Lousioni had pressed her husband's pants and ironed his white starched shirt. Her Mario he must look his best for the meeting with her elder brother, Don Vinchenti, she thought.

Marina was pleased for her husband Mario he had worked hard for many years for the Don and now he was to get the recognition he deserved. She was happy.

Her thoughts went back to the time she and her brother were children and lived in the slums of Milano. As far back as she could remember he had been a cruel bully with no compassion. He had told her many times that his dispassionate attitude was only his way of survival but as time went on and as they grew up together she realized he was different to the other youths, there was something else about him, something sinister that she could not explain. He was unlike anyone else she knew he had an almost inhuman attitude, a total indifference to other people.

She remembered the excitement when the company built a factory in Uganda and Mario became the Don's trusted right hand man. Mario being the head of the facility had talked about the appalling experiments that had been carried out in their Ugandan facility. There they had developed a biological weapon for the president of Uganda, Idi Amin. The product was a virus that broke down the immune system. Amin's men used the virus injecting it into thousands of his political prisoners. The guards had sex with the infected inmates and the virus spread from Uganda across Africa and out of control. Marina was not surprised to learn that all of the scientists that had worked on the project had since died or disappeared under suspicious circumstances. Now only faithful Mario knew the truth.

Marina was indeed proud of Mario. This was to be his special day. He would be acknowledged for his service to the Don, rewarded for his work helping the Don in his rise to political fame. Mario had many contacts in the government, a necessary requirement in bringing the Don to power. Money had worked for some politicians, threats concerning premature family deaths had helped ease the consciences of the officials that could not be bribed.

Marina was sad for herself, but happy for Mario. She wished she could be with him on this day of all days. As it was, without her being mentioned in the communication from the Don, it would be inappropriate for her to go with him. She could however go to the airport to see him off, and this she would do.

Chapter 6

The War Chamber.

While Louisa was changing for dinner Don Vinchenti was about to meet with financiers and investment bankers.

The chamber was dark, full of drifting smoke rising from the cigarettes of three of the five occupants sitting around the long table. Between the shadows cast by the light hanging above the conference table the faces of the men showed signs of strain. Nervous fingers tapping on the polished table was the only sound in the hushed silence. The anticipated arrival of Don Vinchenti held the attention of the men seated around the table including the merchant banker Paul Johnson-Marsh from London.

Paul could sense the anticipation in the room, magnified by the presence of uniformed guards standing menacingly with their backs to the rock walls. He knew they were the hand-picked psychopathic body-guards that the Don called I'Bola, (the executioners). Paul was not surprised that the bankers were more than a little concerned about their meeting with Don Vinchenti. His reputation as a volatile psychotic had been growing after his rise to President of Italy.

Since the election there had been many rumors of the brutal path that he had taken to get there. Certain politicians who opposed him had been murdered. Others had conveniently disappeared. There was no proof of wrongdoing, nor any evidence that the Don had contrived these events, just rumors.

Recently there were more rumors circulating, new sinister stories surrounding him. It was said he worshipped the devil and there were tales of bestiality, pornography and other obscenities being performed at his parties at the chateau. Paul had known the Don for a long time. He had met the Don the first time many years ago. In the early days the bank Paul worked for had made loans to the many companies that the Don owned. Although Paul had not done business with the Don for many years he had continued to remain an acquaintance of the family. In the old days he would be invited to family functions held at the Chateau, the invitations stopped ten years ago, some-time before the Don entered politics. This time it was different he had been invited for banking business.

Paul knew the chamber was somewhere deep in the chateau, as they had been brought down in an elevator the journey had been smooth giving no clue to the depth of the cavernous room. The fact that it was carved out of rock and felt cold and damp gave Paul the impression that it was very deep. He looked around at the others, all sitting in silence in the semi-darkness waiting for the Don to arrive.

The door of the war chamber swung open and the dominating figure of Don Vinchenti entered. He was dressed in a dark blue suit. His black hair was swept back and plastered down with gel. Following closely behind him was a man-servant carrying a set of documents. By the way he was holding them they must be of immense importance, Paul thought.

The sight of the Don gave a feeling of the macabre adding to the increasing tension Paul felt building around him in the room. Paul joined the others, stood up as a sign of respect to the Don as he walked to the head of the table and took his seat.

Then quietly they all sat down and waited in silence. It was customary for the Don to sit with his hands held together and his head bent in prayer for a minute before speaking. This time was no different. As the anxiety built Paul looked at the ring of faces around the table waiting for the man to speak. There was a satanic sensation in the room, an almost tangible substance radiating in the half-light. In spite of the fact that they were all shortly to become joint financers, their faces had the eerie look of ghouls emitting certain malevolence for each other

Then, after what seemed an eternity to Paul the Don looked up and spoke.

"My dear friends" he said in his high-pitched voice.

"Thank you for joining me here today, as you know this is the last part of the financial package that will in the near future save the world from oppression and add a good return to your previous investments.

"I understand that your banks have each approved this final part of the joint loan which will enable our forces to defend the Holy land of Israel in the event of an attack by the Islamic States. An event, I might add, that I have prophesied many times" He stood up and took the papers from his man-servant. "Now, we will sign this historic document which will be the inauguration of the pact."

The Don reached for a pen and pulled the huge document toward him. Then with one sweeping gesture he signed it. The document was then passed around the table and each of the men except Paul signed it.

"You see Paul, unlike your bank these bankers they understand my concerns and are standing strong, err!" He shook his head up and down as if agreeing with himself. "Your bank, should have listened to me, it's a good thing I am doing, and they could have joined err! I gave them the chance didn't I err! err! What do you say Paul?"

Before Paul could answer the Don continued.

"Now, before we go to dinner, I will prove to you all how I, the Son of God, have been given his strength. I've arranged for Mario my brother-in-law, a member of my family, to be here today. He helped me in my rise to power and treated me like his own brother"

The Don motioned to a guard who walked to the door at the end of the room and opened it. All eyes watched as the man immaculately dressed, walked boldly in. A broad smile spread over his happy face as he greeted the Don. First they shook hands and then, almost standing on the tips of his toes, Mario reached up and kissed the Don on both cheeks.

"Mario, Mario, my dear brother-in-law, I have been waiting for you"

"Don Vinchenti" Mario said smiling.

Paul could see that he was happy, in the belief that he was about to have some kind of honor bestowed upon him. The Don stepped back his eyes darting back and forth between his audience and guest of honor.

"Mario, my friend, my dearest friend, you have taken care of my affairs well. You helped me to become the Head of State and now the President of the E.U, I am the most powerful politician in Europe. Now I'm shocked to find you have betrayed me. I understand you have been talking to a Canadian publisher about our affairs in Ugandan."

"But Don," Mario protested. "What you say, I don't understand, it's not what you think. It's not a problem they just whan'a write about you. You know what I mean, your life story. It's no problem."

"Mario, Mario. It is a problem it was an act of treason to bring our company's name into disrepute by associating us with Idi Amin and the terrible genocide of his people."

He paused. "Believe me Mario, I'm a generous man as I recognize your previous service to our country and to avoid the embarrassment of a trial, I am going to allow you the privilege of disappearing."

He turned to his audience sitting in stunned silence. "This act of self-sacrifice on my part will prove to you all that nothing can or will stand in the way of righteousness. I have been given the power from God to save the world and regardless of even family ties I will do the Lord's work."

With that, and before Mario could protest again, Don Vinchenti waved his hand toward the guard nearest to him.

Without a word the soldier pulled out a pistol from the holster in his belt and fired the weapon, there was a crack and smoke rose from the end of the barrel. There was a look of disbelief to Mario's face as he looked down at his crisp white shirt to see a red spot no larger than a small coin spreading and growing in size. He slumped to his knees. His eyes, full of tears began to rotate towards the top of his head. There was silence in the room, nobody moved.

The top of Don Vinchenti's forehead seemed to shine in the flickering light. A glow spread across his face. He looked pleased, as if he were applauding himself.

"You see my friends I have made this tribute to you. By taking the life of my own sister's beloved husband, I have demonstrated that I will stop at nothing in my total commitment to save the world. God bless his soul."

Paul sat in horror, as the initial shock of the brutal murder seemed to resonate in his head. Over and over again he relived the sound of the pistol retort ringing around the chamber and echoing against the empty walls. He looked down at Mario's blood-stained shirt and wondered what danger the world was in, with this maniac in such a powerful position.

Chapter 7

There were six dinner guests seated they all rose as Louisa entered the grand room. Servants in traditional Italian costume stood aside while she walked to the end of the table.

She passed a long carved oak serving-buffet at the side of the room where huge silver salvers waited on steaming warming pans. Bottles of red wine sat breathing in baskets between large stands of cascading fruit. Candles in magnificent silver candelabra lit the elegant room.

The guests stood politely while Louisa was seated at the opposite end to her father. Among the guests was General Bellino, she knew he was her father's pompous blustering foreign minister and right-hand man. He had become intolerable since his rise to power. Also she recognized the revolting Herr Weiner the wart-infested German arms manufacturer who was a long-term friend of her father's. The buttons on his pinstriped vest stretched to hold his inflated stomach in which just added to his ugliness.

Next to him sat another man she recognized from the media the former investment banker Bill Holcombe, his polished face showed a set of white teeth that repeatedly grinned at her, while his eyes constantly leered at her breasts. On Louisa's left was Paul Johnson-Marsh, the English banker and old family friend. He was a handsome man, with long blonde hair and a gently receding hair line. His impeccable dress sense reminded Louisa of his equally good manners. The other two men she did not recognize but from their dress they were obviously businessmen.

Of the six guests Paul was the only person she had met before. Although she didn't know the others she didn't really care for them and felt awkward in their presence.

After a few moments Don Vinchenti rose to his feet. His huge figure brought an immediate silence to the room. He lifted up a large glass of wine in a salute. His piercing voice echoed around the room.

"My colleagues, I would like to toast to the future of our new world and in memory of our dear departed brother. May his soul rest in peace?"

His face ran red in perspiration while the white of his eyes fiery red in color darted back and forth between his dinner guests. They all raised their glasses, and each in their own language joined him in the toast. He swallowed the huge glass of wine down in one long gulp and then banged the table with his fist for a refill.

"Bon appetito"

A servant filled it then quickly backed away. Don Vinchenti sat down, glass in hand. Louisa had no idea what the toast was about, but felt a certain anxiety. The mix of people around the table gave her an unpleasant feeling of apprehension. Why were they here at all she wondered?

Don Vinchenti held the conversation, hardly allowing anyone else to say more than a word or two. After dinner they retired to the drawing room Paul came and sat down next to her.

"Louisa, how are you young lady? It's been such a long time I'm sorry, I hardly had a chance to chat to you over dinner."

"I'm fine, thank you Paul. You're right, it's been some time and in fact I was just thinking about that. The last time we met must have been at one of Mummy's fund raising parties."

She considered this for a moment then said "In fact I think that was the last one she held it must have been ten years ago. I remember now, it was the week before my twenty-fifth. God, how quickly time passes."

"You don't look a day older." He smiled, then, not waiting for a comment, he went on, "I can see your father's in fine spirit. He's very powerful now, and very confident."

Louisa gave him a long look and then said, "He should be but you know Paul, greed has brought him to power, other people's greed. All the hangers-on, the politicians, the church leaders, they all believe he will bring them the same power."

She fidgeted, a little unsure of the ground she was treading and regretted her outburst. She didn't really know Pau,l only that he was an old family friend and she had no idea what Paul's business relationship with her father was, but what she did see was a certain kindness in his eyes.

"I take it you don't approve of your father's position,"

He said in a lowered voice.

"Why are these people here Paul? In fact, why are you here?" She said instead of answering his question. Her sudden change of subject apparently threw him. He laughed and stuttered in confusion.

"My, my, young lady, you really do know how to throw a leading question at someone." Then he just stared at her in amusement.

She smiled at him with an inquiring look, finally saying, "Well, you didn't answer my question."

"Oh just banking business."

"Right," she said, with a slight inflection of anger in her voice.

"No, no, I assure you" His lack of conviction and that he was hiding more was obvious.

"Paul, I can sense something is up. These people shouldn't be in the same room together, let alone eating and drinking with my father."

"I can't talk about it Louisa, even if I wanted to and you shouldn't worry about it either. As I said, it's just a mix of business and politics. What about yourself Louisa, tell me why you have such an obvious resentment towards your father."

"It doesn't matter," she said, angry at his question. She was wary she didn't want to confide in him, if she said anything about Father and it got back to him, well, her flesh crawled at the thought of the consequences. Paul's hand reached across and gently touched hers. She looked into his pale blue eyes and saw compassion.

"Where's your mother?" he asked, practically whispering the words. She was shocked by his perception, how could he know, what did he know, was he just guessing. The fact Mother was not at dinner could have inspired the question, she thought.

"Oh, she's fine. She didn't want to join us this evening. She isn't feeling well, just a headache."

"No, that wasn't the question. I said where is she? It's been a very long time since anyone has seen her."

"She hasn't been well, that's all. Just like you with your politics Paul, I don't want to talk about my personal life"

She had cut him short, and was slightly angry with herself. Nevertheless she had no intention of furthering the conversation. So she removed her hand from his, stood up, and with a departing smile said, "I'll see you later Paul"

She needed air and time to think. She wanted to confide in someone, and would have liked to confide in Paul, but didn't dare. She felt confused she hardly knew him yet something told her he was a good person.

She walked unnoticed through the crowded room past dinner guests who had been joined by many other people. Some of the women she knew were the politician's wives others were the so-called political aides. The men were drinking obscene portions of cognac, and smoking large smelly cigars.

Leaving the smoke-filled room she walked through one of the tall glass doors out into the cold of the night. The stars were so bright that their reflected light gave a blue hue to the magnificent snow covered lawn stretching in a series of terraces down to the frozen lake below.

She had been standing outside for a short time when, without warning, she felt hands placing a garment around her chilled shoulders. Of course, it was Paul he had taken off his satin-lined jacket, and slid its encompassing warmth around her.

Acknowledging his kindness she murmured, "Thank you." She looked at his handsome profile set against the night sky. He didn't speak he just stood quietly gazing into the blackness across the lake to the distant ominous mountains of the Val Gardena.

The stage was set she knew instinctively he would try again, try to reach out to her. It was like standing next to a ticking clock — each second went by as if on elastic, waiting for him to speak, waiting for time to spring back as if no time had passed at all.

She began to wonder, what is time? What does it mean to Mother, locked up, a virtual prisoner? Is time only relevant to your own personal situation? If I were a prisoner, would time slow down—almost stop? What if I was a newspaper editor like Roberto, stressed, making deadlines, does he race against a mechanical measurement such as the distance traveled by the hands of a clock. Or is time imperceptible where by the editor perception of an hour seems to be just five minutes and for the prisoner, five minutes takes an hour. Are the prisoner's seconds, minutes and hours of anxiety infinitely longer than those of an editor are? If so does the prisoner live a longer life than the editor does? What of Mother's time what of her life? It must be abominable, locked away day after day, minutes ticking by slower than other people's hours.

She tried to shake the nagging anguish. At last Paul spoke, breaking the silence.

"I understand you have been helping in the new Balkans conflict."

"Really," she was shocked and surprised how on earth did he know that she wondered? Certainly she hadn't told anyone other than mother.

"It's very commendable." He said.

"It's nothing, considering what those poor souls are going through again. I hate governments, yours, mine, in fact all of them. They don't care about people, they only care about their own self-indulgence. They only care about taxes that support their life style. They care about their friendly arms manufacturers who pay big taxes. They care about the bankers who take obscene bonuses from their failing banks, which are then bailed out with tax payer's money. Then they loan back the money to the government by investing in the government debt in the form of gilt—edged securities and live off the interest. Something wrong with that picture Paul?" she said with obvious sarcasm.

She stopped for a moment knowing she was insulting him as it was the business he was in, but then on reflection she didn't really care.

"The establishment doesn't care a damn about us Paul, we're just fodder in the big picture." She added.

"I guess you and your father don't actually see eye to eye on politics then" Paul laughed.

"That's a pretty good guess," she said then turned away and looked across the valley.

"I know you're troubled about your mother Louisa, I would like to help. I'm sure I can."

"I don't know what you mean"

"I think you do"

"Please drop it Paul," she said without turning her gaze from the distant mountains. It's no good, she thought, there is no way I can confide in him yet she felt he wouldn't be put off. He continued.

"I'll be in London as of Monday. Here's a telephone number. If you change your mind, just call me"

He looked at her with conviction, then said, "Louisa trust me, I really can help. You know, some people are not what they appear to be at first glance. Don't be deceived by the cover of the book, often it's quite different inside" He smiled and pushed a crumpled piece of paper into her hand.

"Please, keep this to yourself"

His tone had an urgency that surprised her. Then she said, "OK, and who knows, maybe I will call you"

He took her hand, gently lifted it, and then kissed the back of it. Without another word he was gone, walking away into the night, leaving his jacket still warm around her shoulders. She looked at the crumpled paper in her hand and attempted to read it in the dark. It was too difficult so she walked over to the window and held it up to the light and saw he had written a telephone number on the scrap of paper. She walked back into the room and handed the jacket to a servant, "Please give this to Mr. Johnson-Marsh with my compliments"

As she took a last look around the room she noticed her father staring at her. His gaze sent a cold shiver through her body. She turned and left the room.

Chapter 8

London England

Paul Johnson-Marsh stared out of the office window into the drab street below, wondering if the continuous downpour would ever cease. He watched the red London buses splash through great puddles of rainwater as they passed by the moving sea of intrepid office workers returning from their lunch-time break, armed against the elements with black umbrellas, each battling through wind and rain toward the shelter of their warm office. Clouds shrouded the tops of the adjacent office buildings. Nelson's statue high on its column disappeared into the swirling mist. Paul turned from the window to look into the questioning eyes of Charles J. Conrad, his boss. The man's in-depth knowledge of world affairs was said to be unsurpassed. His military background with the intelligence service and his specialty, the study of international terrorism, had given him the necessary qualifications for the position. Now he was Paul's superior and the head of the I.T.T.F. or International Terrorist Task Force.

"Well old chap, do you really think she'll call?" The minister asked. Paul walked toward the man's desk. He knew the round chubby exterior and seemingly mild manner of Charles gave no clue to the calculating mind that dwelt behind those jovial blue eyes.

"Actually, Charles, she seemed quite desperate for help, but she was uncertain whether or not to trust me. I think I left her with a feeling of confidence. We shall see"

"So we shall. Tell me, what else happened in Italy?" He waved his hand beckoning him to sit. Paul eased himself into the comfortable leather armchair crossed his legs and begun his debrief from his meeting with Don Vinchenti.

65

"You read my report I take it, so are you referring to the cold-blooded murder of his brother-in-law, and our informer?" He went on. "The man's quite insane of course. The gall of the man, to have him killed right in front of us.

Mario had been with the Bicemco Corp a long time and knew too much, from what I understand the Don found out that he had boasted to the media about their connection with Idi Amin: I am not sure he knew of our connection with Mario, but maybe he did, maybe it was more about us than it was about the media" Whatever it was outrageous and of course he knew jolly well the people at the meeting would do nothing"

"Of course, go on" Charles said dismissively.

"Well the Don signed to receive the closing payment of what seemed a large investment the bankers have with him. As you know some time ago he wanted to borrow money from the I.M. F he'd asked me to help set up the deal through our merchant bank. He even had the nerve to suggest our bank might like to take a position behind the I.M.F for say, an extra two billion. I told him that I couldn't make a commitment like that without a Bank of England license being obtained, and that could take some time. He wasn't very happy, but it kept us in the loop"

"That's good Paul but I suspect he has all the money he needs now, enough to fund the war"

"A war Charles, what war, do you really believe that is the reason for their investment"

"Yes Paul, undoubtedly"

"I never got a chance to look at the papers they signed nor did any of them talk about it afterwards."

"Not to worry dear boy"

"I also think from his body language he wasn't too happy with me being at the signing, I think he felt it was a mistake."

"I am sure your right and yes, we are sure Vinchenti backers intend to instigate a major war, we don't know when, but it is a good bet from our intelligence reports that he is going to stage an attack on Israel and soon.

As he is currently doing his six month stint as the President of the EU it makes him the foremost player in European politics. We also believe he is a member of the Wed group and that is where the real money is coming from"

"Wed Charles, yes I am not surprised"

Charles looked thoughtful before continuing. "You know, I believe the plan is to make the world believe the attack was initiated by the Arabs possibly Iran. Of course then Israel will blast Iran and all hell will be let loose, and Paul it gets worse, today Vinchenti takes over as the commissioner of the ESDP which will give him command of the European Rapid Reaction Force therefore he can legitimately send in the troops without consultation or a mandate from Brussels. This means with a possible million and a half troops at his disposal he can take over the oil states before anyone can stop him. When I say him, I really mean his bosses in the Wed group."

"My God"

"Exactly dear boy"

"Mind you Charles, I doubt if our public will be too thrilled about us getting into anything after the last cockup with the Bush, Blair, Iraq thing."

"Absolutely, then there was Afghanistan, what was that all about you may ask." He stopped for a moment, toying with the rose.

"Yes I know what you are going to say Paul, it was about Al-Qaeda, wrong. It was about oil, which by the way didn't happen and the fact that the drug supply from there had all but dried up is probably another reason. Before we invaded in two thousand and one, the Taliban had held power since ninety six and they had almost completely stopped opium poppies being grown. As you know taking drugs is against their religion and yes I know they are involved in the drug trade now but it is not surprising as it is a way of making money to buy arms, to rid their country of us"

He paused, waiting for a comment but none came so he carried on talking. "Now it looks Paul as if we may get involved in this new Balkan mess." Charles looked intently at Paul for a minute before continuing. "I am sure the Wed group do not give a damn what the public think"

"Ok"

"So you see Paul after the continuing uprisings throughout the Middle East, each country is in turmoil with no hope of a resolution. So they want the Arabs removed wiped off the map, then they can control the oil. This will not be a war, rather annihilation."

"So what you are saying is, what I witnessed was actually an investment in a takeover of the Middle East by the Wed group, good Grief"

"Well the next problem is this, if anybody is going to invade the Middle East and end up owning the oil then I am sure Russia and China will want a stake in the claim. As you can imagine that is the ultimate danger"

"God if they get wind of this Charles" Paul said

Paul had seen this coming. Since a child he had a feeling that there would be a third world war in his life-time. Now it was just around the corner and there was no way of stopping it. "So where does Germany fit in" Paul said returning from his thoughts.

"Arms dear boy, she will be making the arms."

"What a mess Charles"

"Yes. And it gets worse"

"You're going to say India and Pakistan," Paul said realizing they were natural enemies and armed to the teeth with nuclear weapons.

"Exactly"

There was a long silence as the two men sat reflecting on their conversation. Charles lit a cigar. "Anyway, we must keep you on the inside with him. Can you keep in there with the banking business?"

Paul nodded as he watched the smoke curling up toward the high ceiling wondering what was coming next. Now he felt something stirring in the back of his mind. A kind of awareness had come over him. It was as if someone was telling him of his mission on earth.

Charles was speaking. "I believe this to be the most" He paused. "Paul, are you paying attention dear boy? Did you hear what I said?" Charles looked annoyed. Paul pulled back from his thoughts.

"I'm sorry Charles"

"I repeat, I believe this to be absolutely the most dangerous situation we have been in since world war two and it could become totally out of control, if we don't act now."

Paul intervened. "What about the States?"

For the first time ever, Paul saw that Charles was troubled. A sign of stress veiled the Minister's face.

Paul was puzzled. "Is there a question that the United States may not stand with us?" Paul asked with some surprise in his voice.

Charles toyed for a moment with the red rose secured in the button hole of his suit jacket. "No, no, of course they will, but I believe if, or should I say when, war breaks out, after the initial blow they will have their own internal troubles at home, as indeed we may."

He looked down and twisted the rose between his fingers then went on. "After the first strike I think the U.S will probably confine themselves to their own shores for self—preservation and they do have their own oil of course. As you mentioned, ever since the so-called liberation wars which started with the Gulf war mainly for the benefit of Kuwait and then the following fiascoes, I think they lost so many troops I doubt if their voting public will stand for another disaster.

Their inner cities are bursting at the seams with crime and racial hate, it will be just the excuse the radical religious extremists have been waiting for. The country may well explode into anarchy. With their citizens armed to the teeth, it will be chaos. So they will almost certainly keep a large part of the army at home."

He stared at Paul waiting for a response but none came. Paul was looking out of the window again trying to remember when it was that he'd had this conversation before, it was as if he was reliving the whole event or at least a premonition...

He was far from surprised after all the UK also had its own massive racial problems brought on by high immigration and made worse by the European Union treaties and directives. Demonstrations were a daily event and revolution was just a breath away. It had been obvious from the start to Paul that integration on such a vast scale with such economic and cultural differences would not work. He knew that the EU process had been an exercise in expansionism for the avaricious capitalists administered by their own unelected officials who were easily influenced to make polices to benefit the privileged class.

Paul had seen unrest building in the country as the arrogant government even now would not listen to the voice of the people. It seemed to the British public that Germany along with France was virtually running the country from Brussels.

He turned back towards Charles.

"Paul dear boy, please pay attention to what I am saying, which is, unless we can find out the time and date they intend to attack, we will have no way of stopping this happening, if indeed we can" Charles said as he shifted his plump body nervously around his chair before going on.

"Even if we can gain the information and the timing of the master plan and are able to release our anti-missiles from our sub´s in time. It won't be perfect but it might cut Israel's damage

70

down to maybe fifty percent or so. Even then I doubt if it will stop the war from escalating throughout the world."

"Charles, I have a question."

"Go ahead."

"Why not simply kill the Don?"

"My dear boy, what a terrible thought." He smiled. "Actually if it would achieve anything of course we would, but it may not stop the Wed group from their plan to wipe out the Islamic States, with Vinchenti we have a chance of gaining the intelligence we need, anyway it's not that easy we tried to take out Gaddafi and only messed up his house. We've also had a couple of earlier attempts at Saddam Hussein without any success. We found out Slobodan Milosevic was hiding in a certain building in Belgrade, the Americans bombed it, but again no luck, Arafat the same story, although eventually someone did get to him in Paris"

"I see"

"It's just not that easy. Bellino is ready to step into Vinchenti's place in an instant and then where do we stop. Vinchenti is well aware of the danger of assassination and there is a chain of other prospective candidates who would eagerly take his place for Wed if anything happened to him. No dear boy, unfortunately that's not the solution."

They sat silently looking at one another, neither speaking, both men contemplating the horror and magnitude of the forthcoming events. Paul stood up and crossed the room, returning to look out of the window. He gazed out in a dream-like state, staring at the perpetual rain falling into the street below. He looked past the dark, wet, miserable day, and imagined the way life should be. He visualized crowded beaches with happy people and children playing in the surf of crashing waves. The sea covered with small boats their billowing sails caressed by the wind, floating across white capped seas. Parks, fairgrounds, theater's and zoos all filled with laughing crowds. All of this pictured through the gray cloud.

Then, like a changing nightmare he saw the reality, the hideous black metal of the war machines marching into a whirlpool of madness. He could hear the clanking of armor rumbling across Europe again, heading to the last war. Finally there would be the roar of the rockets taking off from the bowels of the earth, excreted from the countries of death. He knew their aim would not be limited to just enemies, but would encompass all the capital cities throughout the world, even neutral countries would not be spared. Warheads would be targeted to cut into the center of commerce leaving the rural areas to the mercy of conventional war machines. With the cities gone, the nuclear rain clouds would continue spreading their dreadful radiation until nothing moved, life had ceased.

Somehow Paul had known there would be something different about this war. He hadn't known what, or even how he knew but now is was becoming obvious.

Finally he turned away regained his composure and walked back to his seat. He crossed his legs, leaned back in the great winged armchair, and threw out a question to Charles.

"Do you think we can really do anything to help, Charles?"

"Don Vinchenti's daughter is the key to this Paul. If she can get us into his chateau in Italy, then maybe just maybe, we will have a chance. Our intelligence department has located a vault containing a safe where we believe his plans are kept. We need to get into it, and soon so we are going to send a small team in, it will consist of an American, a Canadian minder and someone who can open the damn vault. We have agreed to have an American agent on the team, otherwise they would go it alone and God knows what a mess that might be. The agent they are sending is a certain Colonel Matt Stone. I believe you met him some time ago, behind the wall wasn't it?"

"Yes, that's right. I did. Good man actually Charles, fights like the devil"

"So, dear boy, I need you to convince Vinchenti's daughter to get us into the chateau on the pretense of helping her mother to escape." He stopped for a moment. The silence was most discomforting for Paul, suddenly, almost by intuition, he knew what his superior was about to say.

Charles looked him squarely in the eye and said, "I think you can also provide us with the best man in the country to open that safe, what do you think Paul?"

Paul nodded in agreement. He was embarrassed, his superior would obviously know about Paul's relative, or more precisely, his brother-in-law.

"I'll see what I can do Charles" he muttered almost under his breath. Although it shouldn't have bothered him, this left him with a slight feeling of nakedness. Strange he thought, Charles had never mentioned it before even though a few years earlier one of their operators doing staff background check had given his department certain information about his wife's brother.

"OK, good" Charles seemed satisfied, and had the good manners not to dwell on the subject. "Then the most important thing will be to get them in and out of the chateau without being detected. If Don Vinchenti knows we know, he will change his time and date and bring it forward."

Paul sat quietly thinking about the paradox. His duty to his country would seem, on the face of it, to come first but he knew for sure that nothing could be done to stop what had already started, and that his first loyalty was elsewhere. Rather than help his country, he must somehow delay the war. He didn't know where the thought came from, or why he must, only that it was essential. He knew what he had to do, just as if a voice had spoken to him.

"Charles" he said quietly, "I think Louisa will help. Her mother has been locked away in the chateau for a long time, but I think to convince her that we intend to rescue her mother and nothing more may be difficult, she's no fool."

Charles stared at Paul before speaking. He fidgeted in his seat, and then said, "You know of course we can't rescue the mother, that would tip our hand to Vinchenti, so you will need to keep the girl quiet once she has got them in"

Paul's eyes narrowed. "Keep her quiet?" Paul said. Then he paused for a moment before going on. His voice took a sudden turn. "Don't worry Charles I will deal with it when the time comes"

Charles leaned forward in his chair. His round face gave no evidence of emotion. "No no, I don't think you understand, once the others are in the chateau they will need to silence the daughter for us."

"What"

"In such a way, that nobody suspects foul play"

"Silence her Charles?"

Charles twisted the rose between his fingers, while his eyes turned cold, so cold that Paul shivered.

"There is no other choice, dear boy" He paused. "By the way, did you tell her you work for us?"

"Good Lord no! I only gave her my home number but I do think it would be as well for her to come here to Whitehall. I think meeting you will give her the confidence she needs. I haven't told her that I'm an agent but I can tell her that I have connections with a government department who normally arrange the escapes of hostages"

"If you think it'll work, that's fine by me. We don't have time to wait until she calls you, so why don't you call her as soon as she arrives in London."

Charles stood up closing the folder signifying that the meeting was over.

With a departing nod Paul left his superior and walked down the hall to his own office.

There he called the police at Heathrow and asked them to inform him on Louisa Vinchenti´s arrival. Next he telephoned Jill.

74

He suggested inviting her brother Peter Boisey-Smith to lunch on Sunday.

Chapter 9

With the turbine engines humming gently in the background, Matt had drained the last of the cognac from the glass and gently slipped into total oblivion. He sank into a swirling tunnel, bathed in waves of white light, then into a deep sleep.

After a while he could feel the plane bouncing around in turbulence. He began to wake, gradually his eyes opened and for a moment he thought he was still dreaming. Instead of seeing the back of the seat in front of him, he saw the entire cabin of the airliner had changed. It now appeared that he was traveling in an uncomfortably small and bumpy horse drawn carriage. Shivering with a strange chill, he pulled the cloak around him. Cloak, a cloak he was confused and then he looked down at the strange clothes he was wearing. He clutched the hard seat, gripping it in subconscious reassurance. Frantically he looked out of the grubby window, no night sky and no aircraft wing, just a cobbled-stone street and by the architecture of the houses, possibly early ninetieth century London. He heard the snort of a horse, then the call of the driver as he pulled at the reins.

"Whoa boy"

What the hell was happening, was this a dream? Surely he was dreaming. Totally bewildered he bit his lip, and then dug his nails into the skin of his arm until the pain told him categorically it was not a dream.

The carriage came to a stop he heard the driver call down from his perch outside. "Doctor Wiener's residence, sir"

Matt gripped the brass handle and swung the little door open. He climbed unsteadily out into the street, but before he could speak to the driver the carriage moved off, its wheels bumping and clanking on the cobblestones as it disappeared into the early evening mist.

Matt stood still for a moment dazed trying to take in his new surroundings. The dark cloak he wore fitted well, he looked down at the light colored pants and well-kept boots. The clothes were of fine quality. They were probably made to measure by a gentleman's tailor, he thought. He reached up and touched what seemed to be a tall hat balanced on his head, what the hell has happened he asked himself, desperately trying to make sense of the situation? Had somebody slipped him a drug on the plane? Who could possibly have known of his travel arrangements other than the General, the President and of course Oldfield, he would have had the opportunity to read the instructions before handing them over? Even the back room staff would have no idea of his movements as they created documents in such a way that only the designer of the plan General Ichner would know the pieces of puzzle, but Oldfield also knew he had changed his route. Oldfield he mused.

That aside, where on Earth was he? That was the most important question right now. Had they drugged him on the plane, was this just an illusion? No, it felt too real to be a drug induced dream. His mind whirled with questions. Everything was so real, just like stepping back two hundred years. The chilling cold wind driving through the thick cloak assured him of the reality of the situation.

He touched his face it felt normal except for a soft beard, strange I must have been unconscious a long time he thought. He looked down at his hands in absolute horror blue veins were protruding through paper-thin skin like roots of an old tree. They were hands of an old man. Once again his mind twisted in agony as it searched for a reasonable explanation. The street was quiet, only distant cry of a cat disturbed the approaching dusk.

He turned and looked towards the dark house where the carriage had delivered him. There was an oil lamp hanging by the door, under it on the brick work was a worn brass nameplate, it read Dr. Wiener but gave no indication of the Doctor's occupation, doctor of what he wondered?

He found that his bones were unusually stiff as he climbed the worn steps. He lifted the iron knocker. Its loud thump echoed along the desolate street.

While he stood waiting patiently for the door to open, he realized he was being watched by a passing tramp. The man, wrapped in dirty rags, was pushing a wooden hand-cart past the grand house. The cart's creaking wheels broke the eerie silence as it laboured under the weight of the man's worldly belongings. The street cat screamed again in the darkness. Then as the large door ground open, he turned to see an old woman at the door. To his surprise she said, "Do come in Mr. Farthingale, the Doctor is expecting you." Her voice was soft and kind, and had a familiar ring to it, although Matt couldn't think why. He was fascinated how on earth did this woman know him? He racked his brains for an answer as he followed her in. Her acute arthritis became obvious as she lead him down a darkened hallway with the oak floor echoing their footsteps. They passed a tall grandfather clock whose ticking was the only other sound breaking the silence of the quiet house. She stopped at the last door, pushed it open, and stood back with an unspoken gesture for him to enter. The room was warm and comfortable, lit by an oil-lamp and enhanced by a coal fire.

Bent over a large desk was the figure of an old man. The door closed behind him. He was feeling quite weak and slumped down into the nearest chair. Matt Farthingale the benefactor of London's poor, found his memory flooding back.

"I have been waiting for you Matt," the Doctor said without looking up.

Suddenly he remembered where he was, he had been coming to this same house in Hampstead for many years, sometimes for consultation, but more often than not to spend an evening playing chess.

"My God John, I just had a nasty turn" Matt heard himself saying.

The doctor came from behind the desk, eyeing his guest inquisitively.

"The most dreadful thing happened as I arrived here. I found myself standing outside not knowing either where I was, or indeed, who I am" He still felt distressed, and he knew it showed in his voice.

The eyes of the grey-haired man looked over the wire framed glasses perched on the end of his nose. He crossed the room and placed a caring hand on Matts shoulder.

"My dear friend, why don't you come over to the couch, lie down, and tell me exactly what happened"

Matt got up slowly, walked over to an old leather couch and eased himself onto it. He rested his head back until he was looking up at the sculptured plaster ceiling.

"Now Matt, tell me what occurred"

"I was travelling here in the carriage when it seems that I woke from a dream and it took forever to remember who, or where I was. It wasn't until I saw you that I could gather my thoughts, if indeed I really have"

"Really have, what do you mean exactly?"

"Well John, it was as if I was in another time period, somewhere in the future, someplace, where they have these remarkable flying machines," His old voice faltered. "John, I was there. It was so real, not like a dream at all, honestly"

"My dear friend, I believe you please don't worry just relax, stay calm and I'll be able to help you" He rested his hand gently on Matts forehead.

"I think Matt it's time for you to learn more about yourself. I've been waiting for this moment for a long, long time"

The fire flickered in the quiet room. Matt watched the shadows dancing across the ceiling.

"The fact is I have been waiting all these years for a sign"

"What sign, what on earth do you mean John? What you talking about?"

The Doctor held Matt´s gnarled hand and leaned forward, speaking almost in a whisper.

"Matt, your time to pass on has come" The Doctor's long gray hair fell across his forehead as he spoke. His kind voice now more gentle than ever.

"My God John what do you mean? I'm going to die?"

"Yes, of course we all die or, more correctly, I should say pass on"

"But John, the last time you examined me, you said I was in fair condition for my age"

"Undo your shirt Matt I would like to listen to your heart"

"But" Matt head rose from the couch.

"Just keep still for a moment Matt" The doctor proceeded with his examination then stood up and turned away from the couch. "Your body is holding back your spirit, your soul is ready to leave and you have to let it go. As I said, it's time for you to pass on, and to learn the truth about yourself. The next week in the life you are leading in the future is going to be very important. You must be armed with the right information to make the correct decisions"

"This is ridiculous John. Have you lost your mind? What the hell are you talking about?"

He stretched his neck to glare at the doctor's amused face. Gently he pushed Matt's head back onto the couch. Then, taking the oil lamp from the table, he held it just a short distance from Matt's eyes.

"I'm talking about your spirit. I don't know if you can remember, but I hypnotized you once before. Actually it was twenty years ago to be precise, but I was wrong, it wasn't the right time then, but it is now"

Matt tried to get up.

"Stay there, I'm going to hypnotize you. I will endeavor to take you back in time, to your first life here. The regression experience will only last a short while, plus it will take you to some other quite interesting place. The time has come for you to learn why we are all here, and more importantly, why you are here."

Again Matt tried to rise in protest.

"Just relax my friend, and all will be revealed" The gentle voice rang like music as the clouds enveloped him. He seemed to drift for a while, bathed in soft light, listening to the doctor's tranquil voice trailing off somewhere into the distance.

Chapter 10

A grey mist formed, which was difficult to see through, then slowly it cleared and he found himself standing alone on the edge of a desolate cliff with the wind howling, biting into his rugged face. His eyes searched the barren snow-covered wastes stretching out before him. In the far distance a deep red sun hung low, silhouetting the craggy mountains. The animal he had been tracking had left a trail of blood in the new snow. He knew the stake had found its mark so the animal could not be far away. Looking down at the bloody tracks left by his prey, he brushed some of the frozen snow from the crude skin boots covering the dark hair of his legs. Then he pulled at the skin covering his shoulders, bringing it tighter around him. He scratched his ice-covered beard which was mixed with sweat and melting snow and pushed aside the long matted hair that fell across his rugged face.

He stood still, sniffing into the wind, trying to smell the direction of his prey, and then he spotted it lying just ahead.

Just as he moved towards the animal he felt a strange presence, the nearness of another being. It was too late when he heard a movement from behind. There was a crack as the blow to his skull vibrated throughout his whole body. He felt his very life blood draining down his veins, screaming through every artery like scores of ants running wild. The blow sent him reeling, crashing forward, face down into the snow. He laid still not a movement, not daring to breath. Through squinted eyes he watched the pool of blood from his wound grow larger, changing the color of the surrounding snow. He dare not move, he knew his attacker was standing over him, ready to strike the final blow if he gave any sign of life.

His chance would come, and it did. There was a roar, and with it followed the beast Matt had been tracking. The saber-toothed tiger tore at his attacker's arm, ripping at the bone until blood gushed from the gaping wound. The man screamed. Matt rolled over and over, then leapt up and with one tremendous blow buried his stone axe into the head of the preoccupied tiger. The animal shook for a moment and then slumped to its forelegs. Matt swung the axe again this time blood cascaded across the snow in a crimson spray. The beast struggled, trying to stand once more, before finally falling to the ground, dead.

Matt ignored the man lying in agony bleeding to death from his hideous wound. Even though his moaning was almost as loud as the tiger's earlier robust charge Matt had no compassion for him. He took a sharp piece of rock concealed inside the fur he wore, crouched on his haunches and proceeded to hack away at the meat of the beast. Feasting on the flesh and with the hot blood running from his lips, he turned from time to time to glance at the dying man. Finally, taking large chunks of the meat, he wrapped them into a crude bundle made from the fur of the slain animal.

This moment reminded him of his father's cave, and the day his father was killed by a hunter. There was always the danger that another hunter would kill a man, just as easily as he would an animal. He himself had killed many times, for no reason other than the basic fear of the unknown. If he got close to another hunter without showing aggression it would be taken for a sign of weakness, so to kill was the safest way.

He had taken his mate from her father after killing him in a violent contest at the entrance of his foe's cave. Afterwards, he had gone inside to rummage for food, there he found her sobbing in a corner. When he grabbed her she had snarled as she fought like a wild beast biting and scratching him. He managed to sling her under one arm. She was small and light, so he carried her screaming and kicking out of the cave into the daylight. There he

84

held her out in front of him to appraise his prize. Satisfied, he put her back under his arm. Amid her furious struggle for freedom he laboured back through the snow to his own cave. Since that time his affection for the defiant girl had grown, and he knew that she had also formed a secret respect for her hunter.

Now, without another glance at the dying man, Matt began the long climb up the face of the snow-covered hill, dragging behind him the bundle of meat tied to his waist by a woven grass thong. He stopped from time to time to rest, sitting down in the cold snow while mist from his sweating face mingled with the cold evening air. He looked down the steep climb to see if anybody had followed him. The red sun was setting, throwing long shadows across the desolate wastelands. He shivered and stood up feeling stiff from sitting too long after the strenuous climb.

Just before he reached the cave he could smell the familiar stench from the debris of rotting food, old bones and drying skins that surrounded his habitat.

As he approached the girl came running from the cave to greet him. Her long flowing hair although unkempt added to her obvious physical beauty, revealed by the loose animal skin partially covering the darkness of her sensual body. Her deep brown eyes flashed at him as she pulled at the fur containing the meat. He grunted an acknowledgment at her excitement for the arrival of the fresh food. Inside the cave he threw the bundle to the floor and squatted down beside the dying embers of a fire that gave a warm glow to the stone walls. The girl threw some snow-covered branches onto it, soon to be followed by the meat. The wood hissed and crackled from the dripping fat. After eating his fill, his weary eyes closed to the welcome sound of the hissing fire.

It seemed that he had only just dropped off when a piercing scream echoed throughout the cave. In an instant Matt was up. He looked towards the entrance of the cave, the girl lay at the feet of a hunter. The giant attacker roared and growled in defiance, staring at Matt, his eyes were ablaze with hostility. Matt looked frantically around for his weapon but too late he watched transfixed as the giant hurled a pole at him. He felt an explosion, then nothing, just a warm glow a feeling of content, he knew he was dying. A white mist with a bright light swirled around him — then all was still.

#   #   #

When he woke, he found himself sitting on a beach with a young girl she was incredibly beautiful. He looked at her for a while before realizing it was the same girl who had been with him in the cave. Although she looked similar she somehow appeared different, although she had the same flashing eyes that constantly bubbled with laughter, she was more relaxed calm and radiant. She lay next to him resting on her elbows on the pink sand and staring into his eyes. He studied her as the warm breeze blew strands of dark hair gently across her exquisitely sculptured face. He gazed at her body, her skin was smooth and hairless, tanned to the color of light copper. Turning his eyes away, he looked out across the beach where the pink sand melted into the shimmering silver sea. People were swimming, playing and laughing, shrieking with delight. He fell asleep. Later he woke and looked up at the two suns, noticing that they had now moved closer together. Instinctively he knew they were traveling around each other and that by mid-day they would appear to be one. He was home.

Matt looked back to his soul-mate and smiled there was no need for words. With their energies moulding together, they analyzed their recent experiences and lessons on Earth. Afterwards they played on the beach laughing and in absolute bliss for the love of each other. Finally tired, they closed down their minds and slept again.

Matt felt the light on his face and then slowly he opened his eyes. The girl had gone, no sea, no sand, the glare came from the flame of the old oil lamp held close to his face by the Doctor. He was back in the dark room with the Doctor calling his name. The only other sound in the silent house was the grandfather clock ticking outside in the hallway. Matt knew he was back to reality. Or was he? Which state is reality he wondered?

"John, am I going mad, what is going on?"

"No, not at all, what did you think of your first life on Earth, were you surprised at yourself? I mean, being so violent"

"That was my first life on Earth then. No I don't think the violence shocked me, but not knowing who I am and where I am has. Which reality John is the present?"

The Doctor just smiled as Matt climbed off the couch and walked over to the fire-place trying to pull himself together. There was a knock at the door and the housekeeper entered carrying a tray. The Doctor handed him a cup of tea. "There, that should make you feel better"

They sat down facing each other in soft armchairs pulled up beside the glowing fire. The old man's wrinkled features, highlighted by the flickering fire, showed his amusement.

"John, I don't understand" Matt frustration showed in his voice. "I only experienced the final few hours of my life. I don't even know how old I was when I was killed by the most monstrous Neolithic man."

The Doctor laughed with amusement. "You were thirty five years old. That was quite an age in that era."

"Good grief, I would have thought I was a lot older than that, but how do you know all this?" He left the question unanswered and went on. "Anyway, something even stranger happened after that" Matt stood up and walked over to the table where some cakes had been placed.

"Alice made those today," the Doctor said. "Please help yourself they're very good. So, what was so strange?"

"John, I must tell you. I went to a very odd place after my death. It was peculiar I found myself sitting on this strange, yet familiar beach. I was with someone I knew well, I mean, very well" He trailed the sentence off as the Doctor interrupted.

"Come come, don't tell me you didn't recognize your best friend, your soul-mate."

"Soul mate John?"

Matt wondered again if this was all a dream. He could still remember the airliner so vividly, in fact he could remember his military life and his present mission to London in the future. He looked at the Doctor and considered whether or not he could be a little mad, or was it he that was losing it. Yet the experience of being regressed seemed to be incredibly real. Maybe his first thought that he was drugged had been correct all along but if that was the case, then how could he reason it out? He knew that a person drugged would have little or no reasoning powers.

The Doctor turned to study the fire. After a moment, he looked up at Matt who sat with his head back in the chair waiting patiently.

"Each time we die, we return home for a rest. It gives us time to reflect, time to make amends and prepare ourselves for another life. It's then that you would normally choose your next life, what you want to be, and with whom."

Matt looked puzzled "home?"

The Doctor ignored the remark and went on. "If we progress in a lifetime then we move up to another level until we finally graduate."

Matt's curiosity was aroused. "Progress, graduate, what do you mean?"

The Doctor took iron tongs from the coal scuttle and carefully placed knobs of coal one by one onto the fire. Matt watched the smoke until the blue and green gases began to roar from the coals like miniature volcanoes.

The Doctor's voice became a whisper, as if his words might be overheard by the walls. "Our home planet Matt is not here, this is not our Universe, what you see is not the reality you believe it is, to put it simply here we are in a four dimension Universe, run by a computer program that we call the Game.

The computer program is running in a special building in the main University of our home planet in our multi-dimensional or should I say our six dimensional Universe. The designer or creator of the program plus his team, are called Game-masters. As there are no other planets in our own Universe, just the one, they created this Universe for many reasons, not the least being a place to learn from the experience of life, but also to be able to enjoy exploring this Universe that they created.

So they generated a huge amount of energy to create what is known as the big bang. It produced a miniature Universe inside the building which is connected to powerful computers. As each of us is a singular atom of intelligent energy we are able to enter the program, which sends us into this Game Universe and this planet. Everything you see here and in previous lives is made from, or formed from, particles of matter know as atoms, which are the building blocks of this computer-generated Universe. This planet, the Earth, is one of the University planets and being here is the most important part of our education"

"Computers John what are computers?"

"That's too difficult to explain Matt. When we are here we use these bodies as a vehicle. Now as I said each one of us is just a single intelligent atom of energy which means our very nature dictates narcissism. The whole reason for the necessity to live out these lives on a University planet is that instead of us being separate egotistical entities, we will learn to be selfless. That is the reason every so-called sin is in fact an inherent egotistical act of pure self-indulgence"

"Oh, now I understand. So when Jesus said 'Love thy neighbor as thyself,' he didn't mean the modern concept of learn to love yourself first, in order to love someone else. That was already a given. He meant exactly what he said"

"Absolutely right"

"OK. But I'm still confused John, am I to take it that I have returned to a previous body, or life, whatever, in this world or Game as you call it?"

"Yes, well, no, no not exactly. Not returned this is the present but in our past, you and I are also at this moment in a future life, and there is a need to be reminded of these events as your memory of this life was erased in the period of rest we have between death and life"

"How is it possible to be in two places at the same time?"

"In a quantum environment an atom can be in two places at once. Our soul, or the atom of intelligence that runs the complex collection of atoms of our body, can also be in two places at the same time"

"Quantum environment, what on earth is that?"

"When you go back to the future you'll understand it is not important now"

"You mean after I die in this life?"

"Yes"

"Interesting"

"You say you remember the future?" The Doctor inquired.

"I can remember the dream I was having in the carriage if that's what you mean. It was very vivid you know."

"That wasn't a dream Matt. You were there, if fact you are there and you will be going back, very soon."

"I don't like the sound of that."

The Doctor smiled, poking the fire with a casualness of a man about to make a statement of great magnitude.

"As I said, you and I are leading parallel lives at the moment Matt. You and I are both here and in the future at the same time.

In every life we assume different roles, but by and large we stay with the same friends or if you like the same team. We are always trying to overcome our failings, failings which are caused by the great burden of egotism we carry. By becoming altruistic we can move up a level each reincarnation and have more. More can be material wealth, or it may be love from others, respect from our peers for earthly achievements, a gift of one of the arts, or some high social achievement, until we finally graduate, but so often we tend to slip back destroying all the progress we have made.

"And the beach?"

"It's our home Matt. It's where we live, the beach it is on our home planet in the Home Universe."

Matt shook his head in wonderment. "I'm lost John"

For a moment, he considered once again the possibility that his friend could be quite mad. Then he dismissed it, realizing that if anyone was losing it, it was himself.

"John, tell me, what's next? If this is all true, how do you know about it, you've never spoken about this before, why not?"

"You'll have to trust me on this one Matt. I have always known where we really come from. I was born with the knowledge. I have never mentioned it to you before today because it wasn't the right time. Now it is."

"Are you telling me then, that I have some important part to play in a future life? He looked across at his friend's tired face and waited patiently for a reply.

"Well, my dear old friend, where shall I start?" the Doctor muttered aloud. First of all, my level of awareness is of an extremely high category. It allows me to remember all of my past lives and to have some knowledge of the future." He stopped and looked carefully at Matt, waiting for some sign of understanding.

"My mission now is to prepare you for your return home. You are to be given the awareness and the understanding of the situation at a higher level. So I am going to hypnotize you again, this time I will send you forward, to experience the day of your death in the next life you lived after this one. It was after all the most distressing of all your many deaths, after that you will return home and to learn about the next directive for this planet in the Game."

"I don't understand. If I am to return to the home Universe, why don't I just wait until I die in this life, or are you saying I need to die now?"

John never answered the question, he just reached forward and threw the last of the remaining coals onto the fire.

"The future `you' needs you to be informed now. So it was necessary for you to come back and relive this event, and then move on to be told of your mission."

Matt stood up. He still felt a little bewildered, but what the hell, maybe John was a little mad after all, he would pacify him and go along with it anyway. He stretched and smiled at his friend before saying. "Then John, let's get on with it, I'm beginning to feel nervous."

He walked over to the couch and lay back on it. He felt a certain amount of excitement for what was about to happen. He had certainly been fascinated by the previous experience, and he always had a weakness for the unknown.

Once again the Doctor held the oil lamp in front of Matt's eyes, swinging it gently to and fro until Matt could feel himself slipping into an abyss of comfort. That's strange, he thought, I felt my heart stop.

Chapter 11

The morning sunlight filtered through the small bathroom window spot-lighting a single wooden peg on the back of the door. Hanging from the peg was a jet black leather gun-belt with two blued steel guns seated comfortably in their worn holsters.

Matt shook his head. What on earth was I thinking? Some old fellow hypnotizing me in a past life I must have been daydreaming. My God this is not the time to be doing that.

He sat forward on the edge of the toilet seat and looked through a wide scratch in the brown latticework of the painted glass window. He peered down into the street below it was deserted not a movement, no horses, no people. He looked across the street to the window of the store opposite. It was full of spectators, their chalk white faces anxiously waiting. He could see children with their noses pressed hard against the glass their eyes darting up and down the street in anticipation. Matt knew very well why they were there, they were all waiting for the macabre, their gruesome interest in death, his death, it turned his stomach. Hearing a voice call through the door he stood up.

"Matt! You all right, you've been in there a while, they'll be waiting for you." The woman's concern showed in her voice, yet it grated in his ears. He felt annoyed with her, knowing what he was about to face — and why. Yet blaming her for his predicament was wrong, his own weakness had got him into this mess. Reluctantly, he pulled up his pants and buckled on the gun-belt.

"I'm coming Lou, I'm coming, they'll wait." He opened the door to see the back of a dark-haired girl holding a shotgun. She didn't turn from her vigilance of the hallway that she defended.

Matt put his arm around her slim waist and brushed her ear with his lips. "Thanks Lou, I can manage now"

"Matt, you're not going out alone!"

"I have to, if I go out with you and with the whole town looking on, it'll just crush her. I've already done enough damage."

"If you go out alone, they'll kill you" She held the gun with determination, trying to push by.

"Forget it Lou, this problem is mine, I don't want to hurt Mary any more than I already have."

He pulled away, swung around the stair post, looked back at her for a moment, smiled and then without another word descended the staircase of the saloon. His boots echoed on the wooden floor as he crossed the empty bar-room. Then in one movement he swung open the half door and stepped into the bright sunlight.

Hot dust clouds swept along the deserted street. The warm breeze blew against his unshaven face, he pulled his hat down to shade his eyes from the midday sun. Then he looked across to the sidewalk and saw his wife standing in the shadows holding his young son while their daughter was trying to pull away from her toward him. She held the girl's wrist to restrain her.

They stared at each other even now their love flowed across the bare street, tears ran down her cheeks but she didn't move towards him.

He remembered the fateful day he had met Louisa, one of the prostitutes working in the new Bella Union Saloon. It had led into a sexual digression, a depravity that had cost him his wife, his children, his home and soon to be, his life. He had thrown it all away and was now about to pay the price of self-indulgence.

Further down the street two men began to walk towards him. He wiped the dust from his eyes and carefully studied them. He could feel their nervousness and almost smell the fear secreting from their pores. There was no fear in him, just remorse, for this was one battle he could not afford to win.

94

As a gunfighter he was good, very good, some said the best. When he met Mary he retired to the town of Deadwood in the black hills of South Dakota, took the marshal's badge and lived happily until that fateful day he met Louisa. The drunken orgy that followed lasted six weeks. Everything he owned he had lost through drinking and gambling. His own selfishness had let him slip back into his old ways. He had stayed shacked up with Louisa and had not been home in that time.

Again he glanced across at Mary, his wife, then back at the men closing in on him. He loosened the leather thongs on his guns. If he killed these men, one her brother, the other her sister's only son, she would be devastated. They had called him out. In vain she had pleaded with them, but the family shamed, her honor defiled there could be no retreat.

Neither big Baxter her brother, or John Mathews, the young nephew, would be any match for him in a gunfight, but winning would only deepen her wounds. He knew his life was in ruins. There was no option, he must die!

He eyed the drab buildings on either side of the empty street not a movement. The wind blew the dust towards him. A door creaked then slammed shut, but Matt kept his attention directly on the men ahead.

Tears of remorse slowly rolled down his dusty face. When the first of the bullets entered his body he felt them thud into place, but felt no pain. He faked an attempt to fire at his attackers. He dropped to his knees, he didn't look at his wife again it was too painful. He fell forward onto his face then with a mighty effort, tried to rise. Again he heard shots, again he felt nothing as their bullets pounded into him. He rolled over to face the sky. Mary ran screaming towards him. She fell to the ground next to him, cradling him in her arms, she cried out. "Matt you fool, you damn fool! I love you, why didn't you fight? I would have forgiven you, my God, you were forced into it."

His eyes filled with tears as he gazed into hers. Now too late the realization of his great mistake tore the last shreds of his ego into despair.

Her face streamed with tears as she clutched him even closer. He took his last look at her soft gentle features shaded by the bonnet she was wearing. She looked up at the sky, "Oh God, bring him back. I forgive him, oh God! I do — I do."

Lying on his back, he gazed at the sun through a mixture of blood and tears. He cried in self-pity at his own mistakes, knowing he had wasted a life . . . his life . . . and now it was too late.

He looked up past the ghouls staring down at his bloody wreck. His lifeless eyes stared through the ring of moronic faces surrounding the sun. It became brighter and brighter, spinning until its light finally wrapped warmth that was all encompassing. Now he stared back down at his bloody body lying in the dusty street, watched by the gathering crowd. It was then he knew he was going home.

The relief from leaving his body was like a great weight being lifted. The most wonderful euphoric feeling engulfed him. An incredible feeling of well-being and happiness surrounded him, he wanted to laugh he was so happy. Slowly he felt himself float away from the scene in the street into a swirling white cloud, a spinning corkscrew in the shape of a tunnel. Moving fast through the tunnel, he felt no fear, just a magnetism of love drawing him on. The speed he was traveling at seemed to increase, until the white light turned into psychedelic colors flashing by at high speed. Reaching out he tried to touch the sides, but there was no sensation. He could hear singing surrounding him the perfect sound of a choir of children singing soprano in Latin. Their high-pitched voices were pure, as if echoing around the walls of a mighty Cathedral.

Chapter 12

As quickly as his journey had started, it was over. He looked around and realized that was back at the home Planet in his old University and now seated at a round table in one of the Game rooms. In front of him was a computer screen with a numerical keypad. There were five other screens set around the table. In the middle of the table was a large transparent globe inside was a cloud which had the appearance of a small explosion in suspension. He looked around the room, which was full of colorful plants growing up toward a glass roof high above. Rays from two suns sent shafts of warm light down from the high windows. Flowers of all types blossomed around him, filling the room with an incredible bouquet of aromas. Somewhere he could hear the bubbling music of a waterfall.

The last thing he could remember was being in the street where he had left Mary crying, now he was at a Life-Transporter or Game-board as it was commonly termed by the students.

In one of the other seats a white mist began to form in an array of glittering atoms until finally becoming a large ghost-like body. It was Baxter. He looked across at his friend as he stabilized, a strong stocky man, with broad shoulders and a barrel chest, wearing a trimmed beard on a round jovial face. Matt reflected on how strange it was that the human material body they were given to use on a planet was so similar to their true celestial form. Sometimes they would become a little heavier, slimmer, stronger, weaker, but the body and facial features remained relatively the same as their actual form which radiated from that singular atom of intelligence that they really were.

Baxter and he had spent many lives together, often as twins, mainly as fighting men. In Roman times they were gladiators, in the middle-ages they had lived as warriors in many fields of battle. In the eighteenth century they fought as seamen under Nelson.

The lifetime in the Wild West had been somewhat unusual, as they had not been fighting together. Quite the opposite, it had been a life experience that both he and Baxter had requested from the Game-Master. They needed the credits, and so had philosophized that being friends was too easy, learning admiration for an enemy would be more difficult, but of course, as it turned out he now realized he had actually messed up and probably lost credits, rather than gained them.

"I can see you've recovered from your bullet wounds, old boy," Baxter's gravel voice boomed out.

"Well, how did you know that? How did you know that I'd just regressed back to that time? You canny old devil, what you doing here."

"No idea, while I was materializing, I read the screen and looked at everybody's recent history. Seeing as how I am back here too soon, I thought I'd find out why."

"And did you find any information?"

"Not a damn thing. The last thing I remember was flipping through an article on the evolution of man in the National Geographic with fantastic pictures painted by the artist Carroll Jones, when suddenly I found myself here. I guess I must have dozed off, and you Matt, how come you're here."

"I was on my way to London. I fell asleep and woke up in an earlier life. To cut a long story short I was regressed back to a couple of my lives, the one I really messed up in was, as you know, the old west. That experience has left me feeling incredibly stupid? Why do we sometimes foul-up?

"Because, as you say, sometimes we are incredibly stupid, for us to graduate we need practical experience in the Game. Given total freedom with no, or should I say little knowledge of our real alien home, we're bound to screw up."

"Unless I have the strength to conquer my self-indulgence, I'll never make it."

"That's right, it isn't easy though, not with so many distractions on a planet, but the objective is to learn to live life without egotism."

"I have often wondered why they call it a Game Bax, it's hardly that."

"I agree, I suppose someone thought this system is similar to a kid's computer Game." He smiled.

"I think it is anything but a Game Bax, especially as some of the interesting situations that the Game-Masters put us in can be rather disagreeable."

"Yes, like being sent to the planet Earth. " Baxter said.

"Exactly" Matt agreed.

"Why couldn't we have been sent to one of the better University planets in the Game, where people are actually nice to each other, rather than the Earth where most of the players are violent, avaricious and just down right evil? It's like living in a lunatic asylum.

There must be a reason why there is so much suffering on that planet, far more than you would think by chance, what with incessant wars, not to mention the continuous ongoing genocide. Which I might add has been committed by every nation over the planets evolution."

"Bax, my dear friend, apparently the Earth is now considered a sort of prison planet."

"What." He looked at Matt with surprise. "That's a bit extreme."

"I just read it on the screen" Matt pointing at the computer in front of him he went on.

"It's where all the players from the past and the present, who haven't made it, or should I say haven't graduated, have now been reincarnated too."

"Great what does that say about us?"

"Not a lot, no I´m joking, apparently our little group is almost ready to graduate but we are still there in the Game for a much different reason.

"How do you know all this?" Bax asked.

"I just read it on the screen, look," Matt, pointed to his screen again. "Talking of the last minute I wonder what happened to the others, they went into the Game at the same time as us. Normally they arrive back at the same time or at least within a second or two, as one year in the Game is just a tenth of a second here."

"That's normal, but this is different I don´t think we are actually back, just a temporary visit."

"Well Bax, I am going to have a wander around while we're waiting, I'd like to see what's interesting in the laboratories, what do you think?"

"Ok, but I´ll wait here and see if anyone turns up," Bax said as he sat back down.

Matt walked over to the doorway, it slid silently open. He stepped out into bright sunlight and walked without a sound along a path set between rows of flowers and overhanging trees. Small exotic birds flew in amongst the branches.

Walking towards the great buildings of the University he looked up at the tall glass spires sparkling like a giant fireworks in the hot sunlight. It was this building Matt knew housed the main laboratories.

Entering the grand entrance hall he stopped to look up at the spires made of rock-crystal taken from local mines which formed part of the structure extending up hundreds of feet. The light from the crystal roof bathed the whole area in rays of pure blue-white light.

Then he headed across the great hall toward the experimental rooms and old lecture rooms. He walked along the corridor passing by the laboratories where he knew the masters created new animals, plants and other life forms to be used on new planets in the Game. The Masters would pass on to the students the skills needed for creating new solar systems and planets from the gases of space. Eventually as the newly formed planets evolved they would be used for the habitation of the new life forms created by the Masters.

As he turned a corner he almost walked into the translucent body of their old professor and great mentor.

"Professor"

"Gracious me, if it's not young Matt." The professor's ghost like face held a broad smile, his transparent white flowing hair gave him an air of flamboyance. The professor was one of the top intellectuals in the Home University and Matt felt fortunate to have studied under him.

Matt knew him to be a brilliant philosopher. He had played many parts on Earth: Socrates, Leonardo Da Vinci, and more recently, Gandhi.

"I'm just off for a rest in the baths. Would you join me? I'd be interested to learn how you're getting on out there in the field. I hear good things about you"

"I´d love to" Matt said with a smile.

They started walking towards the baths.

"I certainly messed up on Earth, in the eighteen hundreds, the old west, you know?" Matt said, still unhappy about the consequence of his life there.

"Yes, that was a shame Matt, I knew about that unfortunate dip in your advancement, I've been keeping an eye on you. Don't worry," he said and smiled, "all students slip back from time to time, but I understand you made good progress in your last two lives"

"I believe so Professor," Matt said, remembering his recent experiences in the USA.

They walked through the doorway of another great glass like structure. This building held a maze of botanical gardens under the great glass domes. They talked as they walked along the paths of floral bushes until they finally arrived at the baths.

Built in the style used in the Roman era, the huge hall had marble pillars holding up a glass roof deep green in colour which held back the heat of the two suns. Warm springs cascaded through a portal in the wall at one end. Plants, with budding rainbow flowers, hung from moss-covered rocks that edged the sides of the baths.

They stepped into the light green water and sank into it, resting their energy together, spending time chatting as they swam casually round. Matt needed some answers "Sir, May I ask you a question or two?"

"Of course you may Matt"

"I believe we are all given an instinctive knowledge of our true celestial spirit when we are in the Game, is that right?

"Yes, that's right, but you have to acknowledge it, not put it aside as many do when it isn't convenient to one's narcissistic life-style."

"If you don´t?

"You know the rules zero progress will mean eventually being destroyed by the Game-Masters."

"After we graduate and go back into the Game is it necessary to go through the natural birth method or can we create a solid body by attracting atoms in such dense formation that the material body is formed."

"Yes Matt you can materialize, and according to your level, you can choose the age you want to be on your return. We don't use the transfer of life into a fetus using the natural birth method as it is not perfect. It is only used before graduation to experience the total process from being a child onwards"

"I see"

"Matt," the professor said leaning forward, his energy fusing with him. "Before you go, tell me, do you know why you're back here from the Game?"

Matt looked into the professor's eyes. He saw love pouring from the depths of his soul. The old sage had the kindest features he had ever known.

"I think it must be a temporary visit, but no, I guess I don't."

They began to step out of the baths leaving behind the warm and encompassing energy of the water.

"You will very soon," the Professor offered as a remark.

"I guess I had better get back to the Game room then?" Matt said now a little concerned by the remark.

"I wish you well Matt" They stared into each other's eyes. Something of the gravity of the situation swept over Matt and for whatever reason he felt a great compassion and a sadness he couldn't explain. The professor offered his hand as a way to close the conversation.

"It has been a pleasure professor. I hope it won't be long before we meet again."

"I'm sure it won't be," the professor said, smiling with a knowing look. "I'm going to be there in the Game myself very soon."

"Oh really?"

"When it's time I'll walk-in, so to speak, and share a body with someone already on Earth."

"Will it be with somebody I know Professor?"

"Yes."

"Oh?"

"You'll know soon enough," he said as he walked away giving Matt a final wave.

Matt left and headed towards the main building where the Game room was situated. On his way back to the Game room he decided to take a quick peek at the fleet. It was his ultimate goal to graduate and fly with the fleet. Matt knew he wasn't ready to graduate yet although he dearly wanted to. He wanted to enlist in the fleet, to join his peers back in the Game Universe, aboard one of the Intergalactic Light-Ships, traveling and exploring the vast wilderness of space, assisting in the creation of new planets and keeping the peace among the different evolving species.

He took the glass elevator up to the top of the building and stepped out onto the great balcony. In front of him as far as the eye could see were a series of long runways spread out across the desert. He looked across to the huge hangers that contained the latest models of the great Light-Ships all waiting to be transferred into the Game Universe.

Glass tubes connecting the massive hangers carried passengers back and forth between the various buildings. Matt watched fascinated by the technology. Inside the tubes were small transport shuttles in the shape of glass balls. Two passenger seats were situated on either side of the gyro inside of the ball. As each shuttle reached its destination it hit the last one in the row of standing shuttles. Kinetic energy flowed between them sending the forward shuttle off onto its journey. Matt had traveled in them himself and knew the passengers felt no significant movement by the connection.

He took one last look at the scene, then went back to wait for the elevator to return. There were other sightseers waiting to go down, Matt spoke to the one that looked like a tour guide.

"Hi! Are you lot on a tour of the University?" he said.

"Yes, we are" answered the short squat entity that Matt had addressed. "It's these folks first day of the grand tour of the whole facility. Do you remember your tour?"

"It's been a long time" Matt smiled.

"I think you must be from one of the batches before my time?"

"I'm sure you're right, I've been around some time." Matt said smiling at the other. He was curious. "Who are these students anyway? Why are they still in the elementary stage of education?"

"They're new arrivals," the guide said.

"I understood the Game-Masters only created a finite number of souls?"

"Oh no, not quite, he did, but he then found it necessary to create more souls, after so many had to be destroyed. At least that's what I understand?"

"I see," Matt said.

The guide fussed with the elevator button. "I can't believe how long it's taking. Anyway he takes benign atoms, program's them with intellect and consciousness, this gives birth to new souls or, if you like, intelligent atoms like us." The elevator arrived and the group stepped into it.

"That´s the same way we were created." Matt said.

"Yes, of course, except now with each new batch he endeavor's to produce souls with humility. Between you and me, while he allows free will, I don't think he'll ever achieve It.," said the little guide smiling up at Matt.

Matt grinned back in response.

"Nice talking to you," the guide said as they arrived back at ground level. "Good talking to you too." Matt said stepping out of the elevator. He walked back through the hall toward the Game-room.

Chapter 13

Entering the Game room Matt took a seat next to Baxter.

"What's going on Bax?"

"Not a lot so far, but look"

A white mist-like substance was forming in the seat next to him. After a few seconds he recognized the beautiful face of Louisa, slowly her whole body materialized in a sparkling array of atoms. She smiled at him. He was excited to see her but instantly recalled his death in the street.

"It's great to see you Lou." Matt said reaching out and touching her.

"I've just had a regressive experience into the life we led in the old west. It was very distressing leaving Mary crying in the street. I'm so sorry I did that." He paused. "I really did mess up in that life."

He felt her touch his energy as she said, "Don't worry my darling, I know Mary forgave you. I spoke to her when I was here after that life. She has graduated you know?"

"Oh thank God, I'm really pleased for her. Seeing her distressed was awful, it's strange how you never really realize how much you are hurting someone until it's too late."

Matt felt Louisa's energy touching him again. It felt good. They watched together as another entity began to form across the table filling one of the other seats. This time the cloud seemed to pulsate with energy but nothing appeared.

"I think the energy field of the transporter is getting weaker," Matt said.

There was a glittering and sparking in the mist and a strong voice said, "You're absolutely right mate I was stuck somewhere in between. What the hell are we doing back here?"

It was Boisey, one of the traveling companions he had not seen for a very long time. His tough voice was coming from the mist, slowly his translucent body shape materialized. As usual he was smiling.

Then before he had a chance to question him Paul's form appeared out of a similar mist. He looked a little taken back.

"What happened? I don't think I died the last thing I remember was going to bed. So why are we here? Does anyone know? Paul asked.

"I believe we're here to be given some kind of instructions, but I don't know much more than that," Matt answered.

"But I do." The voice came from a mist forming in the last empty seat. It was John, his soft features seemed to be ageless, almost ethereal. Now Matt realized that all of the six team members were present.

John looked round at the others and smiled at each one in turn, then said, "We've been brought here by the Game-Masters to receive instructions from them. Matt was nearly killed on a trip to England by an adversary he is currently lying asleep aboard an airliner. He had to be taken back to a past death through a regression exercise before he was able to return here. The rest of us came the same way of mind dream transportation only our subconscious is here. We are in fact all dreaming this in our sleep on Earth. The first thing is congratulations are in order for, Matt, Paul, Louisa and Baxter. You are all to move up to the next level of awareness, the last step before graduation." He paused to read his screen.

"After we go back to Earth, you will believe this was a dream until we meet, then you will remember this meeting and become totally aware you're in the Game."

Louisa interrupted. "That's something I don't understand John. Why is it that we aren't allowed to know who we really are when we are in the Game on a University planet? I mean after all wouldn't make life a lot simpler if we knew why we're there, when we're there."

"That my dear is obvious, if we knew the truth about our celestial heritage, we'd cheat. There'd be no point to the exercise, we'd never learn or truly progress. Our life would be false, it would be like playing cards with friends knowing the other persons hand. Just a waste of time, like being good because you know teacher is watching, it would hinder our progress. If you are not acting your true self, then your education is a lie." John said.

"Of course, when we go into the Game and are born on a University planet we have a good cryptic knowledge of our real species, which of course most people tend to ignore. After all by accepting the real reason that we are there, and who we are, inhibits self-indulgence, so we push it aside." Boisey added

John's fingers began to type into his keypad while the others watched. After a few attempts he sat back. "I don't know why I can't get in. It must be that the channels are overloaded, no it's coming up on the screen now."

"Dear pupils your team has been selected to help in the next cleansing of the University planet, Earth. Your mission is to make certain that the evil force that has infected some of the players on the planet is destroyed. Secondly and more importantly you must delay the beginning of the cleansing event in order to give the Light-Ships time to arrive there from their current location in the Galaxy Andromeda. The ships will be needed to transport from the planet all the players which are to be saved that have not graduated yet, but have improved sufficiently so they can be returned to the planet after the cleansing. Therefore they will need their human body to remain intact.

There are also many thousands of graduates who have chosen to be reincarnated into the Game to help others through the process. Although it seems there are a great many players who are not interested in being helped, even so the graduates will try to support them right up to the last minute.

For those of you that haven't graduated yet you will hold the temporary position of first grade guide. The upgrade will enable you to be aware that you are in the Universe we created and on a University planet in the Game. The precise instructions of your mission will be given by John your team leader. If you have any questions, with your new grade, John is permitted to answer them for you."

The screen went blank.

"A cleansing" Matt said.

"You do know what that means?" John said.

"Yes of course, it's when they eliminate all of the unsatisfactory students at a particular University planet."

"That's right. It's the time when they destroy some of the student players who have never reached beyond their base level. They are the ones who haven't been able to cope with free will, therefore have not surpassed their own egotism, therefore have failed."

"So the Earth is to be cleansed again. That'll be the second time." Boisey remarked.

"I'm afraid so" John agreed.

"What about Pompeii and Herculaneum?" Matt inquired.

"No, neither does it include Babylon, I heard you were there and how you were lucky to escape from that catastrophe. No they were separate cases this is different, this will be a total cleansing as in the time of Atlanta when only Noah's group was saved."

"Will everybody left on the planet be destroyed? Louisa piped in.

"Yes Lou, as the screen said, everyone that has improved will be removed from the planet by the Light-Ships before the cleansing starts."

"What will happen after the cleansing John?"

"Afterwards, they will be returned intact, and some of us will also go back to pick up the pieces, clean up the mess and get things started again"

Matt stood thoughtfully for a moment. Then looking at the John in an inquiring manner he asked. "John tell me how is it possible to destroy the bad Players. I mean, are we not all just an atom of energy and energy can't be destroyed, can it?"

"No, not exactly destroyed. But we can alter its state" he paused "If for instance a great number of atoms are split at the same time, as in the case of many atomic weapons being detonated in a nuclear war, it will cause a chain reaction instantaneously around the planet which will not only burn all the oxygen as it did on the planet Mars, which of course left the planet lifeless, it will also at the same time split the atom of every soul that is there on the planet. It will separate the nucleus that is the proton and neutron from each other and also their electrons, basically scattering them into dust. The energy, not actually destroyed, but decidedly separated." His voice trailed off.

"You mentioned Mars John was that a University planet too?"

"Yes, but a long, long time ago maybe more than three billion years ago, about a year and a half ago in our time here on the Home planet in our Universe"

"I see but what then?"

Apparently it was cleansed but never rebuilt. With another planet nearby the Earth as it is called now, and ready to spawn, it made much more sense to seed it for habitation. Normally they don´t rebuild a planet when it is cleansed but for what-ever reason the Game-masters love the planet Earth although other University planets in the past have just been discarded after a cleansing. Anyway as I said, about eighteen months ago here in our time, they decided to use the Earth as a kind of laboratory to create different species for future planets. So they put a massive selection of Trilobites on the Earth"

"Trilobites?"

111

"Yes a kind of sea animal which is a good first stage for a planets evolution. After the experimental stage finished they removed them and not long after put the dinosaurs and other life forms including a whole selection of plants onto the planet. Unfortunately the planet took a massive hit from an asteroid and pretty much wiped out all but a few of the mammals and plants"

"Is that when we came in John?" Louisa asked.

"Yes, but it was some time later after the planet went through another ice age, before the Game-masters decided the Earth was ready for habitation. So they tried different types, Neanderthal and other species before eventually deciding on the humanoid form. That was when it became another University"

"While we are on the subject John, how do we enter the Game when we are just an atom, albeit of intelligence, but nevertheless without a physical body form?"

"When we are here at the game board and have materialized our energy we place our hands onto the pads and the program spins our atom into the Game. While at the same time it provides us with DNA which is a double helix code which enables our atom to create a human body to use. Some of the code is used for the genes in the body to function properly, but the main part of the code, which all University planets are led to believe has no function at all, is actually the coding for the particle transporter using light expansion to transfer our atom back here, out of the Game.

"So how many other universities is there John?

"There only just ten now. There are many planets that have been created over the last three billion years and have passed their social evolution. That's when the complete planet stops violent confrontation within the nation states and becomes just one united community."

"Were there many Universities before then?"

"Oh yes, the Game-masters are continually seeding more, as lot of them never get past their elementary stage, although some players graduate before their planet is destroyed.

"Destroyed John"

"I'll explain Lou. They have started many University planets over the last forty three years, that is in our time of course. As you know time is different in the Game, it runs faster, so about thirteen and a half billion years of time has passed in the Game since the big bang was created. That is one tenth of a second of our time equals one year in the Game.

"Yes I understand"

"Anyway the Creator gives each civilization the tool to eradicate the planet if it does not pass its social development stage. The tool the Game-masters provided was the information to create nuclear power which was to be used for technological growth. So if by their voracity and iniquity the different civilization's, or nations, fail to evolve into peaceful union, then sooner or later they would use the nuclear technology in the form of atomic weapons to destroy themselves."

"I take it then a cleansing will mean a total nuclear holocaust splitting atoms resulting in dreadful radiation? It'll be millions of years before the planet will be safe for habitation again" Baxter stated.

"That would be right Bax under normal circumstances, but fortunately now we're able to neutralize the radiation by sweeping the planet with a mixture of uranium and plutonium's antimatter. This has the same effect as a negative and a positive canceling out each other and thereby the harmful radiation remaining after the devastation will be, as I say, neutralized. It takes a little time of course, according to the size and geology of the planet it could take a month or more of local time before we can safely return to the surface."

"John I don't understand. Why don't the Game-masters just wait until the ships get there before starting the cleansing, why do we need to delay the Cleansing?" Louisa asked.

"Well, that's because they don't start it, as you put it. The Game-masters don´t know exactly when a cleansing will start. The actual time day week or even year that it will happen is not exactly predictable, and of course there is always the hope it won't happen. The players on a University planet may change the course of events even up to the last moment. As humanity has such a tremendous struggle against the dark forces of its own narcissistic nature, a reversal seldom happens once the society is on that downward path. Only a small percentage of the player's at this cleansing have any hope of survival, as most are returnees who have not made it even after many lifetimes. With their past record of continual disregard for the laws of the Game, corrupt players from previous lives and other University planets have been reincarnated onto the planet Earth as their last chance. If they mess up this time, as clearly most will or have, then they'll lose their right to eternal life and will be destroyed.

"Are there any more questions? If not we should return." John said.

"Is the Creator one of the Game Masters? Louisa asked looking at John.

"Good question Louisa. The answer is, I don't know." He smiled and looked at each in turn. "OK then, if there are no more questions then I'll explain the plan when we meet on Earth"

John reached forward again and typed into his keyboard. "OK now all hold hands." They reached out to each other, connecting their energies, letting it flow together, until all six became as one. When Matt opened his eyes somehow he felt different, more awake and more aware. He had an inner understanding of the Game-Master's benevolence. It was then a realization came to him that Boisey and John were already at a higher level and must have already graduated. This made him wonder why they would be going back to Earth with them.

With some reluctance he placed his hands on the pads with the others, then rested his head on the back of the chair and looked up at the twin suns through the domed roof above. He had mixed feelings about his journey. There was a sorrow in him for leaving this place, his home. Yet on the other hand, he felt a great excitement with the thought of the forthcoming events.

Slowly the shutters closed, cutting out the brilliant light from above. He thought of Louisa, he imagined her standing naked before him. His deep love for his soul-mate overwhelmed all his anxieties. He wondered where on the Earth she was living and how he would find her when he returned to Earth.

A strong purple light pulsated around the room. There was a humming sound, growing louder and louder, until it surrounded him. A moment later he was back in the spiraling tunnel. In the background he could hear the choir singing, slowly getting fainter until there was just a hint of the serene voices in the distance.

Chapter 14

Deep in the heart of London's East End a light switched on behind drawn curtains. Inside the room Peter Boisey-Smith, MD took off his white coat, pulled on a pair of black cords and a dark-colored sweater, switched off the light and walked back into his surgery. There he took a worn leather bag from the drawer of a cabinet and carefully checked the contents. He selected a leather jacket from a closet, pulled on a cloth cap, walked from his surgery through the waiting room, and out into the foul night.

With his head bent against the driving rain, he hurried along passing by the old Victorian homes in the dark street. Turning a corner, he walked alongside a high brick wall. He took a moment to look around the empty street before sprinting forward and leaping up to grasp the top edge of the wall. In seconds he had pulled himself up onto the wall. Balancing with the skill of a tight rope walker, he made his way along the wall until he came to another wall separating the back yards of the terraced houses. He almost slipped on the wet surface but quickly regained his balance and made his way along it. Suddenly a light came from the back door of one of the houses as a woman let a dog out into the yard. He dropped on his stomach and lay flat along the wall. Boisey's hand tightened on the leather bag, while the other hand grasped the wet bricks. His knees and soft shoes gripped the soaking stone while he inched his way forward.

The rain dripped slowly from the end of his nose which, although broken, added to his rugged yet handsome features.

The dog began to bark. He lowered his head, letting the peaked cap cover his face. Not daring to move, he laid his cheek gently to the cold stone. The rain had soaked through the jacket, through the sweater into his shirt, now it seeped into his underwear. His trousers hung wet and cold against his legs.

The door of the house opened again throwing broken light into the heavy rain. The woman's voice called to the yapping dog. Boisey pressed tighter to the wall. The voice called out again. This time the troublesome animal turned away from the darkness and disappeared into the house. The glass in the door rattled loudly as it slammed closed.

Boisey gave a sigh of relief as the darkness returned. Rising to his feet he balanced on the wall in a crouched position moving past the houses until he reached the rear of a group of old shops. Without a sound, he jumped to the ground, paused for a moment to listen before stepping quickly across the yard to a barred window.

Squatting, he put the leather bag down beside him, pulled a small car jack from it and placed it between the rusty bars of the window. He pumped the jack until the bars gave way, causing a loud crack like a pistol shot. Instantly a light as bright as day came on in the yard, at the same time the door of an apartment above the shop flew open. A short fat man in a grubby dressing-gown came out onto the iron balcony. The light cast shadows across the yard, hiding the intruder as he moulded himself to the wall.

The fat man's eyes strained through the rain searching the yard below, suddenly he saw a gloved hand move against the brickwork below.

The fat man's body stiffened then felt his short legs turn to jelly. Quickly he looked away. "Nothing out here dear," he called loudly, and with a shrug he turned and retreated through the open door.

"What was it, Arnold?" a shrill voice called to him as he pulled the door closed.

"What was it, Arnold," he mimicked under his breath and then called back, "Nothing dear."

"That was a very loud nothing," she fired at him.

"Must have been a cat," he shouted back at her. Then, turning the volume of the television up, he slumped back into his favorite chair and tried to ignore the scene that had just startled him.

"Well," he mumbled to himself, "it's nothing to do with me anyway." His lips turned into a half smile as he thought aloud. "If Fred Jennings, the f 'ing bookmaker, gets himself f 'ing robbed, hard f 'ing luck. Its f 'ing robbery the f 'ing rent he charges me for this f 'ing flea-bag hole he calls a f 'ing apartment."

"What's that dear," his scrawny wife whined from the kitchen.

"Nothing dear... nothing," he answered, then, smiling to himself he reached to turn the television volume even louder.

Boisey moved back to the window and slipped a screwdriver under the wooden fanlight at the same time slipping a piece of flat plastic into place to hold down the alarm switch. In a second it sprang open. He hauled himself up onto the window ledge, reached through and carefully opened the larger frame while slipping another piece of plastic into place. His flashlight shone around the room, highlighting pictures of race-horses on the walls. Finally it stopped at an old safe sitting in a dark corner of the office. He walked across the room and bent to read the name on the safe.

Reaching into his jacket pocket he produced a small book and thumbed through its time-worn pages until he found the name, Milner. He studied the hand-written pages containing instructions that had carefully been researched and collected over the years. Taking out a tape measure he measured the distance between the handle and the keyhole, drew a line vertically down from the handle and then marked the spot. Soon a drill's high-pitched whine filled the air as in seconds it cut a small hole in the door of the safe. Putting the drill down he reached into his bag, pulled out a flask and drank the liquid, quenching his adrenaline-parched tongue. After replacing the flask, he took a small packet from the bag and began to roll tiny pieces of the plastic explosive into balls before inserting them into the hole, working with just the odd casual glance over his shoulder. Moments later there was a muffled bang, he turned the handle of the safe and then opened the heavy door. He gave a low whistle when the flashlight revealed the compartment, full to the top with bundles of used bank-notes.

"My God," he whispered to himself. Taking out a backpack from the tool-bag he carefully placed the bundles of money into it picked up his tools and packed them away with care.

When he climbed back out of the window he looked up to the balcony above. All was quiet. The rain continued to fall. Without a sound he scaled the wall and made his way back between the yards. As he rose to jump off the end of the wall into the street, he stopped short, looking down at the lights of a cruising police car. The interior warmth of the vehicle gave its occupants little incentive to look out of the steamed windows into the filthy night.

After it passed he dropped lightly to the ground, just managing to catch his balance on the slippery pavement below. Then quickly, he faded into the murky night.

Chapter 15

White Horse pub East London.

Dr. Peter Boisey-Smith looked around the bar of the East End pub. He felt at home, this was his heritage and his favorite part of London. He had mixed feelings, a love-hate relationship. He disliked the depravity and corruption, but he loved the people. They were in his opinion the root of the tree, the mongrels of Britain. It was a breeding ground for some of the finest actors, poets, writers, and entrepreneurs that Britain had ever produced.

He never felt out of place here in the East End, although he recognized he was an enigma to most who knew him.

He looked over the rim of his pint glass at the clean-cut features of Jeffery Willis. Jeffery was an old school friend and the most inquisitive person he had ever met, his only interest in life was other people's business, a trait that amused Boisey. Jeffery's insatiable nosiness gave him many opportunities to tease him and lead him on until Jeffery tired of the Game would storm off muttering under his breath.

"What's up Jeff?" Boisey's eyes twinkled in anticipation of the Game ahead.

"What's up Boisey? You know what's up. It's what you have been up to, that's what's up"

Jeffery seated himself in a soft velvet chair opposite his friend. He wiped his mouth with the back of his hand and placed his pint glass down on the beer-drenched table between them. Never once did he take his eyes from Boisey's face. Boisey knew he would be looking for a telltale sign of culpability.

"Come on! Tell your old mate, will yer?" he queried.

Boisey continued staring at him without saying a word. He just sipped his beer, much to the annoyance of Jeffery whose patience was already running out.

"Last night, another bookmaker got turned over," Jeffery blurted out. Then he continued. "Jennings, as if you didn't know"

Boisey ignored the inference and looked across the room to the blonde singer on the stage whose straining voice was almost lost amongst the noise of the bar. She smiled when she caught his eyes staring at her through the crowded room. He turned back to look at Jeffery's agonizing face.

"You mean that old bastard got beat up?"

"No, no, you know what I mean. His betting shop got turned over, e' got robbed, as if you didn't know Boisey!" He said, leaning forward and lowering his tone while glancing around at the sea of faces drinking and laughing.

Boisey searched the crowd of customers looking for a familiar face. Most were young people, dressed well and from the better part of London who preferred to drink in the atmosphere of the old East End pubs.

Jeffery, the great observer of life, nodded his head towards the crowded bar. "Typical" he said. "Saturday night, everyone gets dressed as if they are going to a bloody wedding. Can't tell who's who anymore, it used to be just coppers, car dealers, er´n hoods who wore suits, now look."

Boisey sat back in his chair, sliding down further into his leather jacket, while listening to the profound ranting of his friend while continuing to search the crowd. His eyes casually turned to look at Jeffery in mock astonishment.

"Jeffery old son, what on earth gave you the idea that I would know anything about Jennings being robbed? I haven't heard a thing myself. So what happened anyway?"

"Well," Jeffery said with an air of defiance, "as I am sure you are aware, someone done the safe in Jennings's betting shop and got away with a f 'ing fortune." Jeffery's round face was almost bursting with excitement.

"We're talking retirement money, Boisey. An' guess what? It's got your hand-writing all over it. An' guess what the word is?"

He waited for an answer like a hawk about to strike, eyes ablaze, darting back and forth, almost spilling his beer as he took a quick slurp. Then, unable to contain his self he said, "Jennings thinks it was you."

Boisey looked back across the room to the singer. Jeffery followed Boisey's eyes. "See Bren's still making eyes at you," he said, referring to the singer, Brenda, Boisey's ex-girlfriend. Boisey turned his attention back to Jeffery. He considered the contradiction of the man's ageing face and his balding head. He felt a certain sadness for the poor fellow who lived his life through other people's lives. He knew that if anyone had given the bookmaker the idea that it was he, Boisey, who had robbed him, it was probably Jeffery. Not from malice, but from a kind of misguided hero worship that Jeffery had for him. He could almost hear Jeffery saying, "Mr. Jennings, there's only one man good enough to pull that off, and I bet you know who I mean."

Of course Jennings would have jumped on it. Knowing the rumors in the East end surrounding Boisey concerning his hatred of bookies and pay day lenders, he would naturally think Jeffery knew something, when in fact he didn't. Boisey realized he had taken a chance robbing Jennings. Too close to home, he had thought, but he couldn't help himself. He had despised bookmakers since his younger brother committed suicide after getting into horrendous debt from gambling. So often he had watched the stream of poor fools flow in and out of betting offices. They came to the slaughter from all walks of life, mothers lugging children, unshaven men, despondent teenagers, bank clerks on the knife-edge of embezzlement, young men in flashy suits and old men in rags. All would come with dreams of sudden fortune nearly all would leave in despair. He felt sorry for the poor mothers left at home trying to make ends meet on welfare, while most and sometimes all of the money would have been gambled away by the hopelessly addicted father.

"You ger'na answer me straight Boisey?"

"Me, old son, not a chance I was having dinner with Mr. Ward, you know, from the Serious Crime Squad, we spent the whole evening together."

"Yer, right! Is that the same cosser' you took to Spain last year?"

"Jeffery, what a nasty little thought. I've never bribed an old bill in my life." Boisey laughed.

"Drink Boisey?" Jeffery said, picking up both glasses from the table.

"No thanks, not for me mate. I have to be up early going to the gym, then its lunch at my sister Jill's tomorrow"

Jeffery's face was a picture. "Going to see that brother-in-law of yours Boisey, I thought you weren't too keen."

"I also want to lose some of this," he said slapping his flat stomach. They both stood up and pushed their way through the crowd toward the exit.

"Yer kidding me, you going to Jill's then?" Jeffery's curiosity was obviously killing him. They pushed open the pub door and stepped out into the night air.

"Just to see my sister, not her old man"

"Really Boisey"

"See you, Jeff." Boisey nodded his head at his friend.

"See you Boisey" Jeffery said, acknowledging his friend's abrupt farewell as normal.

Boisey turned the corner of a dark street and listened to the echo of his own footsteps as he made his way to his car. Across the street he noticed a car parked with its engine running. Sliding behind the wheel of his old Jaguar, he sat for a minute studying the other car before turning the key in the ignition then pressing the starter button. The engine of the Jaguar purred to life. Suddenly, he heard the noise of tires screeching as the car pulled out and sped away down the dark street disappearing towards the Mile End road.

In an instant he leapt from the Jaguar and threw himself to the ground, then frantically rolling away from it. He lay on the damp pavement waiting for the inevitable. Then it came, he saw a blinding flash as if daylight had returned. The roar of the explosion rang in his ears until he thought it would never stop.

"Jennings! Bastard." He muttered.

He stood up took a last look at the smoldering wreck then walked back to the Mile End road and hailed a cab. Back at his surgery he unlocked a cupboard to reveal various electronics, putting a selection into an old leather hold-all he pulled the door to behind him and walked back to the main road. There he waited for a cab. A black cab stopped short of where he was standing to let a fare out, he ran quickly too it.

"Ilford mate. Ley Street." He called through the small opening behind the driver. He brushed down his wet raincoat the best he could.

After a twenty minute journey the driver leaned back almost twisting his body to talk through the little sliding window.

"Where do you want me to stop mate"

"This will do" Boisey called out, the cab stopped, he swung the door open and jumped out.

Back in the rain he walked towards a group of small warehouses searching as he went past each building for a name. Finally he stopped at an office, above the door it had the name Jennings Textiles. The office door was next to a set of huge shutters belonging to the warehouse. Within a minute he had opened the door and had slipped in. Instantly he entered the office the alarm bell started to ring. Boisey locked the door again and walked back across the street while the bell continued to ring. He waited under a tree pulling up his collar against the driving rain. After what seemed forever he saw the blue light flashing as a police car eventually arrived.

Two policemen climbed out of the vehicle into the rain, tried the door, flashed their torches through the office windows, drove around the back and promptly left.

Now with the bell still ringing Boisey walked back to the building and entered through the same door. Inside he kicked open the door that led into the warehouse he looked around by the light of his torch and gazed at the mountain of boxes piled high reaching to the ceiling of the warehouse. He began to open them one by one. Reading the labels of each box and muttering out loud. "Xeloda, Gemzar, Avast, Fluorouracl, scum bags, Cytoxan, the filthy greedy scum, all fake fucking cancer drugs, the callous bastards"

He kicked one of the boxes in anger, then knelt down and opened his bag pulling out an electrical device placing it in-between a large group of boxes then he pulled out a block of plastic explosive.

The alarm bell was still ringing as he walked away disappearing into the darkness. It was not long before a police car sped by followed closely by two fire engines.

Chapter 16

As the underground train pulled into Kensington station Boisey ran up the escalator and walked outside into Kensington high street. He looked up to see the dark clouds threatening rain, then pulled his jacket collar up and walked quickly to the elegant building where his sister lived.

She greeted with a hug as he entered the apartment. "Oh my God it's been such a long time" she said not seeming to want to let go.

"Great to see you Jill,"

"Come in, come in, look Paul's in there" she said pointing into the lounge. "I'll be in the kitchen, lunch will be five minutes, and then we can talk. Oh it's so nice to see you." She said with a big smile.

Boisey walked into the room just as Paul stood up. "Boisey" he said almost as a statement more than a greeting. "Would you care for a sherry before lunch?" He said while at the same time waving his hand towards an armchair. "No thanks mate I'll wait until later too early for me."

Then just as Paul reached for the sherry Jill called out "Lunch is ready." He put the bottle back down also the Financial Times he was still holding and looked at his brother-in-law with a smile. "Ready"

"Absolutely mate," Boisey replied.

The conversation through lunch was stilted and sparse, mostly metal touching china broke the silence with an occasional, "be a dear and pass the gravy" as each searched for a mutual subject to talk about. Boisey was now convinced there was another reason for asking him there, something more than a family Sunday lunch.

After lunch they sat in the lounge to read the Sunday papers. Boisey studied his brother-in-law. Paul was a tall handsome man, slim, wiry, he looked in good shape for someone in his early sixties. He was dressed in casual country attire, brogue shoes and corduroy trousers. This would be the usual dress at the weekend for his type Boisey thought. His type, being something in the City, as Jill would put it. Boisey shrugged his shoulders and looked over to his sister who was busy reading a woman's magazine. Her fifty odd years had also been kind to her. She had blonde hair cut short and a neat figure giving her the appearance of someone ten years younger.

He was now wondering why they had asked him to Sunday lunch. It seemed curious that they would want a near stranger to share their precious time. He had seen little of his sister over the past few years, yet strangely she had called at the last minute and insisted that he join them. Well, what the hell he had thought, she is my only sister after all, and if it means that much to her, then I should go even if I'm not so sure of her husband.

Then he thought about the previous night, he needed time to decide which charity to give the money to, there was quite an amount of money which needed to be distributed. The money as such was never the point of the exercise, he saw it as a punishment but nevertheless it would certainly be welcome to the needy of London.

He was already regretting his decision to join them for lunch, as he needed to get on. The apartment was three stories up he gazed up at the rain clouds and watched as the dark chariots of the sky twisted and turned in a death-defying race across the sky. He felt a longing to reach out and touch them, to join them in their silent liberation, fleeing across the roof of the world. Jill suddenly excused herself leaving the room.

"How are the kids Paul"

"They are fine thanks, now they both have children we don't see them so often of course. You're still quite fit for your age Boisey?" Paul said looking at him with a grin.

"I look after myself, mate, you don´t look so bad yourself for an olden," Boisey said, quite impressed by Paul´s strong looking figure...

"I still go on maneuvers with the 21st, you know. So I do keep up to scratch."

Boisey almost stood up with surprise, his hand held on one arm of the chair, now looking at Paul in astonishment.

"The 21st what? You mean The Artist Rifles? Is that what you mean? I don't believe it."

Paul nodded his head in answer to the question.

"You sly old dog, all these years and you never told me you were in anything, let alone the 21st and you knew I did my bit in the 22nd."

"Actually, old chap, I never saw a reason to, not until now, just because you were with the twenty second, quite a different thing actually the twenty first, less blood and guts, more intelligence than anything else."

"So you're in or were in the.... I can't believe it my God." Boisey was surprised and puzzled. True, he had never talked to Paul about his own time with the Regiment and now felt annoyed that Paul had never shared his own involvement in the related regiment with him. Paul smiled in recognition.

"Yes, part-time though. Obviously I'm no longer in the field too old you know."

Boisey sat back with his legs crossed. Although aggravated, he now saw Paul in a new and more respectful light.

"So, my wife's illustrious brother, what have you been doing since I saw you last? Last I heard you were at Guy's hospital," Paul asked, disregarding Boisey's head, still shaking in amazement.

"I thought you knew? I have a small practice in the East End."

"That's not the only thing you do. I hear you have an interesting hobby." Then, standing up, he looked down at Boisey and said, "Shall we talk?"

"Hobby, so what's this you've heard then?" The tone of his voice showed his irritation.

"I hear you're very adept with tools"

"Tools, what's that supposed to mean? I'm a G.P. not a surgeon."

"You know damn well what I mean, and to be honest, as my brother-in-law, I find your dubious hobby an embarrassment," the biting retort came back. There was silence as they looked at one another.

"Oh I see," Boisey said as the penny dropped.

"They also say you're the best. Probably the best the service ever had. They say you could open anything and also an expert with things that go bang, but my dear brother-in-law, you were not supposed to take your special military skills into civilian life."

"Well, what's all this bullshit about? `Eh' Paul?"

There was a long silence while they looked at one another. Boisey's voice, now mellow, broke the silence. "I mean, you must have had a pretty good reason to invite me to lunch and I hope it wasn't just to lecture me for ripping off a few bookmakers and destroying some of the despicable drug baron's counterfeit products and how do you know about that anyway?"

"No, that is not the reason," Paul said ignoring the question.

"Good because it's my own retribution program for the scum and also a re-distribution of wealth, that's what I call it, old son. Seeing as how the old bill seem to have trouble stopping them bringing fake drugs into the country, then I help in my own way"

"No I understand your motive isn't greed. I know you've given everything you have taken from the bastards to charities in the East End, nevertheless."

"I'm all ears, Paul."

"I don't understand why you have kept that dreadful cockney accent of yours, after such a good education?" Paul said as a way of changing the direction of the conversation.

Boisey looked coldly at his brother-in-law, wondering whether or not to answer the impertinent question.

"First of all I'm not ashamed of my working class roots. Secondly, if you must know, I find it better not to pretend to be somebody other than who I am."

"Ok, ok, I apologize I work for the Ministry of Defense." Paul said, continuing on and not taking notice of Boisey's inference.

"Really, Jill told me you were something in the City. So what's that to do with me?"

Boisey feeling annoyed by the whole conversation stood up and stretched. "So how do you know so much about me?"

"Scotland yard, old chap we work closely together."

"So what did they tell you about me?"

"Like I said, no convictions, you're the best."

"That's right Paul, no form. By the way, does Jill know any of this?"

"No, of course not"

"So what does your little firm want with me?"

"Well... we need you to open a safe."

"What! . . . ?"

"Don't get excited old chap."

"I'm not. I just can't believe it. Why me you must have your own experts."

"It's, shall we say, in a difficult place."

"Where's that?"

"I can't tell you just yet. First you'll have to agree to everything."

"Everything what the hell does that mean?"

"We know the location in the building but we don't know the type, or manufacture of the safe"

"Sound's quite the challenge"

"That's why we need you, somebody who can open anything that's there"

"Is there anything else I should know?"

"You'll be with another man."

"I work alone"

"Not this time"

"Alone"

"It's for your protection"

"Protection"

"This place is somewhat difficult to enter"

"Wait a minute, even supposing I agreed, why would you think I'd be interested?"

"It's for your country, maybe even for humanity"

"My God what on earth are you talking about, humanity? Don't you think you're appealing to the wrong part of my character?" Boisey said with a smile.

"Hardly, from what I have been told, I think this is right up your street" Paul said smiling. Then he pushed himself up with the help of a hand on one knee, "Whew! I'm getting stiff sitting here," he said finally straightening up and trying not to show his age.

Boisey shook his head. "Humanity, Paul?"

"What I am about to tell you is highly secret and only a few of us have the security clearance for this very sensitive information, this must not to be repeated to anyone"

"I was in the military, remember."

"Well, you know the situation in the Middle East. It looks as if we're likely to face all of the Islamic nations in a war in defense of Israel. A conflict instigated by the Italian leader, Don Vinchenti and others.

"Others"

"We believe the ruling class so to speak, plans to push the world into war in order to achieve their ambitions, which in this case is the oil."

"Ruling class Paul?"

"Yes the ruling elite, the public wrongly believe government's run the show. These people or should I say this group, are the real

132

thing, the real ruling class. They manipulate the stock market and money markets. They are the silent power behind the Government in this country the US and most of the EU countries.

They are called the Wed group and are our controllers, they are a very small covert group comprised of certain families, leading industrialists, moguls all billionaire tycoons. They call themselves Wed, meaning World Economic Domination. It was founded in the late nineteenth century by a major American family. To give you an idea of their greed, in the last world war they owned factories in Germany and supplied among other things chemicals for Auschwitz."

"Nice bunch of bastards."

"This is almost certainly a move by them, using the Don as a front, to take over and control the oil in the Middle East. The banks that loaned him the capital are almost certainly owned or controlled by Wed.

They own the Mansel Corp which is a multinational conglomerate that own outright or have shares in all the major industries in the West including the media, oil companies, railways, airlines, shipping, banks every major supermarket chain, drug companies, and most of, if not all of the food manufacturers and producers. Their appetite for economic domination has successfully sent the US and the UK into recession by moving their manufacturing bases to the East. Over the last forty years through influencing legislation they changed the effectiveness of the unions to fight for the rights of the working class. The corporation employ lobbyist that pay huge sums to the avaricious politicians, thereby manipulating and controlling each country in the west." He stopped for a minute to let Boisey take it in.

"This is going to be a mess Boisey, it could mean the end of civilization. The brains in London think we're going to be on our own after the war starts."

"What about the United States? They'll be with us, right?"

"Not exactly, they'll be in big trouble at home if this starts, with the religious extremists just waiting for this opportunity to rise into anarchy." He stopped and looked hard at Boisey. "Have you any idea what is happening in China?"

"Yes, I heard they mobilized a million troops last week and with the lunatic in North Korea in their pocket it sounds like trouble."

"We think it's more like three million from the satellite reports the United States has been giving us."

"My God," Boisey said. He stared at Paul for a long time, then in a serious voice said, "I'm in."

Thinking of his waistline after a good lunch Boisey walked cautiously out of the apartment from the back of the block heading towards the West End.

Then he saw a small white van parked with the name Jennings Textiles painted on the side of it. As he walked towards it he undid the leather belt around his waist. He slipped the end of the belt back through the buckle and held it ready in one hand. He stopped for a moment to allow a mother pushing a baby carriage to pass him. Her long legs were clad in dark stockings and tight skirt cut tantalizingly short just covered her strong thighs. Boisey guessed she would distract the occupants of the van and give him the advantage he needed.

As he came closer to the van, he could see there were two occupants. He recognized Jo-Jo's bald head. While the girl walked past the van on one side, he walked out into the road and up to the driver's door. He could see their concentration was on the girl. Opening the door he slipped his belt around the driver's neck, quickly pulling it tight with one hand while snatching the man's gun with the other. Then, leaning almost casually on the door with the other hand he said with a sarcastic smile, "Well, well, I see the boys are up from Ilford then, sight-seeing are we?"

The huge bulk of Jo-Jo McFinn tried to maneuver out of the passenger door.

"Don't Jo-Jo. I'll strangle the little bastard." The message got across just in time, for the eyes of the driver began to pop from their sockets, and his face was turning blue. Jo-Jo slumped angrily back into his seat.

"What are you doing here Jo-Jo? Came all this way to screw with me did you?"

"You're history, Boisey," Jo-Jo said, his bull face bursting red with anger. "Jennings has got the whole East End looking for you, you don't have a chance."

Instinctively Boisey tightened his grip on the belt. He pulled the man out of the car, slamming him on the pavement and then dragged him across the road away from the car.

"If you want to see this piece of garbage again, piss off back to Ilford and tell Jenning's to call this bullshit off. Otherwise I'll reverse the contract and come after him, and you. Meanwhile I'll keep the Weasel, for self-preservation." He shook the belt around the man's neck, indicating he meant business.

He watched as Jo-Jo slid his great weight across the seat and grabbed the steering wheel. With a scowl, he drove the van away, leaving Boisey standing in the middle of the road with the other man hanging by the neck from his belt. When the car left the street he removed the belt.

"I'll kill you if you do anything to aggravate me," he told him. The man stood up holding his bruised neck.

"I suggest you walk down there Weasel" he said, pointing to the Kensington underground station, "and get the train back to wherever you crawled from"

Boisey stood and watched the man stagger off, half walking, half running down the steep gradient towards the station.

Finally satisfied, he turned to walk back toward the west end and then saw Jill standing on the steps of the building. She had obviously run down behind him to wish him goodbye. "Whoops," Boisey muttered under his breath.

"What on earth was that all about?" She said in a voice reeking with anxiety.

"Don't worry love, just a couple of the lads. I gave them directions to St Paul's."

He knew by her cold stare, she was not impressed with his explanation.

Chapter 17

Flight to London

In the blackness Matt could detect a throbbing, he wanted to open his eyes but he was apprehensive. He wondered what the sound could be, it sounded like the humming of a jet engine. Of course I've been dreaming he thought. At that moment there was a scream from a woman close by it rang in his ears and then he heard a medley of voices in a babbling panic. He opened his eyes to see the rear end of pencil lips. She was bending over, giving mouth to mouth resuscitation to the old Italian lady who had been seated across the aisle. A crowd was pushing into him as they gathered around her seat. The steward and pencil lips carried the old lady to the rear of the aircraft, leaving everybody milling around trying to settle down. Heads were twisting and turning between the aisles and across the rows of seats. Their frightened white faces were popping up and down like the ghoulish targets of some eerie fairground shooting gallery.

Matt fell back in his seat, turned away, and looked out of the window. It was still dark outside and the memory of his dream was still strong, so strong in fact, he felt confused.

#

At the back of the aircraft the hostess realizing she must have given the wrong drink to the old lady leaned over the seat and whispered to the man she had conspired with earlier. "I'll tell you straight, I definitely put it in his cognac." The man gripped her wrist, twisting it, he spat the words at her. "You fool! You gave it to that old woman! Can't you see? Look at her lying there. Are you totally stupid?"

"You're breaking my arm Toni"

"I should break yer' neck you stupid bitch"

"I swear I gave it to him. I can't explain it. I watched him die, and now he looks fine" She shook her head. "I don't understand. I just don't know"

The man glared at her back as she pulled away and walked off shaking her head.

#

Matt looked at his watch. It was four thirty London time, they would be landing in two hours. Carefully he pulled the memory stick from his jacket pocket and slid it into the watch. He went to messages and opened the most recent one. It contained a complicated floor plan of a huge house. He scrolled down to the text, it read.

At Heathrow airport you will be met by Peter Boisey-Smith, good Luck.

Stiff from the journey, he stood up and stretched. Then needing to go to the bathroom he walked slowly to the back of the aircraft. There he waited in line behind a broad shouldered, well-dressed traveler who seemed to be drunk. Matt guessed he was probably a young executive or a wall-street trader by the quality of his suit. It was crumpled however, as if he had been sleeping in it, and he held a glass in an unsteady hand. "You all right Guy?" Matt said.

The drunk turned to eye Matt for a moment then said, "What's it to you?"

"Your hand is shaking, that's all"

"So what"

"Nothing, just wondered" Matt said, now wishing he hadn't bothered to ask.

At that moment a young female flight attendant came bustling through the tight gangway. She passed easily by Matt, but the drunk purposely blocked her way. He laughed as she made an effort to push past him.

"Excuse me sir," she said, finally managing to get past him. As she did, he reached down with his free hand and fondled her rear.

She turned around, her youthful face flushed with embarrassment. "Sir, I told you before. I'll will report you if you do that again"

At that moment a bathroom became vacant. Matt put his arm around the man's shoulder, "After you friend," he said. Before the drunk realized the significance of the tight grip on him, he was pushed into the confines of the tight bathroom.

"What the f — " was the last thing he said as Matt head-butted him twice, first in the nose breaking it, then a crashing blow to his head at the same time pushing the unconscious man into the toilet leaving him with the door almost closed. Smiling at the bewildered flight attendant who looked as if she hadn't quite grasped what had happened. He stepped into the now vacant toilet next door. The airline was in turbulence, so he steadied himself with one foot on the seat waiting for the anger to pass. When he stepped out of the bathroom he took a peek through the half-open door, the unconscious man was still there. Satisfied he returned to his seat, with the seat belt securely fastened, he reflected on his dream and the characters in it. They were so real! Yet strangely, the girl had not been his late wife. But he was sure she was someone he knew well, very well.

Sadness swept over him as he recalled the last time he had seen his wife. She had waved him off on a mission almost thirty years before. It was his first mission over the U.S.S.R in the Lockheed SR71 spy plane. He arrived back home after the exciting mission to be greeted by Carol's mother and his three year old daughter Mary. They were both standing on the front steps as he walked up the path towards the house. Carol had been ill with cancer for a long time. Instinctively he knew the worst. He had never remarried. Carol's mother had helped to raise little Mary. Now she is married with a child of her own and very happy. So Matt had made the military his life and at fifty nine, he was stronger and fitter than ever. The years had been good to him, he still had a strong growth of dark hair with high cheek bones, and dark brown eyes. Hidden under his loose-fitting clothes was a body of hardened muscle taking ten years off of his real age.

Matt slept for an hour. When he woke, he pushed up the window blind and saw that the world covered by a roof of white cloud. The deep blue sky shaded into the distant horizon as far as the eye could see. He gazed out of the window, reliving his dream over and over again. Only a dream or was it? He wondered if the old lady had died of a heart attack or something else, for some reason he had a feeling there was more to it.

Suddenly, he realized there was somebody standing looking down at him. "Well, what are you doing here?" Baxter Patterson's voice boomed out.

Matt looked up to see a bearded man dressed in khaki drill smiling down at him.

"Hi Bax," Matt's response came automatically, covering his shock at seeing his long-time friend. Without invitation the large body accompanied by a barrel chest suddenly filled the empty seat next to him.

"So Matt, where the hell are you off to?" His friend's shrewd eyes followed the question. Matt knew this was not just a casual inquiry. Baxter was always digging for something. So he ignored the inquiry, side stepping it with a question of his own.

"You look like you're dressed up for war. What's with the safari kit?"

"I'm just off to the Middle-East I want to be there at the beginning. You know, I only just made it for the grand finale in the Gulf and never got the chance to go to the Iraqi mess. This time I intend to be there."

Matt knew Baxter was referring to the Gulf War, which he had covered in the role of writer for his own publishing company. He had gone into Kuwait city with the troops, and had since written a book on his experiences of that war. The book contained graphic photos and personal accounts in horrifying detail. The one account that stood out the most in Matt's recollection of the book was a descriptive account of the battlefield: He wrote}

I felt as if I had stepped into some horrifying surrealistic Dali painting. The bulldozers that had driven over thousands of Saddam's soldiers, burying them alive in their trenches now lay discarded, covered with windblown sand.

As far as the eye could see, dark clouds of smoke bled into the desert air. The sickening stench of death came from the twisted and charred black metal, interwoven with unrecognizable mangled bodies. The innocent, with their dreams and aspirations, were liquefied together in molten metal, leaving yet another burning scar to add to mankind's own growing funeral pyre.

Then in two thousand and three his publishing company sent a photographer to the war in Iraq. He brought back some eight thousand sickening pictures, describing what Baxter termed as the war of the energy giants. For some reason he never published them. Instead he spent his time caring for the derelicts of Montreal, on call day and night giving support to the drug addicts and alcoholics in their desperate hours of need. Baxter cared about other people's wretched lives, and cared little for his own. Previously, in the summer of '90, after climbing under the barbed wire put up by the army, he had spent five weeks with the Canadian Mohawk Indians to report on a serious situation with the government and local officials. The dispute was over land that had been the Mohawk's traditional burial ground and had been given permission by the local planners to a property company to develop. As the dispute gained ground Baxter stood side by side with them facing the Canadian Military, against odds that might have spelled his own death.

Since then Baxter had traveled the third world countries, going from one war zone to another, reporting on the crime of war, and the misery and deprivation it wrought. Never slanting his reports with political views or for monetary gain, he just gave his own merciful observations of life.

Matt considered how strange it was that finally in this lifetime Baxter had allowed his true nature to be released, he was now cultured with true empathy and sympathy for other's needs. At last he had shaken off selfishness and come to terms with himself, finally understanding the meaning of life on Earth. He was certain that Baxter had found that without the useless burden of material wealth to carry, or to strive for, true peace was attainable.

He wondered whether this revelation was due to his dream, or was he confusing it with reality? He had always felt a closeness to Baxter, one that he couldn't really explain. Even from their first meeting in the military many years ago, Matt had felt an indescribable feeling of knowing him, as if from a past life. They had met in West Germany on a joint N.A.T.0 exercise. Baxter was with the Canadian Special Forces. Their combined mission had brought them together in a smoky beer Keller in Berlin's red light district. That night, after many drinks the bar erupted into violence caused by a group of drunken, brawling, British Soldiers.

Together they had fought their way out of the brawl and had remained good friends ever since.

"The beginning of what, are you alluding to war Baxter? I didn't know we were expecting a war?"

"You know I'm talking about Vinchenti. He is going to get us all involved, isn't he, a'?" Baxter said this while at the same moment turning round and looked sideways at him.

"How the hell" Matt stuttered

"I just know" He smiled.

Matt knew his friend's inquiring instinct would dearly like to know the reason for his journey to Europe"

"It's really bizarre meeting you today. I just had the most unusual dream. You and I were in a familiar place together, but I don't know where. Funny thing is we were discussing an important mission something to do with a war. I guess it was just a dream Bax." Matt said yet at the same time was beginning to realize it was also a kind of reality — that other place.

"No, no, not a dream, something is happening. I had a vision of the future myself." He laughed, seemingly embarrassed. "Strangely enough it also included you."

Then he turned away to grab at the arm of a passing flight attendant. "Could I trouble you for a scotch and water young lady."

She smiled at him, nodding her head in reply. She looked at Matt he shook his head. Baxter carried on. "I sometimes wonder if I even belong here. I mean — with the pain and suffering I see around the world. It's pitiful that the misery is caused by the self-righteous governments, religious zealots and the establishment draped in their own voracity. Why is it, do you think, that such a beautiful piece of real estate as this world, is occupied by so many evil, avaricious, people? I don't know why Matt but my cynical nature is becoming enhanced. Maybe it's because of this damn war we're all likely to get into"

"War Baxter, I don't think so"

"Come on Matt, you know exactly what I'm talking about. If Vinchenti and the others have their way there will hardly be a country in the world that won't be involved some way or other. They're all idiots, like a bunch of squabbling children. Don't they realize what this could lead to?"

He paused for a moment, his face red with passionate anger while he studied Matt, waiting for a reaction.

Then as if puzzled he asked, "You are still with the same outfit?"

Matt avoided the question by looking out of the window. The plane had broken through the layer of white puffy clouds, exposing the vivid green fields of England. Their patchwork design spread as far as the eye could see, covering the land like a beautiful soft quilt.

As Matt gazed out of the window, he felt a strange sensation. First a mist came before his eyes and then it cleared, changing the scene dramatically. He knew he was about to have a vision.

In it he could see fire sweeping across the fields of England. Drifting black embers discharged towards the darkened sky. Everywhere he looked there was chaos. The cities lay smoldering in ruins. Towering columns of smoke rose from their centers. Debris poured into the air like colossal volcanoes at the dawn of time. Slowly, the flames died until there was nothing left, it was over. Life on Earth had ceased to exist.

"I take it you're not going to answer me" Baxter's impatience showed in his voice. Matt quickly came back from the vision and looked toward his friend who held the glass to his lips while sipping his drink. He had to answer, if only to stop further questions.

"Sorry Baxter, I was daydreaming. Yes of course, you kidding me, once you're in, you're in for life. You know that!"

In the background Matt could hear the drone of the flight attendant's monotonous voice giving the passengers the final landing instructions. Then, with a gentle bump, the old 747 landed. It swayed down the runway with engines screaming in reverse thrust before the giant machine slowed to a gentler pace. .

There was a lot of fussing by the other passengers as they pulled their belongings from the overhead compartments.

"Would you like to share a cab?" Baxter asked.

"No, but thanks, I have someone meeting me. Anyway, I thought you had a flight to Tel Aviv?"

"Yes I do, but it's later this evening. So I thought I'd fill the time sightseeing in London." He smiled in a knowing way. Then he laughed, putting his arm around Matt's shoulders. "I guess you've important business to deal with, a' old boy." He gripped Matts hand. "I expect I'll be seeing you soon, a' what do you think?"

Without another word, he turned away, pushing his way along the gangway with the other struggling passengers.

Chapter 18

London

Matt thoughts turned to the message on his watch which he had read on the plane. He was to meet some English guy who would make contact with him at the airport. He walked toward immigration and joined the line. While reflecting on his conversation with Baxter, he noticed a well-dressed, great looking girl, probably in her mid-forties, with dark hair falling partly across her eyes. She had already gone through immigration and seemed to be glancing at him from time to time. She was on the other side of the immigration barrier and obviously waiting for the indicator board to show her flight luggage pickup information. As he looked across to her, she reached down to pick up her hand luggage, tossed her head back flicking the hair from her face, then gave him one slow and final look before turning away. The line shuffled forward, so he bent down and picked up his briefcase, when he looked up she was gone. A strange feeling of recognition came over him, he wanted to talk to her, find out why he felt he knew her. Could she have been the girl in his vision, dream, or whatever it was? No, come on, he thought, this is ridiculous. What am I thinking of?

After going through immigration Matt went in search of his bags. He pushed his way through the crowded luggage area and found the correct baggage conveyer. Suddenly he caught a glimpse of the girl again. It was the girl in his dream, no question. He felt confused. She was staring at him again. At that moment he saw his luggage go past. Quickly he tugged at it, pulling it from the conveyer. By the time he turned back to look for her she had disappeared into the crowd. Damn it, he thought, just suppose she is my soul-mate, that may have been the very moment we were supposed to meet. Then he laughed at himself, picked up his luggage, and went on through customs.

No one had appeared to meet him, so he decided to have coffee in the fast food restaurant. He paid the surly cashier for his coffee at the register and then sat quietly stirring the evil-looking liquid. He waited and watched, fascinated by the crowds bustling by. Gingerly he sipped the tepid drink, and decided once again that the English still had no idea how to make coffee. It's just not possible, he told himself, to get good coffee in London. The Brit's are tea drinkers and beer drinkers, there they excel, but coffee, forget it.

A hand swiped a greasy cloth across the shiny surface of the table while another hand lifted up and replaced the salt and pepper all in one movement. An instant later the intruder had gone, leaving the table clean and wet.

By this time Matt's anxiety level had grown to a dangerous level. He was wondering where the hell this guy could be, or if in fact they were ever likely to locate each other in this melee of people. Then he noticed an older man standing against the wall opposite who seemed to be studying him. His features instantly broke into a smile when he saw that Matt had spotted him. He pushed himself off the wall and began walking towards Matt. When he saw Matt rising in recognition, he swerved away with a slight movement of the hand. It was a signal for Matt to follow through the doors to the outside. More than an hour had passed since he had arrived at the airport. Now as he stepped outside he saw that the weather had changed dramatically. It was just as he remembered England to be, typically overcast with a heavy drizzle drenching the scurrying travelers as they ran to their waiting vehicles.

A London cab splashed its way towards him, pulling up to the side of the pavement. The door of the cab swung open almost hitting Peter Boisey-Smith who then took it upon himself to push

Matt's luggage into the side compartment of the cab. They climbed into the cab and brushed their clothing off. A wet hand reached out toward him.

Boisey's grin gave Matt an instant feeling of warmth. He knew instinctively he was going to like this guy. In fact, as he studied the other's rugged features he felt a strange recognition. Although Boisey was wearing jeans and sneakers, he obviously had good taste. He was dressed in a flying jacket made of the softest of leathers, a shirt with a button down collar that had been cut from the finest quality cotton, and just protruding from under one of the turned back cuffs of his jacket, was a Patek Phillipe watch. His hair was steely gray, cut short on top. His face was tanned and he wore an audacious, permanent smile. This guy was certainly a character.

Their strong hands clasped together like steel, each feeling the other's obvious strength.

"We'd better get to know each other old son! I'm Boisey. Do you fancy a drink in the City?"

Matt was surprised. "It's not mid-day yet," he said, looking at his watch.

"You're right," Boisey said, "but with this traffic, it'll take forever to get into the West End. It'll be quicker if we go south of the water. We'll be in the City by lunch-time, we can have a pint, and then go on to the West End. Better than sitting in this traffic, what do you think?"

"OK, sounds good to me," Matt replied.

Boisey leaned forward and gave the driver the instructions. Soon afterwards the cab turned off the motor-way, leaving the traffic snaking its way slowly towards London. Finally the rain ceased. They passed a long convoy of army vehicles stopped on the side of the road, resting. The drivers were draped over their trucks like drunken statues, draining the last of the smoke from their cigarettes and waiting in sullen silence for the order to move on.

The conversation between them was kept light for the sake of the inquisitive cabby. The journey took them through South London, over Tower Bridge into the City of London with Boisey pointing out landmarks as they passed them. At Bishopsgate they paid off the cab, walked up an alley and entered the Bunch of Grapes public-house. Boisey had told him it was one of the more popular lunch-time haunts for the city people.

They pushed their way into the noisy saloon then fought through the crowd of young office workers to the bar. Men wearing pinstripe suits were standing drinking pints. The girls, painted in high profile make-up, were each exquisitely moulded into short tight-fitting clothes. By the look of their outfits they could have been going out on an evening date but Matt knew this was normal attire for Londoners who regard fashion as a way of life.

The din of the surrounding conversation was too loud for Matt to talk, so he downed his pint of strong flat beer without a word to Boisey. The second pint arrived as the first emptied. He smiled and lifted his glass in salute. After which he looked around studying the interesting faces of the people while at the same time struggling in the apparent race with his opponent to drink a pint of beer in so many minutes, when he caught sight of a man staring straight at him. He probably wouldn't have noticed the man's stare had he not been such a bull of a man, whose head was completely bald and the jowls of his face hung in folds of sagging flesh. The man's shoulders were somehow attached to his head without a neck, while his green pig like eyes that were set too close together, just stared at Boisey like a man possessed. Matt turned to Boisey and shouted above the other voices. "There's someone over there that seems to have an interest in you."

"Where are you looking," Boisey shouted back.

Matt turned to point toward the ugly inquisitor, just as he was disappearing into the crowd.

"I think he must have realized I'd spotted him."

"We'd better go." Boisey's voice had a troubled tone that Matt didn't understand. They left the pub and hailed a passing cab.

"Inn on the Park, cabby," were the only words Boisey uttered until they were well away from the pub. He kept looking out through the back window of the cab, just staring with his face drawn tight until Matt couldn't stand the suspense any longer.

"Who do you think it was then?" Matt asked.

"I don't know for sure it could be something to do with a little on-going dispute I have with someone. I wouldn't have thought anyone would know you're here in England. Even if they do, they wouldn't know why you're here, would they?"

"No, I doubt it," Matt answered. "The only people who would know about this operation on our side of the pond is the President of the United States, my immediate superior, and the staff officer who handed me the instructions, who wouldn't't" he paused, "or at least shouldn't, have known the contents."

Having said that, he sat back and thought again about the fact that he had called Oldfield to change his travel arrangements and the unusual things that happened coming over. Then he wondered if the old lady on the flight had died in his place. Her death could have been from poison meant for him, and given to her by mistake, or had his destiny been changed.

Boisey reached inside his jacket and pulled out a nine millimeter browning automatic pistol and handed it to Matt. "Just in case," he said.

They sat quietly for the rest of the journey. Boisey looked around from time to time, but seemed satisfied that they were not being followed. They rounded Hyde Park Corner and a minute later pulled up outside the Inn on The Park. The doorman opened the door of the cab.

"I'll call you tomorrow morning and arrange a time to pick you up for the meeting," Boisey said reaching out of the cab shaking Matt's hand.

"I'll look forward to it"

"See you tomorrow, old son"

"I'll be waiting for your call," Matt said. Then he turned away to follow his luggage that had been put on a cart by a porter and was now disappearing into the hotel. After checking in, he went to his room jet-lag was setting in, and he needed short nap then a walk in the park before dinner.

Chapter 19

Two days had passed since her meeting with Paul. Now on board an airbus traveling to Heathrow, Louisa sat back in the wide seat and closed her eyes. The quiet calm of the first class cabin gave her the opportunity to reflect on recent events. She tuned the headset to a low volume, closed her eyes and began to think about Paul. Why should he help her? He certainly was charming, but was it false? Could there be an underlying reason for his offer, a more sinister motivation to his proposal of help, she decided not to call him. Slowly she drifted into a light sleep, helped by the gentle swaying of the aircraft flying through moderate turbulence. A while later she woke from a dream with a start to find the journey was over, the moment of tranquility had passed and would soon be surrendered to the hubbub of plane disembarkation.

While she waited in line at passport control she happened to notice a tall man his head held high, his handsome profile suddenly reminded of her dream. He was standing in the line for foreign visitors. He was just a few feet forward of her in his line, so she could only see this side view of his face, but it was someone she felt she knew well.

She just could not think who he was though. At first she thought maybe he was one of the people she had met at Roberto's newspaper, but no, that wasn't it, he was in the foreign visitor's line. If he had been from London he would have been with her in the E.U line. Well, who was it then?

The line moved forward. She felt aggravated, she hated not to be able to put a name to a face. The immigration officer smiled as he handed back her passport. She walked away from the gate, but could not resist a last look. She glanced back at the handsome man still standing in his line. To her embarrassment she saw that he too was looking at her. They stared at one another for just a few seconds, she felt caught in a trap of dilemma, enjoying the eye contact but feeling a need to break away from the tantalizing eyes. It was then she realized she really did know him, yet where from? There was something extraordinary about him, a recognition she couldn't explain, and an excitement she could not explain. Finally, she pulled away from the eyes and looked toward the video screens where she found the number appropriate for her baggage collection. She went up the escalator, picked up an empty cart and made her way to the baggage claim.

Louisa stood watching for her case while every color of the rainbow went by, old leather, new plastic, cardboard boxes tied with string, backpacks, suit-hangers, suitcases bound together with elastic ties, everything except her own suitcase.

In desperation she looked over to the next conveyer, wondering if she was waiting at the wrong one. Then, through the array of moving bodies she suddenly caught sight of the same eyes staring at her. She looked away, scanning the river of belongings flowing past, she stood for a while trying to fight the temptation, when she couldn't resist any longer she looked up, only to find he had gone, she looked back and there was her suitcase she grabbed it and lifted it onto the empty cart. She pushed the cart past the custom officers who were standing as usual with their backs to the wall, waiting to pounce on the oblivious traveler. Outside in the crowded arrival lounge she saw no sign of the man, and so dismissed him from her mind.

She spent most of the day cleaning house. When the phone rang, she glanced at the clock. It was five thirty. Where had the day gone?

"Hi," she said, picking up the receiver.

"Hello young lady, it´s Paul, Paul Johnson-Marsh. How are you this evening?"

"Hi Paul, I had a feeling you might call."

"Perhaps you are a little psychic," he said laughing. "Did you just get in?"

"No, I arrived a few hours ago"

"Oh, I see. By the way, are you doing anything this evening?"

"I've nothing planned"

"Do you know Dominic's in the Fulham road?"

"Yes I do, very well actually."

"Good, how about meeting me there for dinner? Say about nine, nine thirty?"

She thought for a moment then said. "Ok, ok, nine thirty I will be there. Ciao"

Louisa replaced the receiver. She was surprised at her own reaction to his invitation. She was also surprised that he had called so quickly. How did he know she was back? She had not told him exactly when she was returning to London. She sensed an unexplained urgency in all this. There was obviously more to it than met the eye. Anyway, that aside, she was delighted at the choice of restaurant, it was her favorite in Chelsea, and it had been a long time since she had been there. The thought of Dominic's brought back memories of evenings spent there with Roberto. Damn that newspaper, she thought. Then she pushed the irritation aside.

An awful thought flooded over her as she began to wonder if Paul had any romantic interest in her. Although strikingly handsome, he was, after all, at least twenty years older than she was but he had given her a feeling of well-being. She couldn't understand it, or even describe it, yet it was so real she felt she could almost touch the intangible.

Just before nine she telephoned for a taxi. After a few minutes she heard it arrive, the noise of the cab's diesel engine running outside her little mews house was unmistakable. It was one of the many sounds that were so nostalgic to London.

The Fulham road was wet and reflected the evening rain. She paid the driver and ran for the restaurant. Inside she closed the umbrella, then looked up to see Paul seated at the small bar. He smiled at her appearance. "Good evening. You look wet," he chuckled.

"Thanks. I only ran from the cab." She tossed her wet hair back. "It seems the rain in London drowns you even with an umbrella," she said. Taking off her coat she handed it to a waiter who had silently arrived by her side.

"Will you be dining, Signorina Vinchenti?"

"Yes thank you Angelo, I am with Mr. Johnson-Marsh," she said, gesturing toward Paul.

"Very good," he said. Then turning to Paul he said. "Your table is ready when you are." After that he retreated toward the cloakroom seeming a little embarrassed for not having recognized the obvious.

"They seem to know you well." Paul said

"Yes, I've spent many evenings here with a friend, Roberto Capellini."

"From the Evening Journal?"

"God, do you know everyone in London!" she said, wondering whether it wasn't more the case of Paul knowing a lot about her.

"I must say, Paul, I prefer the weather in Italy a lot better, particularly this time of year," she said, making conversation while wondering what she should drink. Then she decided not to drink anything alcoholic which might cause her defense to drop, just in case.

"Would you like a drink?" Paul asked.

"I think I'll start with Perrier water with a twist, if I may."

The waiter returned and showed them to a table. Over Moules Marinieres and a good bottle of French Chablis, they discussed world affairs. Her decision not to drink had been changed by Paul's choice of wine. After a time, it was quite apparent that Paul was gaining confidence. She could sense he was getting ready to broach a subject, and she guessed it would be about her father.

Now she wished she had kept her resolve not to drink. Too late the wine was good, very good.

"I know quite a lot about your father's affairs. I also know about your mother," he said, not taking his eyes from her.

He paused, as if he were expecting a cry from her of mind your own business. She wiped her red lips with a napkin and continued to eat the mussels while waiting for him to go on. She felt a little sorry for him, knowing how difficult this must be.

"Louisa, I know your father thinks, or at least pretends, that your mother is insane. I am sure she is quite normal. If I may be so bold, that cannot be said for your father who is probably not sane at all. Please don't take offense, I am just trying to help."

She laughed gently so as to help hide his embarrassment.

"Don't worry Paul, I agree with you, he is completely deranged but what is it you know about Mummy?"

She studied Paul's kind features but she felt sure he was setting her up for something.

"I spoke to your father about your mother's imprisonment. He told me that since the shock of your sister's death she has been locked away ostensibly for her own safety," he said this with a look of skepticism drawn across his face.

"Of course you know that is bull shit"

"Yes Louisa I am sure you are right," he said while taking the bottle of wine and sharing the remainder between the two glasses. At the same time the waiter arrived with their main course.

After their plates had been cleared he looked once again as if he was embarrassed and about to pronounce the death of his cat.

"I am right, there is absolutely nothing wrong with mother." Then she realized she had made the statement as much for confirmation to herself, as to give relief to Paul's embarrassment.

"My first question is, does your mother want to be rescued from her situation?"

"Actually she said no when I ask her Paul, but I believe she really does."

"Well young lady, what are we going to do about it?" He smoothed the tablecloth, brushing the crumbs of the garlic bread aside. He avoided her eyes, making her wonder if he was hiding something from her. It could be he was embarrassed by the intimate nature of his questions — but there was something else.

The light from the candle set between them cast a warm glow.

It made Louisa feel enclosed with Paul, like a safe haven from the outside world. She wondered whether it could be the wine.

"I can help you Louisa I have certain connections in the M.O.D. I can help your mother escape from the chateau."

She looked into his eyes, searching for any tell-tale sign of deceit, but she saw none. If anything, she saw positive warmth surrounding him, an almost tangible aura of compassion. Then once again she questioned the effects of the wine. Was it clouding her judgment? Was she being too trusting? Did Paul really have the means to help and if so, why?

"OK Paul, what if I go along with you. What's next? What do I do?" she questioned.

"Slow down my dear, all will be revealed in good time as they say."

"Are you married Paul?" She purposely cast the unexpected question, hoping to catch him off guard.

"My word, do you always throw curves at people." He smiled "Well, if you really are interested I'll tell you. My first wife, whom I loved dearly, died in childbirth."

He looked so sad that Louisa regretted asking the question. "Oh, I'm sorry Paul, I shouldn't have asked."

"It's OK, it's just that, although it was a long time ago Louisa, I've never got over it, and I probably never will. It was at the birth of our second child that she died. I was totally devastated. It was years before I could face the thought of another partner. Then, one vacation with the kids, I met Jill. We married after about a year, by that time Peter was six and Cynthia was almost nine. I can't say enough good things about her she is incredible with them, a real mother to them."

He looked down into his empty glass, moving the base around the table cloth in rings as they sat silent for a moment, neither ready to talk. It was obvious that the pain of losing his wife had left a deep scar in his life.

"Paul, I'm really sorry, I shouldn't have asked," she said sympathetically.

He looked up and smiled. "No, don't be, I shouldn't have mentioned it. It still tends to upset me I'm afraid."

She felt a little ashamed of herself for thinking that he might have had any romantic ideas about her. It was obvious now that he had none, but she still had a nagging awareness that there was more to it than he was saying. She saw the waiter heading their way. She beckoned to him. "I'll take a coffee," she told the waiter. "Paul?" she inquired.

"Love one," he said, then as the waiter left he said. "I know tomorrow is Saturday, but how about me sending a car for you and you can meet the man that can help?"

She looked around at the other patrons wondering if there was anyone watching her, she knew her Father and what he was capable of, so her meeting Paul had troubled her. The two at the next table were huddled over a bottle of wine and whispering to each other. The people at the only other occupied table were sitting quietly sipping coffee, seemingly engrossed in their own world. Certainly they didn't appear to be interested in her.

"OK Paul, I would be delighted, and here is my address," she said taking a card out from her wallet," she paused, "thank you for your help Paul." She heard herself saying this although she still wasn't convinced she was doing the right thing. They left the restaurant and returned to the rain. Standing together under one umbrella he hailed a cab.

"Nine o'clock tomorrow morning then," he said as he closed the door of her taxi. She smiled back at him through the window of the cab. This was it, she thought, there would be no turning back.

Chapter 20

Large oaks curbed the inner road through London's Hyde Park. The heat from the morning sun created a mist rising and drifting aimlessly through the corridor of rain soaked trees. Louisa watched a lone jogger splashing his way through the odd puddle with puffs of hot breath meeting the cold morning air. The car rounded the bend at Hyde Park Corner then turned down Constitutional Hill towards Buckingham Palace fenced with imposing iron railings and tall granite-faced guards.

Along the Mall the cab passed blanket-covered horses carrying solemn-faced uniformed troopers of the Royal Cavalry on exercise. Their clean youthful faces with eyes fixed ahead in vacant stares reminded Louisa of porcelain toy soldiers.

The car drove around Trafalgar Square and turned into Whitehall, there it stopped short of Downing St the residence of the Prime-Minister. Louisa knew all the surrounding buildings were used either by the civil service or by the ministry of defense.

She had a certain apprehension about the appointment. How strange that anyone would work on a Saturday in a government department. This also made her consider the fact that Paul's help may be two sided, maybe it was just as important for him.

The car driver smiled. "E're we are Miss, the Ministry of Defense." He said pointing to the tall doors at the entrance of the building.

She walked up the steps, pushed open the door, and entered a large foyer. A uniformed doorman greeted her. His chest displayed rows of ribbons, a colorful story of long military service.

"Morning Miss, how can I help you?" he challenged in a deep Londoner's voice. It seemed loud and ominous to her in the spacious hallway.

"I have an appointment with Mr. Johnson-Marsh my name is Louisa Vinchenti." Her eloquent manner seemed to smooth the doorman's rigid demeanor.

"Miss Vinchenti," he said, sorry to ask but do you have any ID." She was ready for the question and pulled her passport out. At the same time as acknowledging it he pointed with his white gloved hand. "Fourth floor, turn left, last door on the left, but Peter here will escort you." He said this while beckoning to another rather young doorman. "Show Miss Vinchenti up to 405 Peter, they're expecting her."

Together they walked to an old looking elevator whose caged door opened like a trellised concertina. Cautiously, she stepped into it. She hated elevators and watched through the open cage as the floors went by at a snail's pace. Finally along with the escort she stepped out of the elevator at the fourth floor, turned left and found the door as promised. The escort knocked on the door for her then pushing it open he stood aside and waved for her to enter, as the door opened, it revealed two occupants who looked startled by her arrival.

"Oh I'm so sorry," she stuttered."

"No, no, do come in," Paul said. "Louisa, may I introduce you to my good friend Charles Conrad."

Paul ushered her across the room towards the round figure of Charles Conrad. He rose from his seat and walked around his desk, taking a white hanky from his top pocket. First he wiped his brow. Then he took her hand and gently kissed the back of it.

"My dear girl, do sit down," he said, offering her a seat. Louisa sat down, a little bewildered and annoyed by his manner. She hated being referred to as 'girl.' His attitude made her instantly dislike the elegantly dressed overweight man. She looked toward Paul who then said. "Louisa, I have discussed the situation with Charles and to come to the point he is willing to help you with your mother's problem. Charles is a friend who deals in Middle East affairs, mainly helping hostages escape from terrorist organizations. He is certain he can help your mother to escape from her imprisonment."

She was becoming uneasy with the situation more than ever. Why should these people be so interested and so agreeable to help with her problems she wondered. Obviously this had to do with Father and not the escape of Mother. Nevertheless, she reasoned that by playing along with them, it might help Mother anyway. There wasn't anything else she could do and there was something else, something she couldn't explain, she had a feeling or a sense that she was part of an even greater plan something quite different from the plot being developed here in this ministry of defense office. The more she looked at Paul, the closer she felt to him. Strange, it was as if she had known him for a thousand life-times. She had a sense that no matter whatever happened, he would not let her down.

"OK, but why do you want to help me? Is it something to do with my stepfather?"

Charles shook his head. "Stepfather, good lord no it's simply to help Paul. He wants to help you as an old family friend, and as a favor to him, I feel obliged."

He was obviously lying but she decided to let it go, even a slight chance to help Mummy was worth taking any risk. She was committed now anyway.

Charles J. Conrad stood up and went to the window and sat down on the sill which was both wide and low. Louisa watched his flamboyant manner, realizing this was part of his character. The man was obviously an actor. He was playing to an audience, and was about to perform.

"Well young lady, first my team will have to get inside the Chateau." He gestured with his hands apart and palms turned upwards, indicating that it would be a difficult task.

Louisa, having decided she disliked Charles J. Conrad, now found she did not trust him either. So she said sarcastically, "You know, maybe, I can get you in."

163

He seemed to overlook the cynical inflection in her voice. "Good Lord not me dear girl, just a couple of our experts."

"When you say a couple how many do you exactly mean?" She was aghast at the thought. She started to rise to her feet but sat back down after catching a glance from Paul.

"Oh, just two," he said taking a seat on the window sill.

"I don't know about that," she said. "I think one person might be feasible, but two?

"Why don't you work out the details with Paul? As he knows the Chateau, he can help in the planning. If we can get our two experts in with your help we will have another on standby outside to get you out."

She watched Paul for some sign of agreement. He turned towards her and gave her a look that said everything would be all right.

"That'll be fine then I'm ready to give it a go," she said, searching Paul's face. He smiled at her. She felt his awareness across the room and responded with a smile.

"When do you think all of this could be arranged? It will it take time to put such a plan into action, won't it?" She was anxious and worried about her Mother.

"Not too long my dear, just a matter of hour's actually." He slid his weight off the window sill and moved back toward his desk. "Well I think that concludes our business. If you go along to Paul's office you can get started to make the necessary arrangements," he said standing up from the window. Taking the handkerchief from his top pocket, he wiped the imaginary sweat from his neck. It seemed more from habit, than from need, Louisa thought. He walked towards the door, he opened it and stood aside, denoting that the meeting had finished.

"Right Charles, I'll take Louisa later on to meet with the others." Paul said.

"By all-means old chap," Charles said, his face beaming, controlled, even though Louisa could tell something was up.

"I'm sure you will like the people you are going to meet, Louisa," he said with a smile, so unconvincing she knew it was not genuine. Something had gone on before she had arrived that had upset Paul and she wanted to know what that was.

As they were going out of the door, Charles said in a loud voice, "Paul, when you have finished your meeting this afternoon, perhaps you would be kind enough to check in with me." His parting shot hit the spot. She could see Paul was not amused by the man's arrogance.

They spent the morning going over the plans of the chateau that apparently had been provided by the agency. She wasn't particularly impressed when lunch which Paul had promised her when it turned out to be sandwiches brought up by a cleaning lady, but forgave him, as she would forgive anything to help her mother out of her predicament.

The office was small and crowded with shelves of reference books and several filing cabinets. Now she realized there was a sense of urgency coming from Paul that was extreme. He seemed increasingly nervous, as the morning had passed into the afternoon. It appeared to her that there was much more to it than even she could have imagined she needed to know, so she leaned across his desk and stared straight into his eye's, she asked. "Just tell me the truth what is going on. This is more than just about helping Mother and from your body language I imagine it is not even just about Father, is it?"

"I think we have covered every aspect of the plan that we can until we meet the others." Paul said

"You never answered the question, damn you,"

"In a few minutes we are going to Hampstead Louisa, to meet with the others, and then I will explain more, in fact everything. If I tell you now you will not have the entire facts that you need. It is necessary for you to meet the others first, trust me."

"Ok I will, just until then, if I don't like it, I'm going to walk."

Paul looked at his watch, "Ok it's time to go anyway, so let's pack up the plans and get going."

Outside waiting at the curb was a car with a uniformed driver. They climbed into the back. Paul leaned forward and gave the driver instructions, and soon they were on their way through the busy London traffic.

She wanted to know why there had been a feeling of dissension in the air at the office. So in her normal audacious manner, she said, "Paul, I have to ask. What on earth was going on in the office before I arrived? You could have cut the air in the room with a knife as I walked in."

His eyes turned toward her before he spoke. "Louisa, Charles is so self-assured, so ego-oriented, that he has reached the point, like so many powerful people before him, that he cannot distinguish right from wrong."

"For example?" she questioned, intrigued by his answer.

"It's not important Louisa, I can only tell you that it will not affect the outcome. The right thing will be done when the time comes."

"Paul, I really don't know what you are talking about, but for some unknown reason I trust you." She decided to leave it at that.

After a long ride they arrived at a leafy road in Hampstead. Louisa looked out of the window at the large Georgian house. Paul gave instructions to the driver to wait for them. She felt a moment of apprehension, and an uncanny awareness that this meeting was going to be very special to her.

Chapter 21

Hampstead

Matt woke to the sound of the telephone ringing. He opened his eyes and saw the sunshine streaming in through the window. It must be late, he thought as he reached for the intrusive instrument. It was Boisey on the line.

"Good morning. The meetings on, I'll pick you up at four o'clock this afternoon. By the way, how was your first night in London?"

"Boring, I had a touch of jet-lag so I had dinner and went to bed, I guess it was before ten."

"Right old son I'll see you soon." The line clicked off.

True to his word, Boisey arrived on time. Matt walked out of the busy hotel and over to the waiting cab. He opened the door and climbed in. "Hampstead, Mate," Boisey said to the cabby and then he put his finger to his lips as a sign not to talk. Matt wondered why he had done that. Boisey should know being cautious was second nature to Matt. He shrugged it off. Maybe it was because being English he thought others less careful, or maybe Boisey wasn't a regular British agent at all.

The cab stopped in a quiet street of Georgian houses. The pavement was lined with large sycamore trees. Their golden autumn foliage had blown down the street like confetti, covering the ground between the parked cars in mounds of damp, windswept leaves. Climbing the stone steps of the old house Matt stopped, suspended in shock.

"This is really weird," he said.

"What is?"

"I don't know, but I think I've been here before. I mean, well, in a dream at least I think it was a dream."

"Do you believe in dreams then?"

Did the question have an implied speculation in it Matt wondered?

"No, it's nothing, I just had a moment of déjà vu," Matt replied.

When the door opened Matt went cold. Standing there at the door and beckoning them in was Alice, the housekeeper of Doctor John Wiener, his friend from the Georgian era. Things were falling into place or maybe out of place. He followed Boisey into the familiar hallway and looked up.

"There was a staircase here once," he said.

Boisey grinned. "How do you know that? You're right, there was — do you know how you know?"

Matt wasn't sure how to answer that, or even what the question really meant. "I am beginning to think I do.?"

Boisey just looked at him strangely, then without another word followed Alice down the hallway. Matt followed them. Alice opened the last door and showed them in.

The room was familiar. It was John's old consultation room. He stopped quite still, taken back in bewilderment, not by the room as much as by finding the same group of familiar faces that were in his dream. Only Baxter was missing.

Had the dream been real then? Was a dream just another form of reality, as everything is made from atoms formed into dense intricate forms to become material objects then perhaps dreams are the same, they are said to be just sub-conscious thoughts, but they must themselves be built of atoms, and there are millions in our brains, forming into coded patterns, allowing us to experience yet another reality. A place where there is no death no pain, a different and exciting world where the pace is fast and intriguing. If I died now and woke up in some other place, this life on Earth would just seem like a dream. So what is the difference he

wondered is life here on Earth just a dream, if so then which is
reality.

#

An hour earlier Louisa had been introduced to John and felt
some anticipation as they sat quietly drinking tea while waiting for
the others to arrive.

"Who are the people we're expecting Paul?" she asked politely,
again wondering too late, whether she should have become
involved with these people.

John seemed to be a nice kind man. She was surprised that he
could be of any use in this type of covert operation, unless of
course his white flowing hair was deceptive to his ability.

"One is my brother-in-law, Peter Boisey-Smith. The other is
Matt Stone from the C.I.A. He has been sent to help, it's sort of a
combined effort with the U.S.A."

"Why?"

"Why, he repeated her question as if he were stumped for
words".

"Yes, why would we need an American to help us Paul?"

"Well my dear, it's just that the U.S. and our boys are
combining all covert operations at the moment."

She was sitting, scrutinizing Paul, not impressed with his
explanation, when suddenly the door opened and two men walked
in. She recognized Boisey as being the Englishman from Paul's
earlier description. The other person she knew had to be the
American agent, Matt Stone but what she wasn't prepared for was
the fact that she recognized him. A cold prickling sensation
started at the roots of her hair then moved down her body until
she felt her legs go weak. When her eyes met with his she knew

instantly that this was someone special, someone very special. It wasn't just his handsome clean-cut features, or his easy, casual manner, neither was it his magnetic smile. No, it was more, much more. It was like seeing a ghost. It was the man from Heathrow airport. Then at that very moment she remembered a dream she had on the plane coming in from Italy. She was shaken beyond belief. Could he be, she thought, could he be my soul-mate? Can this be the person I travel with each life-time? He walked toward her. She was embarrassed. She stood up, her hair fell across her face, she brushed it aside. His eyes seemed to sparkle full of recognition. "Louise?" he said almost as a question.

"No, actually it's Louisa, and you're Matt? She said, as much a statement, as a question. Then she stuttered, "We meet again."

"Yes, we sure do," he said. "I didn't imagine I would ever see you again after Heathrow. I don't know why I called you Louise, after all Boisey filled me in on the way here. I guess I wasn't paying attention, but I certainly am now." He said seemingly a little embarrassed. Then he continued, "It's amazing I feel as if I know you, I mean, not just from the airport it's as if I've known you all my life. It's, err really quite strange."

Then he just stood holding her hand and smiling at her. Her body shifted with embarrassment and she blushed. She watched him studying her, as if he were breathing in her very beauty, enveloping her in admiration, running his eyes over her like a hand stroking silk, enjoying every moment of their encounter. She was excited at the closeness it was as if they had never been apart. He took her other hand and placed his lips on the back of it, she felt the gentle brush of his kiss her body tingled.

"I know you too," she said.

Boisey looked amused. "You two know each other?"

Louisa looked at Boisey, not really knowing how to answer the question.

"Well, in a manner of speaking. We almost met at the airport." she stuttered, looking at Matt who surprisingly had blushed.

"I think we know each other from our past lives," Matt laughed, seeming to make light of the situation.

"Oh my God you were in my dream." She blurted out, and then felt embarrassed.

"You were in mine too. "

"Which way is the bathroom John? I'd like to freshen up," Louisa said pulling away feeling self-conscious and just wanting to withdraw quickly from the attention.

"Just down the hall, my dear." He pointed towards the door, showing to turn left outside.

She excused herself and left the room.

#

After Louisa left the room Matt turned to greet the others whom he had largely ignored with the shock of meeting Louisa.

"Come and meet John." Boisey said." Matt looked at the older man standing before him. It was definitely his friend John Wiener, the doctor in the vision, and the owner of this very house in the late Georgian era. When John's hand reached out to greet him, it reaffirmed his dream it had all been real. He took John's hand in acknowledgment. John smiled. Matt wondered if the smile told its own story. Were words necessary, did both know each other and why they were there?

"Greetings my friend," came John's gentle welcome.

"Likewise John, likewise."

Even when he realized that it was the same house as in his dream, vision, or whatever it was, he had hardly expected to find him here.

Paul was amused. "I can see that you two also know one another?" John answered the question. "Oh yes we do, but from way, way back."

Matt realized John had the knowledge of their real mission and had now confirmed it, as they had not met before in this life. Perhaps the others hadn't remembered their dream yet. He wanted to ask them if they had a similar dream, but of course that might sound ridiculous. No, he thought, as it wasn't a dream but a real incident it was just a matter of time before they admitted their awareness and acknowledged the real mission. Matt finished shaking John's warm hand, then moved his attention to the, blond, well-dressed man and said, "Hi Paul, old buddy, how are you doing?" Matt recognized Paul from several years before.

Paul stood up putting out his hand, "Fine Matt. It's been a long time." He nodded towards Boisey who was now seated by the window. "I understand you've already met my brother-in-law."

Matt looked over to where Boisey was sitting by the window and said, "Boisey is your brother-in-law? I had no idea he didn't mention it. He's quite er' different, should I say"

Matt thought about the situation: John, Louisa, Boisey, Paul, and himself. Only Baxter was missing from the dream. Now he knew it hadn't been a dream, amazing.

#   #   #

When Louisa returned from the bathroom she found the others talking quietly around the long polished table that was now littered with maps and the plans of her family chateau that Paul had brought with them. She took a seat across from Matt and smiled at him before turning to the others. She was still feeling confused and a little shaken with the incredible meeting with him. How could she possibly meet a person for the first time and act so irrationally? How embarrassing.

First tea was served by Alice the housekeeper. After some polite conversation, John spread out the map of Italy and a diagram of the chateau and began to unfold the plan to the others, explaining in turn, each person's role in the scheme.

"I will provide the transport in and out. I will take you in by car and bring you out by helicopter." Then he turned to Louisa.

"Louisa, could you help by filling in as much information about the chateau as possible. I know you and Paul have pretty much covered everything and he made notes for us, but if you could just go over these plans of the chateau with the others, just to make sure of the details."

"Ok" she said.

Paul then turned to Louisa and said, "I expect you've realized by now that this is not simply a plan to release your mother." He looked a little ashamed.

"I thought that from the start," she said with no emotion showing on her face, she was not amused.

Paul seemed flustered, but went on. "What it is in fact is a plan devised by our two governments to discover the exact time that your father and his associates intend to initiate a war in the Middle East. We need to do this before it's too late." He paused for a moment, perhaps waiting to see her reaction. There was none. She just sat quietly waiting for Paul to continue.

"So, I'm afraid, we have, or should I say I have, not been quite truthful."

"Not to worry Paul, as I said I figured that from the start" she said, looking at him with some distain from the other end of the table. "I know he's power crazy, but starting a war are you sure?

"Very sure, Mario your uncle-in-law gave us a great deal of information that is very sound, I'm not sure if you know, but unfortunately he has since been killed by your Father, we think he probably suspected him of espionage."

"My God what do you mean, are you saying Father killed him or are you saying he had him killed?"

"Louisa, he had him killed, I was actually there when it happened."

"Oh my God that's terrible, that is absolutely terrible, I need to get Mummy out of there now."

John smiled and nodded towards her and said in a gentle voice "Yes, don't worry, we will."

She felt little angry and humiliated by the deception but she wasn't about to show it. It was her reaction to Matt that bothered her more, much more. She could not get him out of her mind. He was tall with jet black hair slicked back and tied in a pony-tail which fascinated her. He was wonderfully attractive, but could he really be her soul-mate? She couldn't explain her reaction to him any other way. It was madness. Why couldn't she take her eyes off him? She watched as he talked with the others about the plan. His handsome face changed from smiles to deep thought, his eyes would flash with fire if he disagreed with one of the others. He would stare with intensity at the maps then, with great thought, give his own point of view. She knew people, and he was one strong, hard, resolute person, but not without compassion.

With their scheme complete, they rose from the table. Louisa walked over to the window and looked out into the street. It was dark outside. A car passed by with its lights dimmed by the night fog. She caught what she thought to be the outline of a man standing on the opposite side of the street. He was staring in their direction. She shivered and wondered why. Maybe it was the thought of going out into the cold night air. Or was it the man across the street? She wasn't sure. Then a voice whispered in her ear.

"How about dinner tonight?"

She turned to see Matt's smiling face.

"That sounds great," she said, then felt embarrassed at her instant reply.

"I'm staying at the Inn on the Park. Where do you live, Louisa?"

"South Ken, number ten Hope Mews. It's not ten minutes from your hotel by cab."

"I'll pick you up about nine o'clock, if that's OK?"

"That'll be wonderful."

John called for a cab. Matt waited for her to say good-bye to the others then walked her to the waiting cab. They shook hands politely. He said, "Nine then."

She nodded and smiled at him. She felt like a teenager making arrangements for her first date, then as the door of the cab closed Louisa slid across the leather seat and looked out of the side window. She looked into the darkness and saw a pair of sinister eyes staring after the departing vehicle.

Ten Hope Mews had been a gift to her from her mother on her eighteenth birthday. Of all the places she had lived, this was the place she loved. She paid the cab then found her key in the half-light of the doorway. The cobblestone mews was deserted, but she had an uneasy feeling as if she were being watched. Then her attention was distracted by the sound of the telephone ringing inside. She pushed the key into the lock and opened the door. Throwing her coat onto a chair, she picked up the receiver.

"Louisa this is your father."

"Oh hi," she replied with a matter of fact tone in her voice.

"I understand you have been seeing Paul, Paul Johnson-Marsh. Is that right?"

"Seeing him is not exactly right, he is just a friend Father. Anyway I thought he was a friend of the family."

"Of course he is, my dear, but why did you meet with him?

"He just asked me to dinner that's all. Why do you have a problem with that?

175

"No Louisa, not at all, I just wondered that´s all, did he mention anything about his visit here?"

"Like what? No nothing, anyway I was going to phone you, I would like to come back soon, if that is Ok. I only spent a little time with mother, as I had to fly back here for a meeting,

"Good, I´ll expect you then"

The phone clicked dead. Strange, she thought. How could he know? Why did he even care? Seldom, if ever, has he been interested in my life. Maybe he is more interested in Paul than me she thought. After showering she walked to her wardrobe and threw it open in desperation. She searched through the great quantity of clothes until finally a garment dropped to the floor. It was a silk dress that had slipped from its hanger to land in a soft pile on the carpet. She bent and picked it up. The fabric felt delicate, right for the occasion. She began to think of recent events. What could it all mean? First there was Paul, who seemed to be so kind, but had it been just a ploy to use her? Now her stepfather seemed to have an unusual interest in him. Ought she to warn him?

Then there was Matt, who is he? How could it be that she was in raptures over a man she had only just met? But she did have this strange feeling that she had known him all her life or even in some other life. She sat down at the mirror, slowly brushing her hair, while trying to piece the puzzle together. What if the handsome Matt is her soul-mate, does it mean this meeting was pre-arranged? Did this mean she was to play a part in some divine circumstance? Could her stepfather be a kind of anti-Christ? She had always taken his, 'I'm the Son of God' bit, with a pinch of salt, but he certainly is evil and possibly a great danger to world peace, there was little doubt about that.

Then, taking a last look in the mirror, she stood up, feeling good. A shiver of anticipation ran through her body.

After Louisa's departure Boisey also left, saying he would pick Matt up in an hour or so. Paul and Matt waited while John took his time to sit down in the armchair by the fireplace. The room was now quite dark except for the flickering of the coals. This brought back the vivid memory of his recent experience in the house. John gazed at Paul who could tell he was about to say something important and waited in anticipation.

"Do you know why we are really here?" John said.

Paul nodded, "To help stop a war. But that's not what you really mean, is it?"

"No, you're quite right, that's not what I mean at all. I was wondering if you feel you may have another mission here, say something more on the spiritual side."

Paul seemed irritated by this and stood up saying, "I really have to go old chap. Charles expects me back tonight with a report on our meeting."

"Just a minute Paul, sit down. I haven't finished."

With some reluctance Paul sat down on the couch. John went on. "I was referring to an understanding at a higher level, an awareness which I believe you have."

"Like the fact that I know our mission is to delay the war, not to try and stop the inevitable," Paul, said.

"That's right Paul," John said. "Then you recall going back, good. I thought you'd remembered when you arrived today. Although I believe you were still unsure until I mentioned it now?"

"Your right I was. I'm sorry. It's just that I find it difficult to talk about but when we met today — I felt somehow different. I've been thinking about it ever since. I have always had a feeling or a perception of the future, one that I couldn't explain. I have often wondered whether the things that I seem to know by instinct, such as life, death, God, reincarnation, the next war, and so on, were just figments of my vivid imagination or whether I really do have a special mission in life. I did have what I thought was a strange dream the night before last but now I know it wasn't a dream, was it."

"Then you do know, you do remember."

"So, we have lived here before." Paul said.

John laughed, "Yes. Yes we have, many times. In fact, we have all experienced one or other of the small Cleansings before. Matt you remember that I'm sure you do?"

"Very much so, we talked about it in the dream." Matt replied.

"Cleansing, what Cleansing?" Paul asked warily.

"Like Matt said, we talked about it in the dream, I think you know Paul," John said.

"You mean Sodom and Gomorrah for instance?" Paul asked.

"Yes, exactly although that wasn't a major global cleansing as in the time of Atlantis when only Noah and his family were spared. It was quite limited by comparison, but nevertheless it was a cleansing."

"It's a little vague John but I can remember being in one of the cities before the destruction and I recall seeing the explosion from a distance. White light so brilliant it burned into my eyes. Yes John, I do remember."

There was a sound of a siren in the distance. "That a siren I hear?" Matt asked.

John's voice seemed indifferent. "They're just testing the emergency equipment. The papers are full of stories of an impending war between the Arab Nations and Israel. I think its propaganda put out by Interpre, you know, the public relations company from Montreal."

"Is that the same outfit that the Kuwait royal family hired to get the United States to take action against Saddam in the Gulf?" Paul asked.

"Exactly, even though the US had given Saddam the green light to invade Kuwait as they were parallel driving into his oil fields. That PR Company did a great job of conning Bush senior into reversing that decision and getting them involved. We believe

178

Don Vinchenti has hired the same company to convince the Europeans into believing the Arabs are starting a war against Israel," John said.

"John," Matt said. "Can I ask you about our time in England when I was regressed by you?"

"Of course you can."

"That time that you regressed me back to other lives, the girl I met there was she Louisa?"

"Yes of course the very same. I'm surprised you had to ask."

"God, then, Louisa is my soul-mate."

"I have another question"

"Go ahead"

"How come you are living in the same house as you were at that time and with Alice your house-keeper, what's more you both look the same?

"We always look the same or similar in each life, but the house, I´m not sure, maybe the computer program had something to do with it, or just luck. I happened to be looking for a house and when I saw the flat was for sale and of course I recognized it as being our old house. Alice, how did we get back together, well that's a long story. Unfortunately as you can see someone had converted it into two flats, rather a shame." John smiled then carried on. "By the way there is another one of the team who should have joined us by now."

"Baxter! Yes of course?" Matt said, remembering his regression. "I just left him at the airport. He's off to the Middle East, well, at least, that's what he said."

Paul rose from his chair. "John I must go." Then he paused and said. "Good luck I will keep in touch."

"Thanks, we need a lot of luck, although they don´t know it a great many players continuing existence depends on it. It's up to these chaps. I'm sure they'll find a way. I've given Boisey a shopping list of explosives to add to his own needs. I think between these two we have the expertise," John said.

Paul shook hands with both Matt and John then walked to the door. "I'll call you as soon as your travel arrangements are made," he said as he left the room.

A few minutes after he had gone John sat down next to Matt and put his arm on his shoulder, "You know there is only a little time left, if we can't delay the war, we'll all perish."

Alice entered the room carrying yet another pot of tea. John poured a little of the hot tea into the saucer, and blew on it. Then, after sipping from the saucer, he spoke.

"The trouble is this Vinchenti character has made plans different from those we anticipated. It takes nearly three weeks for the only Light-Ships we have in the Game to get here as they are traveling from the galaxy Alpha Centauri. It's more than four million light years from here. They left more than two weeks ago so they will be here providing there are no space anomalies within seventy two hours, but if Vinchenti lets loose before that."

"At the speed of light John, that'll take them four million years, no?"

"No, not at all we are in a virtual Universe the Light Ships can jump in and out of space-time traveling inside an envelope of phase distortion."

"Ok John, who is Don Vinchenti, is he the Devil?"

John laughed. "I suppose for want of a better name you could call him that, or at least one of the Devil's disciples.

"You see the Game masters found much to their regret that when they created this Universe the program had some interesting quirks, or faults if you like and in this Galaxy a strange and evil life-form was created. Their home planet is known as Hades. It's positioned about forty light years from here

When they originally seeded this planet as a University they weren't aware at the time that it is in somebody else's backyard, so to speak. The Hades are also a form of intelligent atoms but without compassion, an evil nation of spirits who take control of civilizations by propagating corruption. They are unlike us they have little tangible substance they are more like a virus when they are in their primary form therefore as parasites they must transfer their energy into an alien life-form such as the human mind. They are only able to take control if the soul of that body is a willing party, or more precisely, easily corrupted. Even then, there has to be a mutual collusion on a continual basis for them to keep full control. At any time the recipient can throw the parasite out. They move from planet to planet pretty much the same way as a virus does here on Earth. We don't know how or who brought them here, possibly an alien race stopped here at some time in the past and unwittingly dropped them off, or even a meteorite landed here with the virus, or should I say life form, still intact.

It has been difficult enough trying to bring students through the education period and losing them to their own narcissistic nature, without the added encumbrance of an outside force seducing them into corruption. We believe Vinchenti is hosting one of the Hades and therefore he must be destroyed along with all the players, who have not developed"

John looked at his watch. "It's four o'clock, let's watch Sky news." He stood up, walked over to the television and switched it on.

It had been a long time since Matt had seen British news. It was always a serious business for the English, but this time more than ever. The newscaster was a solemn man whose eloquent voice droned a communication of deep depression.

"Brussels, Paris and Berlin saw another day of rioting. The continuing unrest has now spread to all but a few of the E.U cities. The troubles began again last week when the new E.U directive was announced, the electronic tagging of all new-born babies. This will mean a small chip the size of a pinhead will be inserted into the arm of all new born babies. The law will become compulsory next year.

The violent outcry against this is without precedence, and is tearing apart the very heart of the countries of Europe. Without doubt this regulation is seen by the public to be the last straw. With so many new regulations implemented by Brussels the European population has finally realized the cost it has imposed on freedom, independence and liberty.

Crime is at an all-time high with the continuing widespread demonstrations against the government made worse by the large gangs of National Front supporters roaming our streets fighting day and night against our undermanned riot police. Here like Europe the country is in chaos.

He paused. "In an interview today from his country home in the Italian mountains, the President of Italy and currently the EU Don Vinchenti, made this statement"

The television picture switched to show Don Vinchenti seated in a huge gothic chair. The program broke into the middle of his speech, "time has come for the members of the European Community to stand together. We must be ready in our resolve to defend Israel against the confederation of Islamic nations. As we all know our troubles in Europe have been brought on by their high price of oil which has ruined our economies. The Arab's objective in the Middle East is the complete destruction of the State of Israel, therefore we must be united in our resolve for world peace. "

John switched the volume down.

Matt turned away from the TV puzzled. He looked to John. "What's the deal with Vinchenti? It's nothing to do with the price of oil it's the lack of jobs and shortage of money caused by the grasping industrialists moving their manufacturing assets to China, just like Vinchenti. Also the governments, or should I say the privileged class, intentionally allowed a lack of effective import tariffs just so they and their cronies could further profit from their investments manufactured in China. That John, is what caused the manufacturing base to be devastated in the US and Europe which also added to melt down."

"Yes Matt that's true, but we can't blame China for allowing them to take their assets into the country to manufacture at a very low cost. They needed to grow their economy and were able to pay their workers an incredibly low wage, compared to the basic income necessary to live in the West.

Now because of this, and the lack of employment in the West, the work force has lived within a credit card bubble, trying to maintain a standard of living far beyond what it could currently afford, unfortunately, still believing that jobs would come back from the East, they held onto their instant access to materialism, which has taken them even deeper into financial disaster.

To make matters worse for the poor and this brought them to their knees the already extremely wealthy investors bought shares in the pay day loan companies, whose shocking interest rates were up to six thousand per cent. Which actually made the traditional, house to house loan sharks look virtuous by comparison."

"Yes John I know, greed stalks the world, and of course Vinchenti is one of the wealthiest of those profiteers."

For the next few minutes the television showed graphic pictures of streets full of black smoke from burning buildings. Then the camera swung toward the rioters chased by baton wielding police, while others ran from shops carrying their spoils from among the burning melee. The camera switched to a scene away from the riots, it showed children sitting in apparent squalor surrounded by uncollected rubbish, while drunken adults reeled about the pavement nearby. The pictured flicked back to the newscaster he continued.

"Here at home we are experiencing the same apprehension as we did before the beginning of World War Two."

Then they showed films of people hanging blackout curtains in their windows and boarding their homes. Shopkeepers were cladding their windows with wooden siding, while outside of

London huge machines were seen digging great trenches in preparation for underground shelters to be constructed.

The picture switched to a camera in a helicopter above London. Except for the streetlights the City was dark, almost deserted of cars and people. In the background the commentator was still talking.

"Tonight London is in comparative darkness. As you can see, the city is quieter than it has been for decades, the great blackout of World War Two has returned to London."

John turned off the television. "So you see Matt, things are heating up. There's a feeling of panic in the air. The public are not sure what's going to happen, but they know something is. We need to get into Vinchenti's chateau, find out what we can and create some diversion or cause a situation that will make him delay his plans."

Matt felt relieved that he now knew the facts. Of course it was going to be difficult and he wondered if they had time to pull it off, but John had an aura surrounding him that gave Matt a confidence that he was unable to explain.

The door swung open revealing the smiling face of Boisey.

"Ready Mate"

Matt finished his tea and stood up, "John my old buddy, it has been great seeing you again and I'm pleased, that at last, I know what's going on. I was beginning to think I was losing my mind." He smiled. "I'll wait for your call."

They walked out together Boisey opened the waiting cabs door and said. "Ok Matt I've a little unfinished business to attend to before I can leave for Italy. So if you don't mind we will stop by my office" Then he grinned closing the cab door behind them.

Through a chink in the curtains John watched as Boisey and Matt climbed into a cab. Then he saw a car in the dark opposite the house pulling out behind the departing vehicle. He turned from the window and hurried down the steps to a car parked waiting outside the house. In seconds, it too sped away. John returned to the room seemingly unconcerned. He picked up his mobile phone entered a number then spoke. "George did you catch them up, yes is it, good man follow them, when I saw that car pull out it that's exactly what I thought, so keep an eye on them."

He went to the drinks cupboard and opened the door and poured himself a single malt whisky.

Chapter 22

Death in the East End

Matt watched with interest as the cab drove through the dark streets of London. All was quiet as the cab came to a stop at the traffic lights at Aldgate. Matt noticed a policeman standing alone in the falling rain. He had an enormous respect for the London police walking the streets alone unarmed in all weathers, they were the last true guardians of peace in this modern world.

The engine in the diesel cab rattled as they drew away from the lights. Matt turned to look out of the back window and saw the young policeman staring after the cab as it disappeared into the night followed closely by a black limousine. The dark tinted windows of the limousine told their own story. Matt nudged Boisey giving him a silent message as if to say take a look behind, which he did.

Boisey called to the taxi driver, more in the manner of a command than a request, "Left here cabbie." The cab turned sharply into the narrow street, it seemed even darker than the others did.

"Ok mate," Boisey said then he paid the fare before stepping out into the street. The cab pulled away, leaving the two of them standing on the pavement. Matt looked around, there were a number of drunks littering the pavement, some sitting on the curb others clustered in doorways.

He stared into the darkness and saw that the limousine that had been following them had stopped. As the cab departed it began to move slowly toward them. He motioned to Boisey at the same time reaching inside his suit jacket feeling for the cold metal of the Browning. The limousine came on toward them, slowly, deliberately. Then it stopped thirty feet from where they stood. The lights on the car switched off. Only the purring of the engine could be heard.

Suddenly he felt a hand touch his shoulder. He spun round. The unshaved, stinking wretch stood for a moment with his hand out, then staggered back collapsing in a drunken heap. The moment of distraction had given away the advantage. He turned back too late, a shot rang out, and Matt knew he had been hit. He wiped away the warm body fluid that ran down his face and into his eyes.

Then to one side he saw Boisey take aim at the car he heard the crack of his gun firing, but still the car continued moving towards them. Carefully he took aim at the car as it came even closer but just at the moment he put pressure to the trigger, he lost his sight. Again he tried to wipe away the blood that filled his eyes and then from somewhere near the limousine he heard the great roar of an automatic weapon being fired.

He threw himself to the pavement rolling away from the road while wiping his eyes. Now with his sight restored he could see, but what he saw wasn't nice. He had rolled into yet another drunken derelict. This one was dead and had the stench of a rotting rat.

He looked up at the limousine it had stopped. Nothing in the street moved, the tramps, drunks, and vagabonds had vanished, he saw that Boisey was getting to his feet otherwise the street was empty. They were alone.

Still pointing his gun toward the vehicle Matt stood up. All was silent, except the distant wail of a police car. They walked toward the limousine.

"Shit man what the hell was that, I thought it was world war three, I take it we had back up," Matt said.

Boisey never replied, but Matt could feel a coldness coming from him that he couldn't explain. In the darkness he could see a great mass of bullet holes drilled through the car and shattering the windshield. Cautiously, he opened the car door. There were two corpses inside the car. The driver and his companion were unrecognizable. The cascade of bullets had not only killed but also blasted away their facial details.

Boisey searched inside the car and finding nothing took the keys from the ignition then walked to the back of the car, Matt followed him. Boisey opened the trunk, they both looked down at a bundle, yet another body.

"Jeffery."

The body had been weighted and bound, ready for a trip to the bottom of a river.

Matt looked at Boisey "A friend?"

Yes, a friend." Boisey said as he closed down the trunk.

Matt looked around for the shooter but the street was empty, they quickly walked away from the scene and back to the Mile End road where they hailed a cab. On the short journey Matt reasoned that only John could have known they were followed and must have arranged the protection. Certainly Boisey's gun, had not, or could not create such devastation.

The cab took them to a street near Mile End road underground station, finally arriving outside an old Georgian house. They stepped out into the dark street, paid the cab and walked toward the building. Looking up Matt saw a sign discreetly hanging above the door. It read:

Peter Boisey-Smith. M.D
And
Doctor of Natural Medicine.

Boisey pushed the door open and walked through the crowded waiting room, carefully stepping around the children playing on the floor. He smiled at the young and the old, touching each of them gently on their heads or squeezing their hands as he passed by. Matt followed him intrigued by the complete role reversal.

A slim middle aged nurse with short trim hair, a pretty smiling face dressed in a starched white uniform waited patiently while he took the time to bend and speak to a blind child. Then he walked into his office, followed by Matt.

"Doctor, look at your friends head, my God." She reached up to attend to it. Matt took her hand gently, "its Ok nurse it's just a scratch."

Matt walked over to a washbasin and began to clean the dried blood from his face and washed his hands.

"You're late, Doctor. I was worried. What on earth happened?" she asked.

"I'm sorry Jess, I had an important meeting to attend to in Hampstead then we had a slight detour. By the way," he said putting his arm around her shoulder and kissing her gently on her cheek. "I shall be leaving for a little business trip in the next day or so. I'll need to reschedule my appointments for the next two weeks."

"Oh dear Peter," she said, "That is going to be very difficult darling you're booked up solid, way past Christmas." She seemed very distraught, almost as if he had told her of the impending disaster.

"Don't worry Jess, I'll be able to get someone to stand in for me."

"Peter," she said, "you know jolly well there's not even a remote possibility of that."

"Come on Jess, you're giving me much too much credit. I'll get Dr. Lo from Stratford to stand in for me."

"He's just a Chinese pin doctor. He hasn't your talent."

"Yes he has, Jess. The acupuncture needles are only part of his healing method. Don't worry he has the gift too. Come on let's get on. Who's first?"

"OK. It's Mrs. Haswell. Her son is blind. He's the boy you spoke to on your way in."

She walked to the door, opened it, and beckoned to the mother. Matt sat discretely down in a chair away from the door. Boisey slipped on a white coat hanging on a peg behind the door. Matt could see he felt at home. The woman entered the room clasping the child by the hand.

"Take a seat Mrs. Haswell." Boisey motioned towards a chair set some distance from his desk. She looked at him with surprise. Even though there was another seat closer to his desk, she sat down as instructed.

"What's the boy's name?"

"John. Most call him Johnny though."

"How old is he?"

"E'll be five, next June."

"Has he been blind since birth?"

"E' was born like it Doctor."

"Let the boy come to me," Boisey said in a gentle manner, knowing his voice would comfort the blind boy as well as reassure the mother.

"Doctor, he can't see. I told you, e's been blind since I ad I'm."

"Let him go, don't worry, he can sense my presence."

Boisey moved out from behind the desk and squatted down in preparation for the boy to come toward him.

"Come here Johnny, come towards my voice, don't worry, it'll be fine."

He felt good. He knew it was going well, he could feel the boy already responding to him.

"As you walk toward me, you will see the dark shadow of my body. Don't be afraid. Soon the mist will clear for you. Come now, come to me."

Now he waited as the boy walked slowly, hesitantly across the room toward him.

"Slowly," he whispered, as if to himself. "God is with you." The child carefully crossed the carpet arriving into the welcome hands of Boisey.

"Johnny, I want you to pray to God every night and ask for his help. When you go to bed, lie quietly and think of your body healing itself, think of all the little atoms in your eyes, clearing them of the fog. You can see a little now and every day you will see more."

The boy turned toward to his mother, "Mummy I can see something, I think I can see you."

The mother stood up, she was shaking. She ran to the boy and picked him up. Choking back the tears, her voice thick with emotion, she tried to thank Boisey. Unable to do it in words, she threw her arms around him and sobbed.

"It's a miracle Doctor."

"No Mrs. Haswell, it's not a miracle, the lad could probably see a little before, but he has been told he is blind and therefore his mind and body lived to it. What he needs is positive thought, from you and from him his sight will then improve. The body has its own healing program. It's just that it has to be switched on. Once it has been started, positive faith will maintain its progress. If you help him believe he can see — he will."

She looked at him with tears in her eyes, "You know something Doctor, your right. I've always treated him like an invalid. Thank you, thank you." She took his hand, squeezed it, and without another word walked out of the surgery.

When Jess returned, she was beaming.

"Send the next patient in Jess," Boisey said.

After the last of the patients had left Boisey stood up. He was tired. Taking his white coat off then slipping his jacket back on he said to Matt. "Wait here a moment, I won't keep you much longer, I'm nearly finished,"

With that he left the room and went into the office where he found Jess putting the last of the files away.

He took Jess's hand and gently kissed it. "I have left signed checks for you to post to this list charities throughout London, most of which you already know. I need to go now, the next time I see you it may be in quite different circumstances."

Boisey kissed her, hugged her for a moment, and then walked to the door ready to leave. Jessica almost threatening him, moved between him and the door.

"No Peter you can't go just like that, I know you have something important to do but we've been friends a long time and I've seen you heal many people. You have given all of your time and money to help the sick and the poor. I don't understand why you haven't kept something for yourself I mean what about your retirement? One day you'll need money and you'll have nothing. You must have given away a fortune in the last twenty years." She stopped, looking embarrassed by her outburst, then added. "And I love you."

"Money," he said, "and material things are just an encumbrance Jess, this life is only a learning platform. Everything changes nothing is forever. Have you ever wondered why, after somebody leaves the surgery, it seems as if his or her visit was just a dream? That's because the only reality is the present, Jess. Time is constant. The past and the future for us do not exist. Now is the only reality. When we die, it will be the same for us, just as if this was all a dream. This planet will be a distant memory. Nothing matters except love, the love you have for others and the education you gain while you are here are the only things that you can take with you."

He held her hand even tighter.

"Don't concern yourself about anything that happens while I am away. Trust in God Jess. You'll be all right."

"What do you mean Peter? Do you really think this is this the beginning of a war? I hear a lot of talk about it"

"Jess, you and your family will be saved. I promise, I love you and I promise we will be together very soon, don't worry." He kissed her again.

Then he called out to Matt to join him in the office, there they said goodbye to Jess and without another word walked out into the dark street.

There were no lights to be seen from the houses, the darkness was intense. The Mile End road was almost deserted, interrupted only by the passing lights of police cars and the occasional lonesome taxi-cab. Boisey hailed one, it pulled up just passed where they were standing.

"You better get going I believe you have an important date tonight." He said to Matt.

"I'm impressed with what you did."

"Don't be, I would like to do more, but it's not to be. I'll call you as soon as we know something."

Matt walked toward the cab and as he opened the door he looked back, Boisey had gone.

In the back of the cab he recalled the scenes on the television and began to think how the world had changed. It seemed only a few years had passed when everybody had hailed the demise of the Berlin wall. Like overzealous children the West had grasped at the opportunity of peace with open hands. But Matt knew that Russia needed to recover from near economic disaster, so had cleverly axed her expensive dissident satellite states, leaving them in civil war and ruin. The Russian countryside was devastated by years without environmental control. Siberia, a chemical wasteland as far as the eye could see, with its indigenous population almost extinct. Towns and cities across the republic were seething in sewage, blighted by clouds of acid rain from sulfur emissions caused by nickel smelting. The Black Sea now dead ruined by heavy fertilizer leakage. The Aral Sea had been virtually emptied of water, diverted for cotton field irrigation. Industrial smoke caused birth defects, bronchitis, lung cancer, and leukemia. All this had brought life expectancy in many areas of Russia down to a mere fifty years and the worst case was in the Buryat Republic, where it was as low as thirty years.

So, simulating a changeover to democracy, Russia had regained her economy with financial help from the beguiled West and through the naiveté of the United States business community. She had returned to a form of communism or more correctly collective dictatorship, which of course she had never actually left, just conveniently camouflaged. The old Communist rear guard, of the former U.S.S.R. was firmly back in power. Strong again, but confined to her historical borders, Matt knew she badly needed new unpolluted land and was ready to march for it. March she would, and God help anyone who stood in her way.

Then Matt reflected on Germany's troubles. Although united with East Germany, she had internal problems, economic, political and racial. The right wing fascists, stronger and more determined than ever, had rekindled their imperial spirit.

On another front the Islamic fundamentalist nations loathing the United States and despising it as much as they do Israel had joined together with their traditional enemies, pooling their resources in attempt to take over all the Arab states by force.

He left his thoughts as the cab pulled up under the canopy of The Inn on the Park. The Hotel was in darkness, screens at the windows and doors allowing no light to escape. The doorman, holding a flashlight, opened the door of the cab for Matt. "Good evening sir," he said, walking to the door of the Hotel. Then, pulling open the door for him said, "Have a nice evening."

Matt walked through the entrance. It was like entering another world. The foyer was crowded with exquisitely dressed women accompanied by men wearing black ties and dark evening suits. The elegant couples were all standing chatting excitedly as they waited for cabs to arrive. Then one by one, the various groups, aided by the uniformed staff disappeared out into the darkness. Matt took the elevator up to his room.

Chapter 23

Jennings House

After seeing Matt off in the cab Boisey stepped back into the darkness of a doorway and waited to see if there were any more nasty surprises. He waited until all seemed clear. He thought of Jeffery then Jennings. He knew it was against the rules to kill for revenge, but this was different.

He felt the need to talk about it, but there was nobody that would understand. He wanted to rid his mind of the hatred building for Jennings, but it was impossible. He had to do something. He stepped out into the road and stopped a passing cab.

"Woodford, Mate," he said as he climbed in. The cab driver turned for a moment as if to make some objection, but after looking into Boisey's cold eyes he turned back to face the road and murmured, "Right John."

Boisey gave further directions as the journey progressed until they stopped at the corner of a tree-lined road. He paid the driver and walked away from the cab in the opposite direction he intended to go. As soon as the cab was out of sight, he doubled back and walked around the corner into a quiet road. Tall hedgerows hid the large houses of the truly wealthy. Wrought iron gates spoke of privacy, while the echoing howl of a dog coming from deep in the grounds of one of the homes sent a warning to any intruder.

Finally he stopped outside one of the houses and peered through the gates past the trees before scaling the damp wall next to the gate and dropping into the garden. Treading carefully through the undergrowth, he moved toward the house. He looked at his watch. It was too early, he thought. So he took a seat with his back to a tree to wait until the occupants would retire to bed, meanwhile he would sleep.

Sometime later he woke up to find the seat of his pants wet, so as all the lights in the house were now out he decided that the occupants must be asleep. He stood up and stretched his stiff muscles. After loosening up, he walked quickly across the lawn toward the house. Each window he tried had a locking mechanism set on the inside. He looked at the metal drainpipe and decided that would be his best route in. In just a few movements and aided by the mature ivy vine that covered the front of the house he climbed up to the first floor window, The window opened easily. He stepped in and closed it behind him. The room was a bedroom, fortunately vacant. In the hallway he stood silently waiting to detect where the occupants slept. The sound of snoring came from the room at the end of the hall. Quietly he opened the door and in the dim light he saw two figures lying in the bed. The moon shone onto the faces of the sleeping people. They didn't stir, and the man continued to snore. Jennings fat wife, lying next to him, wore curlers covered by a hair-net. The bedclothes had fallen from her, leaving layers of fat exposed, reminding Boisey of some grotesque Sumo wrestler.

He moved over to the bed and looked down at the sleeping man. Taking out a 357 with a silencer attached he took aim at Jennings temple. Then, as the extreme hatred of Jennings, for the murder of his friend Jeffery, mounted in him, he heard the words,

Thou shalt not kill, thou shalt not kill, thou shalt not kill, repeated over and over again until they were ringing inside his head.

Swearing under his breath he slowly lowered the gun and backed out of the room, closing the door behind him. Cautiously he found his way down the spiral staircase. He had just reached the bottom of the stairs when the grand-father clock struck, echoing around the tall ceilings. He stopped still for a moment to listen, then, not hearing any movement, he continued on into what appeared to be the den. His expert eye detected an old oak cabinet. Instantly he knew it would hold a safe. He smiled. It was a Dudley combination, easy.

The contents turned out to be disappointing. Perhaps Jennings didn't trust safes anymore. He laughed. There was a few thousand pounds, pocket money to a bookmaker, but the bundle of letters he found intrigued him. Why would Jennings put old letters in the safe he wondered? He took a moment to listen. All was silent except for the ticking of the grandfather clock, and the distant snoring coming from upstairs. He started to read some of the letters under the light of his tiny pocket light. After reading the first three letters it was clear that Jennings had been having an affair with the wife of Charley Coles.

Not a bright move, Jennings my old son Boisey thought. Charley, the most feared crime boss in London, is not going to be amused. He grinned as he closed the safe, stuffing some of the letters inside his jacket pocket. Quietly he climbed the stairs and returned to the Jennings bedroom. He crossed the room and carefully placed a few of the letters beside the pillow of the sleeping woman.

As Boisey climbed back over the wall he patted the pocket containing the remainder of the letters, and then smiled. He was thinking about Charley Coles and how he would like to be a fly on the wall when he received a phone call from Jennings wife, and then the post the next day.

Chapter 24

Matt arrived by cab just as Louisa stepped out of her front door. He jumped out to hold open the cab door for her. As their eye's met somehow she knew they were meant to be together. She smiled. They didn't speak on the journey to the restaurant. There was no need, she felt happy, content just to have his hand placed gently on hers.

While the cab sped through the dark streets, she was able to study Matt's facial features by the light of the few intermittent street lamps that still remained on.

He had high cheekbones and a strong nose. His eyebrows were straight and symmetrical and his eyes sparkled, his hair was dark and sleek, tied at the back. This was one handsome man. But were they really soul-mates? That same thought crossed her mind again and again. She enjoyed the warm feeling that emanated from him, and a perception of mental closeness, or was she reading too much into it, she wondered?

The crowded restaurant overlooked the river Thames. When they entered there was a lot of fuss surrounding their arrival. They were given a table next to a large picture window that was draped for the blackout. Louisa took her seat. She pulled the curtain aside and peered out into the gloom. The cold river below was barely visible in the murky night. She shivered and turned her attention back to the warmth of the intimate restaurant.

"Nice table," she said, smiling and giving Matt a look of surprise. She knew how difficult it must have been to arrange this table even though the near blackout of London ruined the view.

He shrugged his shoulders and winked at her. "I often come here when I'm in London. It's a shame about the view, it's normally wonderful."

They gave their drink order to the maître de, then rested back in the comfortable chairs to study the menu.

"Have you spent much time in London Louisa?" Matt said placing his menu on the edge of the table.

"Yes actually I have. I was living with someone for a time, but it didn't work out, so now I live on my own, it's much better. Actually before that I lived with an America lawyer, did you know that?

"No, I know nothing about you in this life. Do you have children?"

Louisa sat back looking distressed, she turned away from Matt. Her features wrenched in despair were caught in the candlelight, he could see that her eyes were filling with tears.

"There was a child, a girl. I miscarried."

"Oh my God, I'm so sorry I shouldn't have asked."

"It's OK. I didn't mean to blurt it out."

"Do you want to tell me what happened?"

"Of course I was a lot younger. We had a quarrel. I left and drove up to Vermont. We were living in the U.S at the time. Anyway I was pretty distressed I just wanted to get away from him. While I was driving I felt it coming on I lost her that night.

It was just at that moment the Italian waiter arrived to take their order. After brushing the crumbs from his vest and struggling with one hand to hitch his pants up over his protruding stomach, he proceeded to take their dinner order in a solemn manner. Louisa had now regained her composure and started to giggle as he left the table. Matt looked at her questioningly.

"What's funny?"

"Just the waiter, I think he believes we're someone special. Didn't you notice how respectful he was? That's really unusual, old Italian waiters normally have an air of nonchalance, he was quite civil by normal standards."

Matt leaned across the table and ran his fingers lightly through her hair. They looked deep into each other's eyes, she felt intoxicated by the moment. She pulled away troubled. There was something this handsome man was holding back. She had to ask, she had to know.

The drinks arrived and she took a sip. "Matt, what's happening? I have a feeling there's more to this than just the threat of war."

"It's difficult to explain," He said cautiously.

She smiled. "Try me."

For a moment he looked at her as if he wasn't sure whether to go on, then he relaxed. "OK. Something strange happened on my way over from the States." Then he carried on telling her about the experience. As he related his story, she began to remember the dream she had on the plane coming over from Italy. Slowly, as Matt told his tale she realized her dream had been almost identical. Her body tingled with excitement as she recalled the meeting in the dream and realized its implications.

As he finished his story the waiter arrived with the antipasto dish and placed it between them. He turned their glasses into the upright position, showed the label of the bottle of wine to Matt. Matt nodded the waiter poured it. She was excited and could hardly wait to tell Matt about her own dream. The waiter put the bottle down on the table and left.

"Matt I have to tell you something," she said excitedly. "I had the same dream on the plane coming back to London. I thought it was a dream at the time, but it wasn't, was it? We were actually back there, weren't we?"

"Yes we were. So you know why we're here then?"

"Yes, yes. I guess I do now, its mind blowing. My God I feel so elated."

They ate their antipasto in the flickering candlelight, both glancing from time to time into the others eyes.

"There is one thing I don't understand though."

"What's that?"

"Where did life start, if it didn't originate here?"

"Well the Game-masters."

"The Game-masters." She inquired.

"Yes they are our tutors or spiritual guides if you like. They are not here, they are on a planet in a different Universe, it's where we come from, and it's the only planet in our entire Universe, but it is our home. The Game-masters created this Universe in a laboratory which is run by a computer program."

"Like a video Game the kids play?

"Not exactly, similar but much advanced and actually when you are here, you are really here, this is reality. Anyway that is why it´s known as the Game and therefore the term Game-masters."

"I see, at least I think I see" she said even more intrigued.

"Everything on the planet either inorganic or biological is made from a collection of compressed atoms. You and I are each one single atom of pure intelligence from our Universe and we use these bodies when we are here to learn and eventually graduate, or not, as the case may be."

"I think I understand Matt. You mean, like a piece of wood for instance, which appears to be a solid object, is in fact a cluster of atoms."

Louisa swallowed the remains of the wine in her glass. She had always had a strong interest in astronomy and a belief in reincarnation, but this was different, quite different. Now she was beginning to understand, and it was fascinating.

"So in fact we're sort of aliens"

"I guess you could say that certainly as far as this Universe and planet is concerned we are."

"By the way, is there one Creator then? I mean one divine person, like God, or whatever?"

"I have no idea, I only know that by the time we graduate and reach the highest level of awareness we will understand."

She studied him, he was so handsome, his manner so composed. He paused and sipped his wine without taking his eyes from her. She watched him in the candlelight, it gave him the appearance of wearing a mask. His face changed a softness had come over it, almost to the point of tranquility. She cut and turned the last of the prosciutto onto her fork, lifting it to her mouth without taking her eyes from him.

The old waiter returned and waited for Matt to put down his fork and then reaching across the table he removed the plates and brushed the crumbs into his napkin. "Another bottle of the Barolo?" he asked, while pouring the last of the wine into their glasses.

Matt nodded.

Louisa eager to hear more said, "Go on Matt, what's next?"

"Well, do you remember in the dream we were told our mission?"

"Yes to delay the war so the Light-Ships have time to get here. But what I don't understand is when we die normally, how do we go back home? I mean, what's so different about this, why do we need Light-Ships."

"Well" he said thoughtfully, "normally when we die for instance we are transported back by a light expansion process. It takes our soul, or if you like, our atom, and spins it so fast that its wavelength becomes longer than that of a photon of light and can be transmitted home in just a few seconds."

The pasta had arrived without her being aware of it. Unconscious of her actions and without taking her eyes from Matt, she lifted the fork to her mouth. She tasted the food. It was good. The waiter came by, poured wine from the bottle and retreated. She felt pleasantly tipsy, and wanted to hear more.

"Go on. So why can't we be transported the normal way? Why the ships?" she asked.

"Well, we need to keep the physical bodies of players, or Souls if you like, that are to be saved this last time and will stay to help and rebuild this planet. Also there are many thousands of graduates who volunteered to be reincarnated back to assist and are here now.

After the first cleansing, at the time of Atlantis, it took years of rebirths to re-establish enough people for the planet to function properly again. So the Game-masters have sent three Light-Ships to lift us off the planet before the Cleansing. The problem would be if the war were to start before they arrive. That's where we come in. First we must find the date and time your stepfather intends to initiate the war and then somehow create a diversion, or some kind of obstruction, that will delay his plans. Also we must make sure he is destroyed."

"Do the others know all this?"

"Before I arrived in Britain, while I was still on the plane, I thought the whole thing was a dream," he said wiping his mouth slowly with his napkin. "As soon as I met John and Paul I knew it wasn't a dream." He leaned forward and held her hand. "They both know. We talked about it, and they both have total recall."

"And Boisey?" she asked.

"I'm sure he must know anyway I think he has already graduated and therefore he is probably a grade or two above us."

"It's funny you mentioned Atlantis, I think I may have been there at that cleansing in one of my first lives."

"Can you remember anything about it?"

"Not really Matt, just this faint recollection of being there. But I would love to have the chance to go back in time and experience that event."

"Who knows maybe you'll get the chance."

"By the way who is Baxter?" Louisa asked. "I remember him from the dream but I don't believe I knew him in any other life."

"He's a good friend. He was in a life-time with us in America in the nineteenth century. I met him on the flight over. I'm sure he knew why I was coming to London, but either he wasn't ready to talk about it, or maybe he thought I wasn't.

As you know from the dream he's involved with us in this mission. It's not surprising, he and I have spent many lives together, even though he's not my soul-mate."

Louisa looked at him with interest as she considered what he was about to suggest. She had to ask, she couldn't help herself, she knew the answer even before he spoke.

"Who is then?" she asked.

Once again he took her hand into his and then reached forward for the other. Holding them together and putting his lips gently to them, he whispered the words, "You are."

She felt her stomach turn as if she had been elevated up thirty floors in a fast elevator. The feeling of love swept in waves through her body, she felt her eyes filling, she could hardly see Matt through the tears that gently rolled down her face. It was then she knew for the first time. This was the real thing. She wasn't going out of her mind. No — she had met her true soulmate.

"I feel as if I am sitting on someone's shoulders, looking down, truly understanding about life and death for the first time. Wow!" For a moment she relived her dream and reflected on the situation.

"So what will happen to us when this is over? Will I come back here?" she asked, wiping a tear away with one finger and hoping her mascara hadn't run.

"Well, we may have a choice, I'm not certain," Matt said, dragging the words out slowly. "I would like to join the fleet."

"The fleet Matt, what fleet?"

"After we graduate when this is over we then we go back to our home Universe we will have many choices. For instance if we want to travel in the Game we can help pioneer a new planet or we can choose to work aboard one of the interplanetary vessels, that's what I would like to do."

"Are we Angels then?" she joked.

"Not Angels no wings, I believe when we graduate we will have an enlightened status though, maybe with some extra senses."

"You know Matt, I think, when I graduate and have a choice, I'd like to come back here. I love it here, it's a beautiful world, but the violence and the greed, it's such a mess. I can understand why it has to be cleaned and I'd like to help rebuild it."

She stopped for a moment, remembering an incident that sprang to mind. "You know the other day when I was walking through Hyde Park, I watched a dog playing with a ball. He would run with it, throw it, bite it, grab at it with his paws, chase it and then pick it up and run again, just having the best time. He was totally happy. Wouldn't it be wonderful if everybody in the world could be that happy? To be able to enjoy life without the encumbrance of materialism, to be like that little dog who owns nothing, has no material possessions, except maybe his collar. Yet he's completely happy with nothing other than the mutual love he shares with humans. Isn't that a sobering thought?"

"Yes it is, and that's the whole point, there's nothing wrong with materialism. Happiness can be achieved with or without it, it's the abuse of it that's wrong.

"When we as students reincarnate into a new life-time, if we have progressed and reached a higher level of awareness we are given a further challenge, another obstacle, material wealth, or power. This is when some people screw up. For instance, if you look at some of the players that have reached that level and have been given that challenge, such as pop stars, film stars, sports stars, politicians, wealthy families. They mess up by conveniently putting aside the awareness of their real origins and believe they are a cut above others, which is the beginning of their downfall. It's a difficult to reach the higher level and even more difficult to maintain it, only the strongest of students manage it." He finished the last of his wine, carefully placed the glass on the table and in a soft voice said, "Let's go."

Louisa sipped the last of her wine while Matt paid the check. When they left the restaurant it was still raining. Matt threw his raincoat over her, hailed a cab, and gave her address to the driver.

On the way she told him of her father's telephone call. "Maybe your father suspects something is up. Possibly he wants to question Paul."

Matt kissed her on the cheek and said, "Don't worry, everything will be fine."

Chapter 25

That night they sat together in her small kitchen and talked until it was almost dawn. Matt looked at his watch, it was six in the morning. He bolted down the last of his coffee and told her he would call later. After he left, Louisa felt tired and could hardly stay awake. She went to bed and immediately fell into a deep sleep.

It seemed as if she had only just dropped off when the phone rang. It was Matt. "It's on for tomorrow afternoon. Our flight is leaving from Heathrow at two o'clock." He paused. "I was just thinking there's so little time left. I'd like to see the English countryside one more time before they destroy it. How do you fancy doing a picnic?"

"A picnic, are you serious?

"Yes," he replied with a hint of laughter in his voice.

"Matt, there's a war about to start and you want to go on a picnic. You're impossible." Then she laughed and said, "I'd love to, what time?"

"I'll hire a car and I will be there by ten thirty."

"Great," she said looking at her watch. It was only nine o'clock she had been asleep just three hours. "I'll be ready."

Although it was November, it felt like a warm summer's day. Louisa packed a small picnic basket and was ready as the car drew up outside. She put the basket on the back seat of the car. Then as she was about to climb in she hesitated then ran back into the mews cottage, reached into the refrigerator and seized a cold bottle of Puligny Montrachet 1983.

They drove off toward the Essex and Suffolk border where Louisa knew of a great spot where they could picnic.

Matt wore short sleeves. For fun Louisa had chosen a Victorian floppy hat made of straw with a thin pink ribbon and dried flowers tied around the crown.

They left the car and walked through fields inhabited by butterflies of various colors, with the occasional summer bees buzzing noisily by. Eventually they arrived on the edge of an escarpment that overlooked the rolling landscape. Matt sat gazing out across the fields. He could smell the sweet bouquet of the countryside, with the combination of wild flowers ferns and bracken filled the air. The greens and yellows of the fields were mixed with the red earth colors and still wore the last remnants of their summer attire.

Without even looking he could sense Louisa's presence. Then he turned to gaze at her. She too seemed to be taking in the beauty of the moment. He studied her. The way she was dressed she could have stepped out of a Victorian magazine.

He leaned over to her and ran his mouth, partially open, across her soft neck, lingering for a moment to collect the scent of her starched cotton dress. It reminded him of his youth, the smell of her hair, the softness of her skin and the exciting sensation of prohibited desire. He lay back on the grass. She turned to lean over him. She brushed her lips across his cheek, slowly working around his forehead. Pouting her lips she kissed the other side of his face, before moving across to his waiting, anticipating, open mouth. She smiled, as if she knew he was aroused. He looked away for a moment and laughed, slightly embarrassed. Drawn back to her eyes he gazed into them, hypnotized.

She sat up, putting her arms around her legs and resting her chin on her knees. Her soft dark hair fell across her face, she flicked it back revealing her laughing eyes. He caught a scent of her breath, exciting, and tinged with the aroma of passion.

She lay back down on the grass, staring up at the passing clouds. His mind reeled in tremors of delight as he studied her exquisite curves. She was still looking up at the clouds above as he ran his fingers gently across her stomach and down, crossing lightly over the tops of her legs. Slowly his hand stroked lighter than a feather, up over her body, crossing the same path until the tips of his fingers barely touched her face again. With great veneration and tenderness, he caressed her breasts. She moaned. A smile of tranquility spread across her face he leaned forward to kiss her breasts through the cotton fabric. Gently he kissed her cheek before lying back on the grass. At that moment he sighed, then took her hand. "I love you, Louisa."

"I love you too." She paused. Then, in a profound voice, she said, "Like I have never loved before."

Filled with love for her, he wondered if it would ruin the moment to conclude this intellectual lovemaking with an encounter of physical sex. Lifting his muscular body over hers so as not to rest his weight on her, he held the provocative pose almost as a suggestion of desire. He waited. With her eyes soft with love and passion, she pulled him to her. When she was ready, he entered her warm body. She gripped him tight. They moved passionately together, with the methodical breathing of long distance runners. Finally they rose to an ultimate climax. At that instant Matt knew they were immortal, and were now joined forever in eternal love. Their union consummated they fell back onto the grass.

Matt lay looking up at the sky watching a lazy gull drift high in the rising thermals. The bird hardly moved, gliding in the same position above him, rising up and down, back or forth, swaying in the wind. He wondered. Had it watched them? Was it aware of them? Did it care that they even existed? Did the bird live on another plane, maybe another dimension? Was it in fact above them, not only literally but also in terms of awareness? A few moments passed and he fell asleep.

The sun was getting low on the horizon when he woke. He turned to Louisa she had her eyes closed. Gently he kissed her lips.

"I think it's time to get going if we want to get back to London in time for dinner." He whispered.

Matt picked up the picnic basket and took Louisa's hand. They walked back toward the car through the high grass. Louisa took her straw hat off and dragged the brim through the tops of the cat-tails. She held her face down in a child-like shyness. Matt wondered what she was thinking.

"Louisa, you look as if you're embarrassed? I'm sorry if I have offended you in anyway," he said in a gentle whisper.

She looked up at him smiling. "Oh no, oh no, you crazy fool. I'm in love."

That evening was spent at her mews cottage. She cooked. They talked through supper and on through the night, periodically making love until it was almost dawn. Then they slept.

Later, she woke to find that Matt had already left. The coffee was on, and there was a note beside the coffee maker.

Darling,

As we arranged, you will travel with John. He will meet you at the departure gate. Your ticket will be at the British Airways desk.

Love you. Matt

She poured a coffee walked over to the front door opened it and picked up the newspaper from the step. She sat at the table in the tiny kitchen. The front page story was about her stepfather. The headlines read Don Vinchenti warns, Arab invasion of Israel imminent. She pushed the paper aside and slid open the patio door that led out into a small enclosed courtyard. There was a tree growing out of the paving. Flowers were blooming in the old wooden tubs set against the red brick wall surrounding the miniature garden. She sat and listened to the birds as they sang their morning chorus and considered for a moment about the birds and animals of the world. Were they also players in the Game who had chosen to reincarnate into a different form?

214

Could they be on a higher level, after all except in certain circumstances, as in hunting for food or defensive action, most of the animals on the planet have a social behavior that is far less violent and aggressive than humans. Would they be saved too?

She needed to do some last minute shopping, and was getting ready to leave when the phone rang. She picked it up. The voice on the other end was faint. It was her stepfather. Without speaking she replaced the receiver. The last thing she wanted was to speak to him. She was embarrassed by her action, even though she knew it was the right thing to do. When the phone rang again, she ignored it, put on her coat and left the cottage.

Chapter 26

As Matt's cab arrived at Heathrow airport it passed lines of tanks, soldiers walking in pairs and military police directing traffic

He stepped out of the cab to find the place in chaos. Outside at arrivals refugees fleeing from the war-torn Eastern Europe sat wrapped in yards of colored material guarding their pitiful possessions in cardboard boxes tied with string. Their sullen faced children, fingers in mouths, stood looking in awe at the multitude of passengers passing by.

Inside, everyone was in a frantic state. Matt waited in line to be checked in. Surrounding him were people with huge carts of baggage and uncontrolled children running and screaming between the carts.

After checking in, he walked through immigration, through security, and then followed the signs to his gate in the new European terminal that was still under construction. He had wanted a coffee, but remembering the airport coffee on his arrival, he decided against it.

At gate twenty-two he sat down, opened his newspaper, and looked around the lounge for Boisey. They had all arrived independently of each other, and was each sitting alone among the other passengers waiting for the same flight. Suddenly he saw someone who shouldn't have been there, it was the man from the London pub, the very man he had seen staring at them the day he arrived in London.

He felt shocked, was it coincidence? Or could someone else know of his plans? Casually, he placed the paper down and caught the attention of Boisey who was standing only a few feet away chatting to a female flight attendant. Matt discreetly pointed a finger at the man.

Boisey saw his signal and said good-bye to the girl then with a relaxed stretch of his arms walked towards the bathrooms and with a quick glance behind disappeared inside. A few moments later Matt followed him in. The bathroom was under construction and appeared to be empty.

Mystified by Boisey's disappearance, he turned ready to walk out. It was then he looked up and saw that Boisey had climbed the workman's scaffolding and was balancing just above the doorway. He was steadying himself by holding onto a water pipe above his head, thereby hidden from anybody entering. Boisey unnecessarily put his fingers to his lips.

"Not so fast," a voice boomed from the entrance as two men Matt had never seen before came through the door followed by the bald headed man. They were each carrying guns.

"I don't believe it Jennings must have paid a fortune for this hit." Boisey said looking down from his elevated position.

"He's a very unhappy man Boisey," the bald man said now looking up to where Boisey was perched.

"I should think he is, I almost feel sorry for him Jo-Jo, what with him losing that money and Charley finding out about his little affair."

"You might think it´s funny Boisey but Jeffery soon lost his sense of humor when we showed him the mistake of being a friend of yours." Jo-Jo boomed. One of the men walked to the door to prevent anyone else coming in.

"I told you if you came back into my life I'd have to kill you, Jo-Jo," Boisey said.

"Kill me you idiot? What do you think this is?" he said waving his gun towards Boisey. "You give me a bleeding headache, that's all you do." He raised his gun, now pointing it directly up at Boisey. "Get down from there," he said shouting up at him.

"God, you're so dumb, Jo-Jo. I don't know why Jennings employs anyone as stupid as you." Boisey said.

"You're mighty flash for someone who's just about to die." Jo-Jo said, his neck turning red with anger.

Matt looked at the man nearest to him whose attention was on Boisey he was raising his gun and about to fire. Matt grabbed him by the arm, swung him around as if he was a child's toy doll and crunched his knee up into the groin. As the man creased up in agony, he seized him by the head and smashed his knee into his face. He left him to crumple to the floor and flew across the room toward the other gunman who was holding the door closed. Matt heard a muffled pop as a gun equipped with a silencer fired just missing him. He pirouetted and his outstretched foot kicked the weapon from the gunman's hand. Like a spring, he jumped and kicked the man in the head. Landing, his foot lashed out again, catching him in the chest and dropping him to the ground.

Meanwhile in the first few seconds, Jo-Jo's attention had been taken away from Boisey who took advantage of the moment and moved like lightning, swinging down from his position, and with both feet together in the air, kicked the giant in the head. Boisey landed nimbly on his feet. Jo-Jo had gone down almost without a sound. When Matt looked around he saw the hulk of Jo-Jo on the floor and Boisey standing over him.

"Neat Boisey, very neat," Matt said. "You're not bad for an old guy"

Boisey smiled then a look of concern spread across his face. "Hey, I believe they're boarding our flight, shall we?" He gestured towards the door and at the same time bowing in a joking gesture. As they walked away Boisey took a silver coin from his pocket and casually tossing it into the air.

"What's that?"

"It's my lucky charm, my old mate." He said as they walked out of the bathroom passing other people who were now entering the bathroom.

Matt looked back in amazement to see people were actually walking around and ignoring the prostrate bodies in the middle of the room.

Later, on the plane and over a drink, Boisey explained the incident by telling Matt that there was a question of ownership of a certain bookmaker's ill-gotten gains. All of which Boisey had donated to worthy causes and charities in East London.

"No problem with the police?" Matt asked with a smile. He was beginning to like Boisey-Smith.

"Funny thing is, in all the years of my indiscretions, they never bothered me once, most peculiar."

Then he looked at Matt, winked, and with a sideways grin, downed his vodka and tonic.

Chapter 27

Matt felt the tension building while cramped next to Boisey in the trunk of the limousine as it drew up to the gates of the Chateau. It was driven by John dressed in a chauffeur's outfit with Louisa seated in the back. A guard walked out from a side gate to look inside the vehicle, recognizing Louisa and without a word he waved to the guard box for the gates to open. The guard sauntered around to the back of the vehicle and was just about to try the trunk when the great iron gates opened. As John moved forward Matt felt a certain excitement at the vulnerability of their situation. A short way up the winding drive the car slowed almost to a stop, Matt heard a switch flick open the trunk. He dropped to the hard ground and was instantly followed by Boisey. They both rolled away into the deep snow, disappearing quickly in the frozen undergrowth.

When the vehicle pulled away over the crisp surface toward the chateau, Matt stood and listened for a moment while looking through the trees at the building. There were many cars in the parking area. The front of the building was ablaze with light coming from huge spotlights directed up from the surrounding perimeter. He watched as the limousine carried on to the door of the chateau. He saw Louisa snuggled in her fur climb out and walk up the steps leading to the grand entrance. He felt a chill in his bones as he watched the door of the chateau open allowing the warm air of the building to escape condensing into a white mist as it mixed with the cold night air. The limousine turned back towards the gate.

Boisey had gone ahead, moving through the deep snow without a sound. Matt followed shouldering his way quietly through the snow-covered bushes. He caught up with Boisey to find that he had found a dark corner away from the lights and was already preparing to scale the wall. Matt looked up to the high balcony above, it was not the same one as the plan which now he could see was lit up by the lights. This would be easier and safer. Boisey began the climb. Matt watched as the expert effortlessly moved up the stone wall of the fortress, skillfully hugging it like a magnet. He waited in the cold, glancing up from time to time and wondered if he would be able to follow the agile man.

The bitter cold froze his face, he was so cold he began to shiver. He wondered whether the shivering was due to the cold, or to the excitement of the moment. After his climb Boisey had disappeared over the balcony. Matt waited, but still nothing happened. The sound of dogs barking began to disturb him. Something in the darkness touched his face like the wings of a butterfly; it was the end of a nylon rope that had been lowered down. He took hold of the rope and carefully climbed the wall. When he finally reached the balcony he clambered over the side then slipped, falling backwards in the deep snow on the balcony floor.

He looked up at Boisey who was attempting to stop himself from laughing. Matt had a hard time not laughing himself. With a big grin on his face Boisey turned back to the window and began to wipe away the snow surrounding the frame. Matt kept watch, taking a moment to glance towards the dark mountains silhouetted by the bright moonlight. From behind the peaks the light of the moon created long black shadows across the frozen snow. The spectacular moon-light view of the Val Gardena reminded Matt of an Alistair Grimshaw painting.

From behind him, he heard the sound of the window opening. He took a last look at the scene as a cloud drifted across the moon. Somewhere in the grounds a dog began to bark. In just a few seconds they had both climbed into the room.

"Damn dogs, I'm plagued by them" Boisey whispered, while slowly closing the window behind them.

Matt's eyes took a moment to become accustomed to the dark. When they did he saw they were in a bedroom. He froze as he heard a sound coming from the direction of a four poster bed situated at the other end of the long room. He looked toward Boisey who was standing motionless.

Hardly daring to breathe, Matt strained in the darkness until the light from the moon reappeared exposing two lumps in the bed. The occupants had the sheets pulled firmly up over their heads. To Matt's horror, he watched as a champagne bottle began to roll in slow motion across the bed. It reached the edge, stopped suspended for a moment, then fell, landing with a clamor on the wooden floor. There it continued to roll assisted by gravity, across the sloping floor, until finally it stopped just short of his feet. The noise of the bottle rolling on the uneven boards still rang in his ears, and now a deathly silence hung in the air. For a moment Matt looked down at the offensive bottle deposited at his feet. The silence was broken when a giggling noise came from underneath the bedclothes. Boisey carefully opened the door and they both slipped out into the hall, leaving the occupants of the bed cavorting under the covers.

They walked carefully down the empty hallways, stopping from time to time to listen to music and laughter coming from somewhere deep in the chateau. Matt studied the map in the dim light cast by the flickering candles held high in the wall sconces. Finally Boisey pulled out his flashlight.

"Good thinking," Matt said.

After many turns and down a flight of stairs they found the doorway shown on the plan. It should have been the entrance to the room containing the vault, yet it looked different to the plan. It had three deadlocks. Then he noticed another identical door farther down the dark hall. This door had only one lock. He tried the old brass handle of course it was locked.

"I don't know. What do you think Boisey?" Matt said mystified.

"Hell, let's try this one first." Boisey said as he moved towards the door with the three locks. He pulled out a set of thin wires and began to work on them. In a few moments he had the first one open then after what seemed like less than a minute the other two locks were opened. Boisey turned the knob on the door very cautiously. Inside the dark room Matt switched on his flashlight and then stopped in horror as the light picked out a bed covered in cobwebs. Lying in it were two skeletons. They took a closer look. The occupants had both been shot through the head. It seemed from the position of their remains they may have been making love when they were shot. Matt switched off the flashlight to end the terrible picture. He felt sure that this was Louisa's sister and her husband. Louisa had told him about her sister's accident and for some reason he'd had his doubts about the story of their deaths. Now the truth was clear. Matt reasoned that only Don Vinchenti could have taken their lives. For some demented reason, he had killed them both. Only he could have organized the elaborate cover up. Maybe he ordered the ski guide to be killed, then had this room in the chateau locked and sealed. Perhaps Louisa's mother knew the terrible reality of the event, and that would explain her captivity.

They closed the door of the room and moved cautiously down the hall. Boisey began to work on the lock of the other door.

"I don't believe what I just saw. God, that was awful! Someone's very sick around here," Boisey said, not turning from his work. Before Matt could comment, the lock sprang open. This is it, Matt thought. The two flashlights swept around the room, stopping at places of interest in their search for the entrance to the vault. It was a grand room, a baroque desk sat centered on a fine Kashan carpet. The walls were lined with bookcases, between them hung large masterworks in oil.

"I guess we know where some of the world's most famous stolen paintings ended up," Boisey whispered to Matt as he studied a Paul Gauguin.

"I wish I was here on my own. I think I might relieve him of one or two of these," his voice whispered again in the darkness.

At the end of the room, almost covering the whole wall, hung the largest Brussels tapestry Matt had ever seen. He watched Boisey running his hands over the walls, along the edges of the bookcases and around the sides of the old steam radiators. Suddenly and without a sound, one of the bookcases Boisey was examining swung open, revealing the vault door. It was not as big as Matt had imagined, and it was obviously old. Boisey turned the flashlight onto his own face and winked. Then he placed his old leather medical bag that he had insisted on bringing for luck on the floor and delved into it. Matt looked at his watch and wondered about Louisa. There was little time to waste. Boisey had no trouble opening the strong room door. They may just as well have left the key in the lock, Matt mused.

When they entered the musty vault, Matt saw the solitary safe standing against the wall like a huge refrigerator. He heard a whistle from behind him.

"Oh hell!" he heard Boisey exclaim. "It's a custom built Chubb. How long have we got?"

"Not long, we allowed fifteen minutes for this part of the operation," Matt said, looking down at his watch.

"That's bloody impossible," Boisey said. He sounded discouraged by the magnitude of the task set before him. "I'm good, but not that bloody good."

"You've got to open it, there's no option." Matt said agitated, as he had mixed emotions, a feeling of panic joined his frustration with the time restraint.

Matt watched as Boisey sat on his haunches, his thumbnail in his mouth, staring at the safe. He reminded Matt of a child deciding which way to cut the birthday cake. Minutes ticked by. Matt was agitated. "Come on, come on," he whispered in the darkness. He felt Boisey's cold stare coming back at him even though he could not see his features. At last, after measuring the safe twenty or more times, Boisey commenced to drill a small hole an inch from the handle. Then he took a piece of plastic explosive from his bag. Rolling it into tiny balls he pushed them one by one into the small hole. This seemed to take an eternity to Matt, who sat patiently waiting and watching as the minutes ticked by. Finally, Boisey pushed a small silver detonator into the last of the plastic leaving it just protruding from the hole.

Boisey stood up. "Matt, quick help me, I need the carpet that's under that desk in that room."

They walked quickly back into the grand room. Matt struggled with the desk, lifting up one end while Boisey pulled the carpet out from underneath. They dragged the carpet into the vault and proceeded to cover the safe with it.

"You had better stand outside," Boisey said.

"What about you?"

"I'll be out in a moment."

He waited, but Boisey did not reappear. There was a thump. Matt rushed back into the vault to see Boisey bending over holding his hands between his legs. Matt reached down, picked up the fallen flashlight and shone it onto Boisey's hands. He could see blood slowly oozing from between the man's fingers.

"What the hell happened?" he asked. "Come here, let me see." Matt pulled Boisey's hands apart. At first, because of the bloody mess, he thought that both hands had been injured. Then as he cleaned away some of the blood he realized the wound was confined to one hand. He quickly slipped his own jacket off. Then, with a knife meant for killing more than cutting, he cut off a piece from his shirt sleeve, and applied the strips to the bleeding hand.

"What on earth happened? Your hand is a mess!" he queried again.

"I forgot to bring the damn fuse wire. I had no option but to whack the detonator with that." He kicked a bronze figure lying on the floor.

226

"You dummy! You stood there and hit the detonator with that thing, knowing what it would do. You're crazy!"

"I didn't have any bloody choice, did I?"

Matt turned to the open safe and started to search for the invasion plans. There was a mass of papers to go through finally Matt said, "My God Boisey! The invasion is set for tomorrow at midnight but I can't find anything with the launch sites marked on it." Matt said holding open a map he had taken from the safe. Boisey studied the map for a few moments before saying, "Every major city in Israel has been targeted."

"That's bad look at this Boisey. This is part two it looks like they have targeted just about every Arab country in the middle-east as well. Then what, I hate to think? Boisey put down the map ready for Matt to scan.

"Interesting" Matt said, pulling out the wire on his watch. He scanned each map in detail and all of the documents from the safe. There were certainly enough clues with the safe being blown to tell the Don that someone had seen his plans and now it was too late for him to bring the war forward so it should delay his invasion plans. Matt put a small roll of microfilm on the floor near the safe, just to establish that the motive was not robbery. It was then he remembered the memory stick. He pulled it out of his pocket and slotted into his watch he then went to messages, it read,

Enter the invasion date and time on your watch, press transmit. Then silence the girl.

Kill Louisa: sick bastards leave no witness, no evidence. Whatever, he wasn't going to relay the information. If he did then the U.S would take action and that would start the war. Then he said loudly "Bastards."

"Who´s that?"

"It doesn't matter we had better get a move on."

They locked the door behind them and moved back into the hallway. Suddenly they heard the sound of footsteps ringing out on the stone floor. Someone was coming towards them. Matt noticed the open door of an elevator. "Let's go," he said.

Boisey glanced at his watch. "We're running out of time."

They entered the elevator. Matt pressed the first button his fingers touched and then realized the elevator was going down "Shit we are going down."

"No kidding" Boisey sarcastically remarked.

After an obvious descent, the board above the door brightened at what appeared to be the basement level. Matt felt tense, not knowing what to expect. The doors opened silently in front was a passage carved out of rock they walked cautiously along it until they came to a metal grid overlooking what at first appeared to be a huge natural cavern. Water dripped from the roof above, and the place was damp and badly lit. Matt felt a hand grip his arm and saw Boisey's bandaged hand pointing down to the cavern floor a thirty feet below. He was looking at a huge round wall enclosing a dome built on the cavern floor. It seemed very odd, so out of place for these otherwise natural surroundings. Again he felt Boisey pulling at his arm. This time he was pointing to a metal ladder leading down to the ground. Nodding in agreement he joined Boisey slowly climbing down the ladder hand over hand.

They reached the bottom of the ladder and stopped to listen but could only hear the continual drip of water hitting water. Carefully, they walked over to where the huge dome was. Boisey climbed onto the wall surrounding the dome and grasping Matt hand, pulled him up alongside. It was then Matt could see that the dome itself was made of metal. He had visited enough rocket sites in the United States to recognize a silo when he saw one.

"Boisey do you know what this is?" Matt said. He was having a hard time believing it himself. Then he carried on. "It's not a normal rocket silo it's far too big. It's about the biggest one I have ever seen. It looks like a Russian Soyuz shuttle with a two stage cell attached. How the hell did he get hold of a damn shuttle? I'd swear it is one of theirs. They must have lowered it down here and covered it over. You know that's exactly what they did. This is not part of the building, I bet its right under the lawn." they both looked up "and this cavern isn't natural at all. Now if they fire this while we are down here, we'll be blown to pieces. Of course they won't because you can bet this is his escape vehicle." Matt stood for a moment looking at the forbidding dome and then jumped down.

"Let's find the control center. It must be back up the elevator inside the chateau. No one would want to be near this baby when she goes up," Matt said.

Now he was worried about Louisa. Had she found the key to her mother's apartment? He looked at his watch only ninety minutes to go. They entered the elevator in darkness. With the aid of his flashlight Matt pressed the button to the next level. Nothing happened. Boisey unscrewed the plate from the panel. "Someone has turned the power off," he casually observed.

"Now what?" Matt said, looking at his watch again. Already minutes had passed since he had last checked the time. He frowned. This was serious.

"Let's get out of here, there's something wrong," Boisey said. He looked up at the inspection panel in the elevator roof then tapped Matt on the shoulders, indicating he was about to climb onto them. The agile man hardly seemed to rest on Matt's shoulders for more than a moment before he had pushed the inspection panel open and was swinging by his elbows from the hole.

"The only way you'll be able to get up here is to hold my ankles and I'll pull us both up," Boisey called down. Matt grabbed Boisey's ankles. Boisey straightened his arms, straining to take the great weight of both their bodies. His powerful legs came up to his chest, giving Matt enough room to grab the edge of the inspection door and pull himself through after Boisey.

"That must have hurt your hand," Matt said, remembering the blood soaked material covering Boisey's hand.

"Just a scratch, old son" he replied.

"They must know someone is down here, Boisey."

"Maybe, but it could be a security move if they found the vault open."

In the darkness they began the long climb up the side of the shaft, using the bolts on the girders as steps for their boots. When they reached a set of doors, Boisey moved a small metal bar that released the lock. He was able to slide open one of the doors.

Bright light flooded into the dark shaft, blinding them for an instant. They looked up to see a young girl dressed in a black uniform. She looked down at them and let out a scream. Then turned away and ran down the hall Matt called to her in Italian, she didn't stop. In an instant Boisey had leapt up from the shaft, and was in pursuit.

The door sprung back, leaving Matt once again in the dark. He fumbled around looking for the release bar, his hand touched on something warm, a rat "shit" he let go, the rat squealed and he almost lost his grip on the girder. He swayed out for over empty space while holding on with one hand before finally gaining his balance.

Just then light came flooding back into the shaft. He looked up to see Boisey smiling down at him. To his surprise Matt saw a pair of sleek legs, clad in black stockings, lying on the floor beside Boisey. He could see that they belonged to the unconscious body of the girl.

"Come on, old son, can't stay down there all day," Boisey said with a wink.

"We'll have to do something with her," Matt said as he climbed out of the shaft. He pointed to a bright red door marked, Fuoco. They dragged her to the door. Matt opened it and searched the wall for a light. "I can't find the damn light."

"Here," Boisey said offering the flashlight.

Matt shone the light around the room. Reels of hose with old brass nozzles filled the room while fire-fighting suits hung on pegs like monster ghouls.

They bound and gagged the girl and left the closet without a word. Walking cautiously along the hallway they found a door which led to another long corridor. Matt was beginning to feel concerned that they may be lost. He had a map of the main building but there was nothing on it to indicate that the maze at this level even existed and Louisa had not mentioned it either. He looked at his watch. Only one hour fifteen minutes before the helicopter would arrive. They walked quickly past room after room that each held arrays of computers. Where were the people, Matt wondered? All the screens had been left switched on filling the corridor with the hum of electricity. It seemed as if the whole place was suspended in some freak time-warp waiting for the controllers to return to their complex equipment.

At the end of the long corridor Matt carefully opened the last door. One look at the vast room told him that this was the main control room.

"Boisey," he called, "in here."

"What the hell?" Boisey said as he peeked around the door, his face a picture of surprise. "This reminds me of my old ship Crystella."

"Crystella?"

"Nothing mate, nothing, I just get these flashes from a previous life sort of déjà vu, you know," Boisey said, looking a little agitated.

This was the first time since they met that Boisey had admitted to the existence of another time frame, or of their past lives.

"So, you know why we're here then? I mean the real reason," Matt said, wondering what kind of answer to expect. Boisey's blue eyes seemed to light up. They turned brilliant, almost translucent, shinning in the half light of the room. Matt wondered if he was seeing things.

"Of course, Matt" He looked at Matt in a strange way, as if to say, you kidding.

"I didn't know if you knew. You hadn't said anything."

When Boisey laughed Matt felt a little foolish he had obviously been aware of the whole thing from the start.

"Why the hell didn't you say something before?" Matt asked.

Without turning his head Boisey continued to move around the room, taking a closer look at the vast network of screens on the surrounding walls. "Because, my old son, nobody ever asked me and as I graduated a long, long time ago I saw no point in mention it. Anyway, how many of these screens do you think there are?"

"I guess there must be over a hundred. Do you know what their function is Boisey?"

"No do you?"

"Yes these are live videos cameras, operating all over the Middle-East. Look there that's a street is in Tel Aviv. These cameras have been set up in every capitol city of every Islamic state. I know because this Boisey is our own system. However look there, that's the White House and that is one of our supply dumps in New Jersey. I can't believe it, this is certainly our IVPS, but somebody has added a lot of extra cameras sighting them in European and US cities. How the hell did he get into our system?

"What did you call it, IVPS?"

"Yes Integrated Visual Progress System it's basically a satellite network. It collates all of the information from the pre-set video cameras streamed up to a set of satellites. Then also using the images it can translate them into binary or hex language, making any troop movements world-wide into a computer generated graph. It will also give a minute by minute report on our position in any war situation and as you can see the war can be watched on television screens from the comfort of a nuclear shelter or right from here," Matt said walking over to the control panel.

"But how the hell did he get access to your satellite system?"

"Beats me, anyway why don't you set a little surprise for Vinchenti here" he said pointing to the central control panel. "I think this'll be the perfect place to put a timed device. If we destroy the wiring trunk of this network, it'll take days to put it right. That'll certainly delay his plans."

Boisey walked over to the panel, bent down and looked underneath. "Looking at this I'd say this is the control panel for that little bird he has down below. If we blow this it'll be impossible to fix it in time for him to get off the planet."

"Great."

"Right, just give me a moment, when do you want it to go off?" he said. Then, delving into his bag he took out a small explosive device.

"The sooner the better just in case someone finds it."

"OK, how about an hour?"

"That'll be good. We should be away from here by then."

Boisey knelt on the floor and reached under the control panel. Matt waited anxiously, glancing at his watch from time to time until finally Boisey stood up. He was looking pleased with himself. "What's next? Oh damn," he said.

Boisey was staring over Matt's shoulder. Matt felt the hairs on the back of his neck react when he heard the sound of a rifle being cocked. He followed Boisey's actions by raising his hands above his head. Then he turned to see a dark skinned youth in uniform pointing a rifle at his head. His mind raced. The situation was grave; he could hear feet running toward them. He thought of Louisa, the helicopter, the time. He had to think. Boisey looked ready to spring when the door burst open and what seemed like the whole of the Italian army poured in.

"No, Boisey," he called, but too late. Boisey had already launched himself at the soldier with the rifle. There was a noise like a clap of thunder as the weapon's blast filled the room. Matt watched the scene as if in slow motion. When the soldier pulled the trigger, he saw Boisey's hand already on the stock, pushing it to one side. Then, in one movement, he took the rifle, pulled it around the man's throat, and snapped it back, breaking his neck and letting the body slide to the floor.

The small army pouring into the room stopped in awe at the spectacle. They stood mesmerized, watching Boisey. He in turn stared back at them, his eyes once again glowing, sparkling as if they were on fire. Matt stood amazed, as the soldiers seemed to be hypnotized by him. With a steady hand and a casualness that surprised Matt,

Boisey still holding the rifle in his bloody hand, walked over to the nearest of the men and took away his weapon.

"Come on mate, lend a hand," he said.

Matt began taking the weapons away from the bewildered soldiers.

"They look as if their brains are frozen, Boisey. What on earth did you do?"

"Oh just a little trick I learned in the past. I'll tell you about it some time." They threw the guns into the hallway then pulled the door closed behind them.

"How can we lock them in, we haven't a key," Matt said, holding the door closed with his back. Realizing what he had said to the master of the keys he laughed. Boisey gave Matt a sideways glance and then took out a wire from his pocket. In seconds the door was locked. They moved back down the hallway toward the elevator. Matt peeked into the closet where they had left the girl.

"She's gone!" he said in a whisper. "I think we'd better start climbing." Matt was worried things were going wrong. They entered the shaft and started the climb up to the next level. When they reached it, Boisey had trouble opening the doors. Suddenly, without warning they slid open. Boisey looked back down at Matt, pulling a face as if to say, what happened?

Before he had time to pull himself from the shaft a soldier's face appeared looking directly down at them. Boisey looked up into the barrel of a rifle gripped firmly in the man's hand.

"Not our bloody day, old son," Boisey was quick to point out. Out of the corner of his eye Matt saw Boisey reach into his pocket.

"Do you speak English, mate?" He said to the dumfounded soldier. At that moment a silver coin spun from Boisey's fingers up into the air. It took just that second of distraction as the man's eyes followed its path upwards for Boisey to grab a leg pulling the man off-balance. The soldier let his rifle drop then tipped forward, rolling over Boisey's shoulders and with an extra nudge fell away into the black abyss of the shaft.

The clatter of the soldier's rifle hitting the floor next to the elevator had been louder than his short scream fading down the empty shaft. They climbed hastily out and waited, but nothing happened. Matt realized they had arrived back at the same place they had started. He looked at his watch fifty seven minutes to go. Where was Louisa? The plan had been to either meet her outside the room were the vault was located or go on to her mother's apartment.

"Boisey," he said, gripping his arm in the darkness. "We need to find Louisa, she must have gone ahead by now."

"Perhaps you're right."

"Yes, it's a possibility they've found the safe open and they know we're here. Let's find out if there's been anybody in the vault."

"OK, let's go." He quickly walked to the door and tried the handle it was locked. They had purposely left the door locked to give them a little time. "It's still locked so I don't think they've discovered it yet."

"Still I have a feeling something has happened and I don't like it," Matt said.

"What the hell do we do now?" Boisey said.

"It's possible that Vinchenti has Louisa. Then there's only one thing to do," Boisey asked.

"What's that?"

"Find the Don."

"You're crazy. He's probably surrounded by bodyguards, and there's no guarantee that he's got the plans with him."

"You've a better idea?"

"Yes. I'll go to the kitchen Boisey, you go up to see if Louisa is in her mother's apartment."

"Right O` mate."

They turned to go in their different directions then stopped frozen. There was a sound of boots running toward them from both directions. They both looked down the hallway toward the elevator.

"You go, you go I´ll hold them here." Boisey said, at the same time opening a door where he was standing.

"Too late" Matt said. Then he turned toward the first soldier that had arrived. He whirled around, his arm and hands moving faster than the eye could see. The soldier staggered back, falling unconscious into his colleague behind him. In the confines of the narrow hallway Matt was moving like an organized machine with his bare hands cutting and chopping down the troops one by one.

He took a second to look around at Boisey who was protecting his back from the oncoming assault coming from the other direction. Although he knew the soldiers wouldn't use their weapons for fear of killing one another, it was still a hopeless situation. Far too many soldiers, Matt thought. There is no possible chance of us fighting our way out of this hall and no hope of helping the others, only a guarantee of death.

With his arm wrapped around the throat of a terrified Italian soldier, Boisey backed up against the wall, dropped him to the ground. Then with his eyes blazing he just stared at the other soldiers. They seemed shocked at the slaughter of their companions in such a short time. Boisey's obvious control of the situation had alarmed them sufficiently to hold them back for a few crucial seconds.

"Get out of here." He shouted at Matt.

Matt looked at Boisey wiped his sweating forehead and shrugged. With one more final kick he dropped a man who was swinging the butt of his rifle at him then sprinted back into the lift. As the door closed he saw Boisey with his back against the wall, his hands held high above his head and the clatter of metal as ten or more rifles were cocked.

Chapter 28

Louisa had gone to the kitchen in search of the housekeeper hoping to find the key to her mother's apartment there. When she entered the kitchen she discovered Carlo. He was sitting at a long wooden table, cleaning an old brass dish. The room was lit by a single candle she tried to retreat.

"`A, Louisa, can I help you?" he slurred.

He had obviously been drinking. His blood red eyes frightened her she wanted to run. Instinctively she knew it was a dangerous situation, but decided to front it out. There was no other way, she had to have the key.

"Do you have the key to Mother's apartment?" She asked with staged arrogance.

Carlo looked at her for a moment and then walked across to a cupboard in the corner of the kitchen. After a moment, he returned with a bottle of wine and an additional glass. He refilled his glass, poured wine into the other and offered it to her saying "I'll find you the key Miss Louisa."

Thinking it best to appease him she took the glass and drank without another thought. She watched him as he searched for the key among dozens of others hanging on a board attached to the wall. She was just wondering why it was taking him so long to find the key when she felt a gradual dizziness coming over her and a need to lie down. Then it struck her, Carlo must have drugged the wine. Through the haze she felt his strong arms pick her up and carry her over to the hard wooden table. He dropped her down onto it as if she were a rag doll. She felt the weight of his heavy body bearing down on her, the mixture of garlic and alcohol on his breath made her feel sick. The kitchen was situated behind the main dining room. She could hear a great deal of noise coming from behind the doors she knew it would be futile to cry for help, even so she wanted to scream, but nothing could escape from her paralyzed lips.

She could feel the heat flowing from Carlo's body while his clumsy hands fumbled with her clothes. He held her down by her hair and pushed his decaying teeth into her lips, she felt sick. He ripped off his shirt and tore open her blouse. With both hands he broke apart her bra, exposing her breasts then rubbed the filthy matted hair of his chest onto her bare skin. The heaviness of his body caused her backbone to rub against the scrubbed surface of the table. She was crying. He lifted her like a bag of potatoes, turned her over, and slammed her back down on her stomach bent over the table. He pulled up her skirt. She could taste the blood from her bleeding lips. Hardly daring to breath, she gritted her teeth as his rough hands grabbed at her body. Then, just as he gave out a sensual moan, the door burst violently open, letting bright light pour into the room.

Carlo turned and screamed in Italian at the intruder. The drunken man at the door may not have understood the vile oaths, but he certainly got the message. He stood and stuttered pathetic apologies in reply to Carlo's train of guttural obscenities. The man backed out and closed the door leaving the room once again in semi-darkness.

#

Matt now frantic to find Louisa left the lift at the next floor and searched in each of rooms pushing each door open in succession looking into the fine examples of eighteenth century architecture, with high painted ceilings and walls decorated with colossal paintings and murals. Most of the rooms were crowded with people, some in Military uniform others in macabre costume. Loud music was playing throughout the building with everyone in a party mood. He almost made the mistake of walking straight into the main dining room but stopped short at the doorway and looked in. An orgy was in full swing. The corruption of young boys and girls was evident among the drunken melee. The guests in this room were dressed as witches, skeletons, goblins, hunchback dwarfs, monsters and the like, their costumes representing one or another of the dark side of mankind.

Servants dressed as devils drifted through the crowd carrying large vessels of wine. A group of revelers were gathered around the far end of a long table. Matt entered and moved cautiously through the crowd to gain a closer look. The group were cheering in the candlelight as one of their number, a man dressed in the manner of a priest proceeded to copulate with a young girl. The girl was laughing, as she lay spread-eagle across the table amongst the remains of a feast.

Matt's stomach turned at the grotesque sight. There was nothing he could do, as the girl herself seemed to be in collusion with the act, so he moved back toward the door. A hand touched his arm, he turned to look at the man whose grip held him, it was a drunken servant who stood spilling wine over himself from a large silver jug. Steadying himself, he offered the remains of the contents to Matt who pushed him aside without even an acknowledgment. He looked at his watch, fifty minutes before John would arrive with the helicopter. He jostled his way out of the room and back into the darkness of the hallway. He stood for a moment deciding which way to turn, he wondered where the kitchen would be and if Louisa had managed to get the key from there. Then he spotted a chambermaid coming toward him.

"Mi scusi," he said in his broken Italian.

"Si sigore"

"Dove si trova la cucina?"

She pointed down the hallway indicating the way to the kitchen. Matt just nodded.

#   #   #

Louisa felt warm vomit on her back as it dribbled from the drunken man's mouth. She started to retch herself, her stomach contorted violently as she fought to hold him back twisting and turning away from him. Then suddenly the door flew open again and light came flooding back into the room. She felt the weight of Carlos lifted from her. Before she could even move from the table she heard his wild protest ringing in her ears, a scuffle and then silence.

Louisa pushed herself off the table, scared. She turned to look at the new intruder.

"Matt" she gasped "Thank God"

Carlo lay in a heap on the floor. He began to rise, Matt moved quickly, stamping on the back of the man's neck with his boot. There was a loud crack; she knew he would never move again.

Louisa picked up her torn clothes and held them to her chest then, sobbing, she clung to Matt.

"Good Lord Lou, did he rape you?"

"No, thank God, but it was damn close. If it hadn't been for you," she said wiping the tears and mascara from her face.

She picked up a towel from the floor. "Matt, wipe that filth off my back," she said, still shaking. He obliged taking the towel and a lot of water from the kitchen sink he cleaned the vomit from her back. Afterwards she tucked her blouse back into her skirt, picked up her jacket and went to the sink where she washed her face and her hands. Even then she felt unclean and shuddered at the thought of the filthy man.

Matt opened the door to the hallway. Without another word she walked past Carlo's body giving it a kick for good measure.

They climbed the stone staircase leading to her mother's apartment then walked along the hallway and stopped outside the door. There were voices coming from inside. She could hear the high pitch of her father's voice he seemed to be having an argument with her mother. Matt pushed open the door and entered an empty room. Then they saw that the bookcase at the end of the room had a secret doorway and the door stood ajar.

Quietly they walked across the room to stand by the open bookcase. Louisa stood closely to the opening so she could hear the words clearly it was her Mother.

"You killed my Gina. You shot them both and I've spent ten years locked up for your insanity. You murdered Gina and Mario, now you want to kill my Louisa. You're sick, you're very sick your warped mind is trying to justify the killings but it can't."

"I am the son of God," Don Vinchenti screamed.

Horrified, unable to believe what she was hearing, Louisa gasped. Then she stepped back almost falling into Matt. How could this be? Was it true? Was her stepfather so evil was he completely insane? Oh God, please don't let this happen, it can't be true. She felt her world tumbling. Her whole body began to shake out of control. Tears of anguish streamed down her face. Why hadn't her Mother told her the truth? She felt confused. She ran her fingers through her hair tearing at the strands. Unable to contain her stress she looked at Matt reaching out to him, he took her in his arms and held her close. At that moment the door flew back revealing Don Vinchenti's huge body stood silhouetted in the doorway with his own bodyguards close by. "So who the hell are you?" He screamed at Matt. Then he gestured to the guards. "Bring them in here."

She looked at Matt for help, and then turned to run. Matt caught her by the arm pulling her back. "Don't Louisa, he'll kill you." Holding her gently by the wrist, he led her through the doorway into the room beyond. Like the rest of the chateau, the room was built of stone. In one corner there was a tiny cell. Her father stood by the open door. She walked to the door and found something that appalled her. Her mother, hardly recognizable was sitting chained to a wooden bench. Her normally well-groomed hair hung in a tangled mess. It clung unattractively to her damp face, and her clothes were pulled around her body in disarray.

"Oh God" Louisa screamed. "What have you done to Mummy?" She pushed past him into the cell and threw her arms around her mother. At that moment the Don looked at one of the guards standing behind Matt. The look was obviously a command. The man stepped forward and smashed his rifle butt into the back of Matt's neck. Without a sound Matt fell into the cell as his knees buckled under him, he landed heavily on the stone floor. Louisa dropped to her knees and gently touched the back of his bleeding head. "You bastard," was all she could manage.

"Your other friend will be joining you soon," her father sneered, his fat cheeks pulled back like a grotesque circus clown.

"She has to be taken care of, my dear," he said, referring to her mother.

"You know she's quite mad. You two have a lot to talk about." He laughed, the iron door slammed closed, leaving them in semi-darkness.

Her mother was sitting with her face between her chained hands still sobbing. Her bloodshot eyes looked up to Louisa. Then she smiled "It's OK dear I have to put on an act for him, I'm quite all right. He is evil and mad Louisa," she said pulling herself together while wiping away the tears. "I'm sorry that I never told you that he killed Gina but if he suspected that you knew, he would have had you killed. I know I've lived with that evil man for all these years. He told everyone that I'm mad so that he could lock me away and keep the truth hidden. He killed Gina himself, shot them while they lay in bed."

"My God why did he do such a terrible thing?"

"He was insane with jealousy. I don't know if you are aware of it, but he had sexually abused Gina since she was a child. He couldn't stand her being married; it cut him off from his sexual perversion."

Instinctively she felt compassion for her mother. She had heard it said that her stepfather epitomized the very depth of depravity, but this revelation was beyond belief, although typical of a degenerate mind she thought.

Distracted for a moment by the worry of her predicament she knelt down and took a closer look at Matt. She cradled his face with her hands and stroked his hair his breathing was very shallow. She glanced around the cell. No chance of escape then she looked at her watch. Oh no, thirty minutes to go, then what? Where was Boisey she wondered? God what a mess her head felt like it was spinning.

"Lou, what is it?"

"I don't know where to start, Mummy. It's such a long story. The thing is I do have another friend here in the chateau."

"Why don't you explain what's going on darling?"

Kneeling next to Matt and still holding his head in her hands away from the hard floor she said, "Well Mummy, I met this wonderful man. He came with me partly to help you escape and also to disrupt father's plans. When was it I met him? I've lost track of time, maybe two days ago? Well, you remember Paul don't you? Paul Johnson-Marsh" she said, while removing her jacket and slipping it under Matt´s head.

"Yes, yes, of course I remember him Louisa, although it's been years since I've seen him."

"Well Mummy he was here the evening I came to see you, I think on business at the request of father. After that we met again at his suggestion in London and after some discussion he promised to help rescue you. He introduced me to Matt and another person named of all things Boisey, very strange, anyway he is also here now, somewhere in the Chateau, I hope." She looked down at Matt, "I fell in love with Matt the moment we met."

"This all happened since you were here just a few days ago?" Her mother said, smiling again.

"Well it's sort of difficult to explain. You see, I've known Matt in another life," she said wondering what her mother would think. After all, it was less than a week ago when they talked about her meeting her soul-mate.

"Do you know he's your soul-mate, Louisa?"

"Yes, I know it seems ridiculous that I should meet him so soon after discussing it with you, but I did."

"He is your soul-mate darling. Matt is your soul-mate."

Louisa shivered. She was cold. Her mother seemed strangely calm now that was good but she had to think, why would she say such a thing about Matt how would she know? Mummy had often talked about such things, but to say it with such conviction, how very strange. Maybe being locked up for a number of years gives one divine perception, she thought.

"Yes I know he is but how do you know? What on Earth made you say that?"

Her mother smiled, "I'm afraid there is no time to explain now darling, it's quite complicated."

There was a noise coming from the other side of the cell door, Louisa waited in anticipation for something to happen. Her mother drew closer. Louisa stood up and put her arm around her, comforting her. She heard a key turning in the lock. The door swung open. A guard backed into the cell dragging a body by the feet. Louisa's heart sunk when she realized it was Boisey. He had his hands tied and looked as if he had been badly beaten. The door closed, leaving the cell once again in semi-darkness. She ran to over to Matt as he was seemed to be gaining consciousness.

As Matt woke, Louisa was looking at him obviously alarmed at his suffering. It took a minute or two before he could remember where he was. He lifted his head and in the half-light he saw the smiling face of Louisa. He began to talk, the words difficult to get out. "Hi Lou, I must tell you something," he said through bleeding lips.

"What is it Darling?" She said with pity in her voice.

He licked the blood with his tongue. "The plan," he said.

"The plan, what about the plan?"

"It's not going well," he joked.

"You are a fool Matt. I think that's pretty obvious. God you hit your head when you went down it looks awful. Is there anything I can do?"

She stroked his forehead and ran her fingers lightly over his bruised face. Then gently, she bent forward and kissed him on the cheek.

#   #   #

Looking up into the semi-darkness at a carved rock ceiling Boisey wondered where in the chateau they were. He felt the cold from stone floor seeping into his battered body. He took inventory: his face felt swollen, and there was a constant pain coming from his groin. All the bones in his fingers felt as if they were broken, and his ribs were at the very least badly bruised.

Then he tasted blood from his broken teeth and that brought the memory flooding back. He remembered the rifles pointed at his head as they marched him into the room he had been about to open. Boisey knew the men were angry from their earlier humiliation and wouldn't think twice about killing hm. First the soldiers tied him to a chair and then what appeared to be an argument broke out between the soldiers and their officer.

"What are they saying? I don't suppose they're particularly amused with me," Boisey said to the officer.

"You're right. They intend to kill you, I want to take you to the Don but the others don't, and I think I am losing the argument."

"Charming, could you ask them if I could have a say in the matter?"

The words had just left his lips when there was a thunderous report of a gun being discharged next to him. It left a deafening ringing in his ears. He turned to see the officer taking a rifle from the hands of one of the soldiers. Then the squabbling started again. The argument stopped. One of the soldiers left the room. The others now stood quietly pointing their rifles at their prisoner.

Then the officer turned to Boisey and spoke in excellent English. "I have sent word to the Don, they," he said referring to the soldiers, "as I said, want to kill you but I don't think it's appropriate, not before the Don has had the chance to question you. Who are you anyway an English spy?"

Before Boisey could answer, the door flew open. The towering figure of the Don arrived dressed in black military uniform with a solid gold artifact of a horned goat hanging from his thick neck.

Following close behind him was an entourage of people dressed in macabre costume.

"Jesus! The devil in person," Boisey whispered to himself.

The Don stood before them, his face running with sweat. "So, who are you?"

"I am just a friend of Louisa," Boisey said.

"What are you doing here in my house?"

"I told you, I am a friend of your daughter."

"What do you mean friend? I don't know you." He said with a smirk on his face.

"I came here to pick her up, to take her to London for the weekend. No big deal" Boisey said.

"Oh no big deal, eh, I think you come here to kidnap my wife, and then we find you snooping around the lower levels of my Chateau. 'Eh? Explain that?"

"I keep telling you I was with Louisa and I got lost somehow, the troops frightened me, and, I err, protected myself, that's all," Boisey said.

"With great competency, I understand."

"Bit of luck, old son, that's all,"

Suddenly Don Vinchenti turned and screamed, "Bring me a drink."

Hardly had the words left his lips when a servant came running through the doorway carrying a flask of wine and a large silver goblet. The servant's nervous hands poured the wine into the goblet and handed it to the Don. Seizing it he took a long drink while studying his prisoner out of the corner of his eye.

"You're a liar, I know you're here with an American spy, Colonel Stone and your luck has just run out." He wiped his lips with his cuff.

"I've had Stone followed from the start, thanks to my friend, or should I say deceased friend, Oldfield. I knew you were coming here, but I don't know why. Was it to kill me?"

Boisey never answered his thoughts were on Matt whether he had managed to find Louisa. It was obvious that the Don was fairly drunk, and his condition was clouding his mind, he appeared less concerned than he ought to be. This also meant they hadn't discovered the vault yet. They had left the bookcase closed but the carpet was missing, thank God nobody had noticed he thought. He began to wonder how it was that a man like this could become such a powerful politician. It was obvious though, the same way as most other world leaders in history had gained power, through bribery and violence and corruption. The Don swallowed the last of his wine before speaking again.

"Unfortunately my guards, they don't have a good way with words. But they do have a way of getting people to talk with the butts of their rifles. Think my friend before it's too late."

Boisey could sense the depravity surrounding the Don. He wondered if the beads of sweat emanating from the man's skin were droplets of some perverse disease. He could smell the aroma of smoke on his clothes, as if he had been standing beside a log fire. Or was it, he speculated, the reek of burning embers straight from the fires of hell. He laughed to himself at the thought.

"I expect you will tell us everything we want to know." Were the Don's parting words as he left."

As the Don left, the blows had come fast and furious. Only the first ones hurt. Then his body took over, it went into shock. He became numb. He felt, no pain, just realization that he was close to death and that he must hold on to life he was needed, he must hang on.

#   #   #

Louisa put her arm around Boisey who was now sitting up. "What happened, she said gently?"

"We came across some of your countrymen. They must have thought I was an English football fan and decided to kick the shit out of me"

"No don't joke this is serious you're badly hurt. God, I'm so pleased to see you though."

Matt looked at Boisey lying next to him, he looked in worse shape than he felt himself. He was just wondering how the hell they were going to escape when the door of the cell flew open. The backside of a guard came through the entrance, followed quickly by a second guard hurtling through the air soon followed by Baxter Patterson's large form. Without losing the big smile on his face, he picked up one of the soldiers who was reaching for a sidearm and slammed him back on the ground breaking the man's neck.

"Where the hell did you come from?" Matt gasped.

"I could hardly trust you to come here on you own, Anyway, I thought there would be a good story in it for me."

"How did you get into the chateau?" Matt asked, still in a state of shock at his friend's timely arrival.

"That was simple. The man is so in love with himself, he's a sucker for publicity. So your lot got in touch with my lot, they needed someone who knew you to look after your backside. So my publishing company in Montreal set up an interview with the Don. So here I am.

"I'm supposed to write his life story. It was set up for me to have another meeting with this guy called Mario he is the Brother-in-law. Anyway when I arrived here they said he was unavailable, I insisted on seeing the Don and he fell for it, he's incredibly vain."

Matt laughed. "So as far as this mission was concerned you knew what was going on when we met on the way over, but you never let on?"

Bax winked at Matt in a knowing way and said, "True I have been working with this Mario character for some time, and believe it or not I also had an unusual dream on the plane. After that I slowly began to realize who we really are."

"Why on earth didn't you say something when we met on the plane?

"I was still coming out of the mist so to speak. It wasn't until we landed in London that it became crystal clear."

Matt looked at his watch. "We have to go," he said. He tried to stand up, but he was still weak so he sat down again.

"Not me, I'm here to do the story on the Don and the main event, Armageddon and all that." He laughed.

Matt knew he was making light of the situation. Baxter obviously had a further undertaking that he wasn't sharing.

Boisey groaned as he unsteadily stood up. With the help of Baxter and Louisa, he picked himself up and sat down next to Louisa's mother.

"How do you feel Boisey? You OK?" Baxter said, putting his big hand on Boisey's sore shoulder.

Boisey flinched. "I'll be fine thanks," he said, smiling.

"Can you undo Mother's chains?" Louisa said to Boisey.

"Of course, if someone undoes my hands," he replied.

"Of course silly me" she said untying his hands.

As soon as his hands were free he reached into his pocket with his good hand, searching for a wire.

"Oh I'm sorry, let me help," Louisa offered, seeing him struggling with one hand.

"No, no, it's all right. It's just now my fingers are a bit sore, that's all." He found his wire and seconds later the chains were undone.

Baxter walked to the door. "Well, I'm off, I'm going to find the Don. I might be able to keep him busy, gain you some time, a?"

With that he opened the door and was about to walk out when Matt, still shaking his head, managed to stand up. He took Baxter's hand. "You be careful, you old goat," he said.

Baxter grinned and left without another word.

"I don't think he wanted to leave. I believe he would rather have been going with us," Louisa said.

"If we don't get a move on, we won't be going anywhere. The helicopter will be on the lawn in eight minutes," Matt said.

"How do you feel Boisey?" Matt said bending to help him up.

"Like shit." He said, putting his arm around Matt.

"Come on then." Matt said. "If we've only a few minutes left, we had better get going."

With the aid of Matt's arm, Boisey was able to make his way to the door. Matt was feeling a little better although he still felt sick he had managed to pull himself together enough to help Boisey out of the cell.

Louisa's mother stood at the door for a moment. She looked at the others and then turned to her daughter and announced, "I won't be coming with you darling. This is where I'm needed."

"Mummy what on earth do you mean? Why not, what do you mean? It's ridiculous after all of this, now you don't want to come with us?"

"I have work to do, Lou. Matt will explain." She stared deep into Matt's eyes, almost hypnotically.

It was then Matt realized the truth and who she was, but still he couldn't understand why she had to stay. He had to know.

"I know who you are, but I don't understand why you can't come with us now?" he said addressing Louisa's mother.

"I have to be here Matt. I have to make sure he is here on Earth when it happens. You see, he has the capability to leave the planet from down below here." She said pointing to the floor. "I must be here to make sure that he doesn't do that, I must be sure he is turned to dust."

253

"Ok right, I see. It's that huge silo down in the cavern. Wow! I was right it is a shuttle then. Now it all makes sense." Matt said now realizing the significance of the situation.

"That might be so mate, but if we don't get a move on, we are going to miss the boat as they say. Incidentally I have left a little explosive surprise, when that goes off he won't be going anywhere, trust me." Boisey said this looking at Louisa's mother with a smile..

"I understand, but I'll stay for a little while longer, just in case." She said.

"Mummy I don't know what's going on please tell me what's going on, why do you need to stay here? This is absurd!"
Her mother reached out and put her hands gently to Louisa's face her manner seemed to change, radiating calm from within. "Darling, don't worry. Matt knows. He will explain. Now go on before it's too late." She released her and said, "I love you Louisa."

"She has a point." Matt said, "how are you going to get off, won't you be destroyed too?"

She appeared not to have heard the question for she turned and walked back into the cell. Smiling at him she slowly closed the door and said, "Maybe."

"No!" Louisa screamed and grabbed at the handle of the door. Matt took her by the hand and gently pulled her away.

"Come on, don't worry, I'll explain later." Then to Boisey he said, "Let's go."

Resting his arm on Louisa's shoulder, he walked her away from the door.

They moved cautiously through the open bookcase and out of the room that had held her mother prisoner for so long.

Soon they were out in the hallway and climbing down the stairs. Suddenly Boisey stopped turned and said to Matt, "I have to know. Who was Oldfield?"

254

"He was the officer who handed me my orders," Matt said.

"That explains a lot," Boisey said then continued on down the stairs.

Matt looked at his watch, just a few minutes to go. From the plans of the chateau he knew they were near the west wing, the spot where John was due to arrive any moment. He turned to Boisey. "You take Louisa and go ahead. I'll wait here in case anybody comes after us.

"OK," Boisey said.

Without another word he clasped Louisa by the hand and headed along the hallway toward the west wing.

Matt looked at his watch and let two minutes pass before he followed reaching the west wing without an incident. With no sign that Boisey and Louisa had been stopped on their way, he pushed on through the crowds of drunks. With the party still going on it was considerably easier for him to move unnoticed along the packed hallway. Without warning a soldier obviously drunk suddenly turned and slammed the butt of his rifle into Matt's chest. Spinning the rifle around, he stuck the tip of the bayonet into Matt's neck, pushing him against the wall until he could hardly breathe.

A crowd of drunks mainly soldiers in high spirits gathered around, their curiosity aroused by the commotion. The soldier thought it was funny. His black tunic stained with vomit, his face red and bloated with alcohol leered at Matt in amusement. He realized the man was obviously drunk and just having fun. He also knew from the color of the uniform, that the man was one of the Don's personal guards, a sadistic brutal soldier who might just kill for the hell of it.

The laughing crowd took the soldier's attention away for a split second. Matt hand came up and smashed into the man's neck. Instantly he crumpled to the ground, his rifle falling on the floor went down. The crowd hushed. The next soldier moved forward, Matts hands flew around the man's ears slapping them so hard and so fast that the man collapsed before him. He felt a sharp pain in his back as another soldier smashed a rifle in between his shoulder blades. He twisted around grabbed the weapon with one hand, then using the leverage of the rifle bent his arm back until it snapped. As the next soldier moved forward Matt dropped to the floor in one movement brought both feet up into the soldier's stomach and tossed him over his head while he continued to roll over backwards then bounced up onto his feet in one rolling movement. The crowd stood aside, Matt left the scene bulldozing his way through the crowd until he found the kitchen. The body of Carlos was still on the floor, as he passed by he kicked it then opened the door to the outside and stepped out into the welcome cold night air.

Feeling a great sense of relief on leaving the chateau, he pushed his way through the bushes until finally he was out in the clear. Then he saw the others crossing the frozen lawn. He called to them, and started to run toward them. A black shadow launched itself at him. Instantly, he felt the jaws of the animal biting deep into his flesh, holding him tight like a vice. The teeth tore at his sleeve. The weight of the animal dragged him down onto the grass. With no weapon he felt helpless, and screamed out at the top of his voice, "God help me." As the jacket ripped the animal let go slinking away into the darkness. Matt wondered whether it was the shock of him screaming out or help from above that made the animal whimper off. It didn't matter either way the animal was gone.

Holding his bleeding arm he managed to stand and run towards the place he knew the others would be waiting. Hoping to see John arriving with the helicopter he looked up to the clear night sky. To his surprise he saw lights stretching high across the sky. He stopped dead in his tracks when he realized they were too high and covered too much of the sky to be lights from a helicopter. The intense beams of light streamed across the sky like huge searchlights. They waved gently back and forth changing intensity while totally lighting up the northern sky. Matt had seen the aurora borealis many times in North America and knew that it was impossible for it to be that phenomenon here in Italy. In the distance he heard rumbling of thunder, yet surprisingly the sky remained clear of cloud. He started to walk towards the edge of the lawn. What the hell could it be he thought? The sound of thunder became louder and louder, moving closer. Blast, it must be a storm that could mess up John's arrival in the helicopter.

Then he saw the wall. A wall of light seemed to cover the whole north side of the horizon. It looked like a huge fence made from blinding forks of lightning striking the ground and stretching from east to west as far as the eye could see. Lighting the mountains like daylight, the powerful lights continued to sweep the sky above the moving phenomenon.

The noise was deafening. Matt stood in awe of the spectacle, before gradually it dawned on him what it was. It was of course, a Light-Ship taking a low pass across the planet. The lightning was produced by the static electricity in the atmosphere generated by the anti-gravity engines of the great ship. He knew that even at the ship's height, the noise that sounded like the rumbling of thunder was coming from the main propulsion units of the colossal vessel as it strained to position itself against the pull of the Earth's gravity.

He staggered on until he finally reached the other two who were standing at the edge of the lawn staring into the sky.

He put his arm around Louisa and kissed her. She responded with a loving hug. "My God Matt I was worried about you. What is that?" she asked, pointing into the sky.

"It's a Light-Ship. They made it. They've arrived in time."

"My God Matt, it's incredible. How big is it?"

"Pretty damn big I'd say."

"You're not kidding. What's it doing, it's very low?"

"It's not actually. Its way up there, it just appears close, it's just so big."

Suddenly, every light inside the chateau came on. At the same moment they heard the swishing of the helicopter blades as it came in low. It was John. The black form of the helicopter came throbbing out of the darkness with its searchlights blazing. It touched down some distance from them, they ran towards it, Matt looked back. Soldiers were pouring out of the doors of the Chateau and were now running toward them. Together they stumbled across the open gap amid gunfire and great flashes of light that now seemed to surround them.

John jumped out of the helicopter and helped Louisa aboard. Matt reeled, hit by a bullet in the back. John hauled him onto the platform and then reached for Boisey who was struggling to climb aboard. John jumped into the pilot's seat and in a moment the helicopter lifted a few feet from the ground. It hovered for a moment before rising slowly away from the chateau. Then a hail of bullets tore into the craft. Matt looked down Louisa was holding her arm, trying to stop blood pouring from a bullet wound. He pulled her towards him. The blood from her wound felt hot and sticky. The craft seemed to sway and stagger, Matt could tell John was having trouble gaining altitude.

They were only a few hundred feet or so in the air when Matt looked out from the doorway of the chopper to the chateau below. He saw a flash of light lift from a bunker in the grounds of the building. Instantly he knew what it was. Then a moment later the missile smacked into its target. He felt a shattering jolt and experienced a blinding light as the helicopter exploded into a huge fireball.

Inside the inferno a light as bright as the sun, surrounded them. It encompassed them and seemed to hang in the air while time stood still. Matt looked at Louisa lying in his arms. Transparent bubbles were forming over her body, surrounding her. Slowly the bubbles lifted her out of his arms, up and away from the roar of the explosion. He looked at the others. The same thing was happening to them. Their bodies began to rise upwards surrounded by bubbles like a scuba diver rising from deep in the sea. He called out. "Louisa, don't leave me. Don't go without me. I love you."

The light from the explosion still surrounded him. Then came darkness, nothing, not a sound. Then unafraid he closed his eyes.

Chapter 29

When Matt opened his eyes he knew he was aboard one of the Light-Ships. He looked around at the cabin-walls they were glowing with pale blue light. It was then he saw Louisa. She was sitting across on the other side of the cabin gazing toward his arrival couch. She looked thoughtfully at him; her own transparent aura was glowing with love as she spoke.

"Matt finally, I was beginning to think you would sleep forever." Her gentle voice was like music to his ears.

"God, it's good to see you Lou. The last thing I remember was the chopper exploding,"

She stroked his forehead. "It's all right darling. At the moment we died, they locked on to us and transported us up here. I've been waiting hours for you to wake."

"How did the others make out?" Matt said rising from the couch.

"They are all fine Matt. I've talked to some of the officers. The other ships will be here soon and they're sure it's not going to be a problem to get everyone off the planet in time.

Matt wanted to talk about the last few moments on Earth, but there would be time for that later. For now he was safe and warm, and soon his energy would return. "So, did they tell you what's going on down there?" he asked.

"Well, I haven't heard much, I was too concerned about you I've been waiting here most of the time. Although they did say China is marching toward its western borders. Did you know John and Boisey had already Graduated?"

"I know Boisey has and it did cross my mind that John was also a graduate."

"Well darling, John went up to the bridge with the other officers. Before he left, he gave me some wonderful news." She stopped, paused as if on a brink, then said, "Baxter, you and I have graduated and even more exciting they have given you a post on one of the inter-galactic Light-Ships here in this Universe."

"But" . . . Matt began.

She put her fingers to his lips. "I know what you are going to say, but it's what you really want. I want you to take the position. We will be together again, we have the whole of eternity."

She moved closer to him, she was beautiful. Then she said, "I love you Matt, I will be with you forever but when it's time I want to go back down and help them rebuild the planet."

"You can't, you've lost your body."

"Oh yes I can, now I have graduated Matt, I can recreate my body, by materializing atoms into a density the shape of the body I just left. There will be many players going back down who have not graduated but been given another chance to see the light, so to speak. I will be there to help them."

He experienced a feeling of happiness that was overwhelming. She paused, looking at him, allowing him to see she was filled with love. He could feel the warm flow of electricity emanating from her.

"You're right it's not a problem darling you can do that and now that I have graduated I'll also be able to create my own material body when I go aboard a light-ship."

"Of course, but I don't know how to do it."

"I don't think that'll be a problem Louisa, you'll soon learn."

"Matt do you think there's a Game-board on the ship?"

"Of course, why?"

"Well, I was thinking, John said it could be as long as three or four weeks before I can go down to the surface, I'd like to use the Game-board to go and look back at an event in past."

"Oh?"

"I missed an opportunity."

"An opportunity?" he inquired.

"Well, it was a horrible experience, when I lost my child. I'll tell you more about it when we meet again," she smiled and looked at him with love in her eyes.

She smiled, showing her deep love for him.

"By the way, do you know who my mother really is? She stopped, waiting for him to answer.

"My mother is also your Professor, one of the Grand Masters," she said.

"I know darling," Matt said, "although I only realized it at the last minute I just didn't have a chance to tell you."

"Do you think, she, I mean, he, will get off before the Cleansing? I truly love her, him, you know what I mean."

"Don't worry I think Baxter is there to make sure that the professor gets off the planet in time."

"Oh, that's right Matt. I forgot to tell you, Boisey went back down. He said he intended to help Baxter bring Mother up to the ship. Do you think he can really help without a body?"

"I'm sure he can." He stopped, there was something else he wanted to know. "What happened to your natural father?"

"I thought you knew. Gina and I were the children from Mummy's first marriage. I don't remember much about my father, all I know is that he was a scientist who worked for my stepfather and he was killed in Africa when I was very young.

"What will happen to Vinchenti Matt? Will he really be destroyed when the cleansing happens?"

"Yes, absolutely as long as he is there on the planet when it happens. Like us he can only leave the body through death. Unlike us, who leave at the point of death and are transported back out of the Game to the real Universe, these beings of Hades are only inhabitants of this reality. So instead they have only an incubation period of several days after the body dies to find a new recipient, normally a new born child. That's why it's so important to make sure Vinchenti is on the Earth when the chain reaction occurs, so he will be turned to dust for sure. It's almost certain that he will try to leave the planet by using the shuttle that's beneath the chateau. With the world about to have a major nuclear war he will want to leave and take the shuttle into orbit for a while. After all, the whole purpose for him being on Earth was to help pollute the world into its own destruction. I don't think he did a bad job actually. By the way, we think his previous existence was in the body or should I say the mind of Hitler. "

Just then the door of the cabin flew open to reveal the laughing face of Boisey his body was now glowing in its transparent form. He was followed through the doorway by Baxter, still in his original physical body.

"There's no need to worry folks, we got the Professor off. The old master has gone roaming the ship, said something about looking around the transfer decks," Boisey said. "Apparently my little box of tricks blew the command panel for the escape shuttle to smithereens and there's no way they can rebuild one in time to get the Don off.

Unfortunately though I have some bad news for you Matt," he smiled.

"Go on?"

"Baxter and I are going to be serving with you on the same Light-Ship. That'll be interesting, don't you think?" Again he smiled then said, "Good luck Lou." He walked to the door followed by Baxter.

"See you soon guys," Matt said as the door closed silently behind them.

Chapter 30

Now alone again they moved closer to each other. "Matt, I want to join with you; I want to experience the feeling of being as one. Just for a few minutes"

He felt her encompassing warmth. He sensed, rather than saw, her beauty. Now she enveloped him. Her energy tingled, charged with static electricity.

"Louisa my darling, you are the most wonderful soul-mate in the Universe. I'd love to join with you and experience the emotion of being one." Although the words were only thoughts, it was as if he had spoken.

She responded by reaching out, pushing her hand into the haze of energy particles that represented his body. Then she whispered into his mind. It sounded like the gentle music of bubbling water. He recognized it and was the harmony of pure love. Slowly his own mist intermingled with hers, their minds joined together until finally they molded into one being, one singular pattern of purity, and one entity.

Locked together in love, with their energies combined, the now singular entity moved forward across the cabin to look out through the window. At that moment the view became obscured by the arrival of a huge Light-Ship passing between them and the planet. The ship continued on its path slowly curving around the planet, until it finally disappeared over the horizon taking up a position on the other side of the revolving globe. A moment later another great ship appeared, the last of the Light-Ships had arrived.

While the enormous vessels began their task of taking on board the players that were to be saved, the entity reflected on the beautiful planet and how insignificantly small the blue spinning ball is, relative to the vastness of the Universe.

It pondered on God the Creator of the Game and empathized with His sorrow, for this his creation that had, once again, been so thoroughly defiled.

Now it was time, the rising mushroom clouds developed across the surface of the planet, exploding like little white puffs of cotton wool, until they covered all the land and blue of the sea.

The entity stood and viewed the scene in pity and in awe at the absurdity of man. It cried in frustration, and wept for the souls that might have been saved.

The fools, it thought. The stupid, stupid, fools. If only they had listened.

If only ---they knew.

To be continued